Grace's Saving

Seven Unsuitable Sisters
Book 3

BY MAEVE GREYSON

ARE YOU SIGNED UP FOR DRAGONBLADE'S BLOG?

You'll get the latest news and information on exclusive giveaways, exclusive excerpts, coming releases, sales, free books, cover reveals and more.

Check out our complete list of authors, too!

No spam, no junk. That's a promise!

Sign Up Here

www.dragonbladepublishing.com

Dearest Reader;

Thank you for your support of a small press. At Dragonblade Publishing, we strive to bring you the highest quality Historical Romance from some of the best authors in the business. Without your support, there is no 'us', so we sincerely hope you adore these stories and find some new favorite authors along the way.

Happy Reading!

CEO, Dragonblade Publishing

Additional Dragonblade books by Author Maeve Greyson

Seven Unsuitable Sisters Series
Blessing's Baron (Book 1)
Fortuity's Arrangement (Book 2)
Grace's Saving (Book 3)

The Sisterhood of Independent Ladies Series
To Steal a Duke (Book 1)
To Steal a Marquess (Book 2)
To Steal an Earl (Book 3)

Once Upon a Scot Series
A Scot of Her Own (Book 1)
A Scot to Have and to Hold (Book 2)
A Scot To Love and Protect (Book 3)

Time to Love a Highlander Series
Loving Her Highland Thief (Book 1)
Taming Her Highland Legend (Book 2)
Winning Her Highland Warrior (Book 3)
Capturing Her Highland Keeper (Book 4)
Saving Her Highland Traitor (Book 5)
Loving Her Lonely Highlander (Book 6)
Delighting Her Highland Devil (Book 7)
When the Midnight Bell Tolls (Novella)

Highland Heroes Series
The Guardian (Book 1)
The Warrior (Book 2)
The Judge (Book 3)
The Dreamer (Book 4)
The Bard (Book 5)

The Ghost (Book 6)
A Yuletide Yearning (Novella)
Love's Charity (Novella)

Also from Maeve Greyson
Guardian of Midnight Manor (Novella)
Once Upon a Haunted Highland Mist (Novella)

Chapter One

En route to Broadmere Manor
England's Lake District
Early June 1822

LADY GRACE ABAROUGH, fourth sister in birth order to Chance, the sorely frustrated Duke of Broadmere, hung out of the carriage window and breathed in the sweet air of the countryside. The clean, earthy scent of crops flourishing and wildflowers blooming made her spirits sing. They had finally left London to enjoy the wonders of summer that Broadmere Manor and the Lake District always supplied.

She waved to the next Broadmere carriage in line behind them. Jasper, the driver, grinned and tipped his hat. It was a glorious day, sunshine bathing the world. The four carriages and assortment of wagons it took to move the family, the household's servants, Grace's beloved hounds, and the enormous conglomeration of trunks and supplies clipped along at a jaunty pace. She couldn't wait to arrive and behave most inappropriately by shedding her stockings and wiggling her toes in the cool, lush grassiness of the manor's gardens.

"Gracie!" Serendipity, the eldest Abarough sister, pinched the underside of her arm, just hard enough to make it sting. "For the hundredth time, would you please sit and behave like a proper young woman of one and twenty instead of a wild hoyden just escaped from the nursery?"

Not about to be subdued, Grace sat back and nudged her

sister. "Pinch me again, and I'll make sure Gastric sleeps under your bed after eating everything known to make him break wind."

"That is not fair." Joy, the next sister in line after Grace, shuffled the small deck of cards she always brought along on lengthy journeys to keep herself entertained. "My bed is on the same side of the room as Seri's. If that hound of yours unleashes his artillery under her bed, his poisonous fog could suffocate me as well."

Felicity, the next-to-youngest Abarough sister, opened the hamper at their feet and withdrew a carefully wrapped cloth bundle. "Poor Gastric can't help himself. He should not be used as a weapon, nor should he be made fun of. Biscuit, anyone? Cook and I worked out a new recipe, making them lighter and even more scrumptious, if I do say so myself."

"We are nearly there, Felicity. We can enjoy them with tea. Later." Serendipity gently took the bundle of biscuits, returned them to the hamper, and firmly latched it. "And please remember what the modiste said—she can't let out your gowns further. New ones will have to be made, and we aren't due back in London until late summer, early fall." She gave Felicity an affectionate pat. "Self-control will win the day. I know you can do it."

Felicity went quiet and bowed her head, obviously hurt by the stinging reminder about her love of food and the results of her indulgences.

"Leave her alone." Grace elbowed Serendipity again. "I know of at least two modistes in the village. If she needs new gowns, we'll simply get them there."

Merry, the baby of the family, leaned across and patted Felicity's knee. "Eat your biscuits, Fellie." She fixed a narrow-eyed glare on Serendipity. "Mama would never be so cruel, and you know it, Seri. You should be ashamed of yourself, dousing the generous spirit of our sweet Fellie."

Grace gave her baby sister an approving nod before turning back to her eldest one. "You really need to stop spending so much time with Chance. His relentless nattering to hurry and get us all married off so he can finally get the full of his inheritance is making you mean-spirited. Or has he promised you extra coin for your dowry if you help him in his quest? You do realize he'll turn on you? After all, no matter how bossy you are, you're still one of us and have to marry for him to prove to Mr. Sutherland that the requirements of Mama and Papa's will have been fully satisfied."

"*You* are the mean-spirited ones." Serendipity glowered at each of them in turn. "You are like a pack of wolves. Always turning against me when my suggestions are only meant to help you."

"I think we have all been trapped in this carriage too long." Felicity once again retrieved the biscuits from the basket and opened the square of linen protecting them. She passed them out, even giving one to Serendipity. "We are not usually at each other's throats so viciously."

"She makes a valid point," Grace admitted. Uplifted and filled with generosity because of escaping the confines of Town, she reached over and squeezed Serendipity's hand. "Truce. I know you promised Mama to take care of us all until we married. Just try not to be so…"

Serendipity arched a golden brow. "So…*what*, dear Gracie?" she asked in a snappish tone. "It appears your peacemaking skills need polish."

Grace gave a disgruntled snort. It would seem she needed to put her older sibling in place. Fine. There would be no truce. She made a mental note to ask Cook for a plate of eggs and beans for Gastric. That would arm her precious dog's belly with enough flatulence to last all night. "Try not to be such an odious harpy, Seri. You should always side with us about this Marriage Mart business. Not Chance."

"I was not discussing the Marriage Mart," Serendipity said. "I was merely addressing proper behavior and appearances."

"Marriage Mart," the rest of the sisters said in unison.

Serendipity eyed them as if seeing each of them for the very first time. "Have I truly been so horrid to you all?"

"Most definitely," Grace hurried to say. "Especially after the success of getting Blessing and Fortuity happily married off. It's almost as if you smell blood and can't stop yourself."

"You have been rather sharp," Felicity told Serendipity in a quiet, apologetic way.

"Definitely a harpy," Joy said, sounding distracted as she laid out her cards on the small lap table she had commissioned from London's finest woodworker.

"Merry?" Serendipity asked. "Have you no disparaging words with which to fling at me?"

"Yes." Merry pointed at the beaded tassels of her reticule. "When you borrow my things, will you please take better care of them? There is an entire strand of jet missing from this corner. I shall have to have it repaired before carrying it in the future."

Serendipity closed her eyes and pinched the bridge of her nose, just as Mama had always done whenever they had collectively worn her patience to its thinnest.

Grace almost felt sorry for her sister. Serendipity had assumed Mama's role as matriarch of the family after their sweet mother had died after a long, torturous battle with consumption. Then a short six months later Papa had died from what they all decided was a broken heart, leaving Chance, the firstborn and only male of the Abarough brood, as the fifth Duke of Broadmere. And that was when the madness of marrying off the sisters in true love matches had begun. Because until all of them were happily married to husbands they loved, their brother had to survive on an allowance—an entirely too modest allowance, according to him. Grace could just see her beloved parents up in heaven, laughing until they were breathless at the game they had set in motion.

But Grace was also well aware that Serendipity was not above feigning a bit of drama and hurt feelings to turn circumstances in the direction she wished them to go. However, since Grace was still in a generous mood, she would attempt to make amends.

"We sisters have spoken, Seri. All you need do is have Merry's jet bag repaired and refrain from any Marriage Mart machinations until after summer's end. Then, once again, you will find yourself in our good graces."

Serendipity lifted her head and turned to fully face her.

Grace recognized that familiar wariness lurking in her sibling's sapphire eyes. "What have you done?"

"You do realize Chance intends to fill this summer with garden parties, outdoor dinners, and formal picnics?" Serendipity's judgmental eyebrow that always gave her away slanted higher than the other. "Just because we do not find ourselves in the heart of London's Polite Society, does not mean the search for suitable husbands can't continue."

"Oh, Seri." With a long-suffering groan, Grace slouched against the side of the carriage and propped her elbow on the ledge of the open window.

"Posture," Serendipity said in the same singsong way Mama had always done.

"Just stop, Seri. I am in no mood. You have successfully placed a dark blight upon my day. You should have been born a storm cloud. Happy?" Her elbow still propped in the window, Grace rested her chin in her hand and tried to console herself with the view of the lush green countryside. Blessing and Fortuity had both warned she would be the next little Abarough goose that Chance would hang in the window to attract suitors. Not that he wouldn't just as happily marry off one of the others first, but for the moment, the blissful unions appeared to be happening in birth order. Except for Serendipity, who had sworn to remain unwed and look after everyone else until their fates were settled at the altar. Not even Chance would cross Serendipity. She had pushed him out of too many trees when they were children.

That memory made Grace smile. All of them truly had been blessed with the most wonderfully indulgent childhoods. She sent a silent *thank you* to her parents, positive they still watched over their lively brood.

As the carriage rattled through the land adjoining theirs, she noticed activity at the landowner's manor house that had remained vacant last summer. "Wolfebourne Lodge is being opened. What do you know of it, Seri?"

"It is my understanding," Serendipity said, her eyes narrowing with the effort to recall every last detail, "that the new duke thought the countryside might provide a much-needed change of scenery for his charges." Serendipity always knew the latest *on dit*. When their mother had become bedridden, she had made it her duty to keep up with every last detail to keep Mama entertained.

"His charges?" Grace leaned farther out the window to keep Wolfebourne Lodge in her sights. "What *charges*?"

"A much younger brother and sister from one of his father's later marriages."

"How many marriages did his father have?"

"From what I have gathered," Serendipity said, "the old duke died on his way to the altar to marry number five."

Grace pulled herself back inside the carriage and stared at Serendipity. "What happened to the first four?"

Her sibling wrinkled her nose. "The first died in childbirth after bringing forth the current duke, the next two from illnesses. And the last…"

"And the last?"

Uncomfortably shifting in place, Serendipity cleared her throat. "He had her legally severed from himself and the estate. Divorced." After pursing her lips tightly together as if the words she was about to say tasted terrible, she whispered, "On the grounds of adultery."

"Oh my." Grace couldn't fathom such a situation because their parents had been absolutely devoted to one another. "And was she the mother of the new duke's charges?"

Serendipity nodded. "Ran off and left them when they were tiny little things, but at least they are still considered legitimate and are hopefully provided for financially, since they are the duke's siblings."

"Yet and still." Grace couldn't imagine the turmoil of being a child caught in the middle of such a mess. "I hope the new duke isn't a heartless devil."

"Gracie! Language!" Serendipity resettled herself again. "But I quite agree. I am unsure of the children's ages, but their mother's behavior is not their fault, and they should not be made to pay for her ways. Sins of the father and all that, you know?"

"Hopefully, the new duke has a kindhearted wife who will ensure the children have a proper home filled with happiness rather than worries from the past."

The air of victory rolling off Serendipity made Grace realize her error too late. Her sister smiled a wickedly delighted smile. "A reliable source informs me the Duke of Wolfebourne is quite handsome as well as quite without a wife."

Grace nodded at Merry sitting across from her. "Merry loves children. Sounds like a perfect match to me."

Merry pointed at her. "You are next on the chopping block, remember?"

"I possess no recollection of reading a rule book regarding the order in which we are to be married off to the highest bidder," Grace said.

"True love matches, and you know it," Serendipity corrected her. "And who knows? Perhaps he and Merry will hit it off. She is eight and ten now. A little on the young side, but not overly so."

The carriage lurched to a stop.

"Thank heavens," Grace said. Without waiting for a footman, she threw open the door, gathered her skirts in her fists, and leapt out.

"Gracie!" Serendipity shouted, but Grace ignored her.

Instead, she hurried to the carriage that she and Papa had refashioned to transport her beloved hounds without cooping them up in boxes or unsafe open wagons. Papa had loved their dogs as much as she did and hadn't hesitated when she asked to gut an old carriage and make it perfect for the transport of their puppies whenever they traveled to the countryside. She threw open the door and was greeted by happy barks and howls. "My babies! How did they do, Carson?"

Carson, the Broadmere huntsman for as far back as Grace could remember, nodded from his well-cushioned seat of honor among the dogs, who were wriggling on their pillows that were secured in shallow boxes. Custom-made leashes and harnesses, also designed by Grace and her father, kept the pups safely in place. "All are fine as can be, Lady Grace, fine as can be, but they be needing a good run now. Especially Lucy's pups."

"Let me help." Working together, Grace and Carson freed the dogs from their tethers and set Lucy's seven plump little puppies on the main house's front lawn, well clear of the servants unloading the wagons and carriages.

The canines' excitement about fresh grass to run and roll in filled Grace with joy and made her itch to race across the meadow and maybe even roll around in the grass a little herself. She waved down her maid, who stood with the other maids supervising the unloading of the sisters' trunks. "Nellie!"

The middle-aged woman in the white ruffled cap hurried over and curtsied. "Yes, my lady?"

"How terribly difficult would it be to find and air out my *country* clothes so I might wear them today?" Nellie didn't approve of Grace's scandalous attire of buckskin breeches, an old linen shirt and jacket, and scuffed boots that dearest Papa had always allowed her to wear whenever riding on their property. But what the maid didn't understand was that Grace always kept the promise she'd made to her father. When dressed in her favorite *adventuring* clothes, she stayed on Broadmere land, never went anywhere near the road to the village, and also avoided the neighbors. Buckskins were just so much more sensible than a riding habit, and with her long blonde braid stuffed up in a ratty old cap, if she was spotted from afar, most would simply think her a lad taking care of the master's horse.

Nellie deflated with a heavy sigh. "No trouble at all, my lady, since I felt sure you would wish to wear those dreadful things as soon as we arrived. Before we left last summer, I wrapped them in paper and stored them in your main wardrobe. They should only need a good shake before you put them on."

"Wonderful!" Grace felt like dancing a jig. She so loved the countryside. "Let's hurry so I can get changed and out into the meadow with Gastric and the boys. I am sure they are all ready for some exploring after our long ride. Poor Lucy will have to stay behind with her pups, but Carson knows to give her and her babies the run of the side garden."

"Yes, my lady. Shall I tell Jasper to ready your horse?"

"Perfect!" Grace caught up her skirts and started up the stately flagstone path to the front door.

"Gracie!"

"Drat," she said under her breath before turning to face her brother, striding her way. "What?"

"Do not be surly with me," he said. "I wanted to speak with you about your riding attire while we're here this summer."

"Papa always let me, and you know that."

Chance raked a hand through his stylishly cropped whitish-blond hair and looked everywhere except directly into her eyes. "I know Papa always let you, but you were younger then—not of an age looking to marry."

"What would Papa say at this very moment? You know he and Mama are watching over us." Grace jutted her chin higher. Chance wasn't a bad sort. He merely needed reminding that even though his sisters stood between him and the entirety of the Broadmere estate's coffers, he loved them and would never wish them unhappy. She poked him in the chest. "Well? What would Papa say?"

"Papa would remind you that there is a time and a season for everything, and that perhaps your season of scandalous dressing should be set aside—much like you set aside that wooden sword of yours that bruised the dickens out of my shins when we were children."

"The only reason I set aside my wooden sword is because

Mama took it away when she realized I had grown stout enough to cause you real bodily harm. You know they always let us sort our differences on our own as long as no one was endangered."

"Gracie."

"Whining my name will not convince me to wear that ridiculous riding habit that does nothing but get in the way when the pups and I go exploring. I wear the silly thing in London or if I ride into the village, where anyone will see me. That was enough for Papa. It should be enough for you—or are you saying you are a better man than Papa?"

From the deep amethyst hue of her brother's eyes, she had succeeded in stirring his emotions as planned. Chance might be the head of the household and hold some sway over what she and her sisters could or couldn't do, but Mama and Papa's memory and the requirements of their will were powerful weapons in and of themselves, and she had no qualms about using them. "Well? What say you, brother?"

He bared his teeth and growled, thrilling her immensely. "If anyone of importance sees you, your inappropriate attire goes into the dustbin, and you will restrain your manner of dress to your acceptable riding habit, or you will not ride. Is that understood?"

If he tried to put her favorite outdoor wear into the dustbin, she would purchase another wooden sword and beat him with it. However, since she was quickly losing daylight and eager to be riding free with the wind in her face, she jerked a curt nod. "I shall follow the same rules Papa gave me: stay on our land, stay away from the road to the village, and hide from any neighbors or passersby."

Chance threw his hands in the air and turned away, heading toward Serendipity and the other girls while grumbling under his breath.

Not about to waste the opportunity to escape, Grace rushed inside and hurried up the right side of the dual staircase with its elaborate gilded banisters and mahogany steps that made the marble entry hall even grander. She found Nellie in the sisters' shared dressing room, shaking out and brushing the scandalous clothing that was the most comfortable attire Grace had ever been blessed to wear. Men had no idea how fortunate they were to escape the curse of stays, elaborate layers of petticoats, and endless amounts of ribbons, pins, and buttons.

"Your boots are free of spiders or vermin." Nellie nodded at the worn pair of knee-high boots that Mama had ordered from the local cobbler with the instructions that they be perfect for riding and mucking about in the fields. With low, sturdy heels and thick soles, the boots from Mama were one of Grace's most cherished possessions.

"I missed you, old friends," she told the boots as she picked them up and hugged them.

Nellie shook her head and quietly clucked like a disapproving hen, but didn't say a word as she helped Grace change into her unorthodox adventuring apparel.

"No one ever sees me, Nellie," Grace assured her as she shrugged on the jacket plagued with snagged threads and sleeves with frayed edges. "And my horse and dogs do not judge me by my apparel."

"I would never judge you, my lady," the maid said as she sorted Grace's hair and helped her secure the weight of it up inside a tattered old cap. "But there is word that the new Duke of Wolfebourne will be about this summer. He may be looking for a wife."

"I have four sisters from which he can choose." Grace stepped into her boots, then straightened and adjusted her braces. She didn't want her buckskin breeches to sag so much in the backside. With a jaunty tap of her hat, she offered her fretting maid a reassuring smile. "Besides, here in the country, the *ton* is always a few days behind on the latest gossip. For all we know, the man is already married. Stop worrying and enjoy the fresh air."

"Yes, my lady." But Nellie looked far from convinced or pleased to find herself in the country.

"I shall bring you some fresh wildflowers," Grace called out as she skipped from the room, took the back stairs down to the kitchens, and exited the house through the servants' entrance. Some members of the aristocracy escaping London for the summer had been known to drop by unannounced when they noticed the larger manor houses were once again inhabited. The joyful return to her adventuring clothes would be short-lived indeed if she used the front entrance and was spotted by anyone whom Chance considered a threat to the Broadmere reputation.

Keeping to the shadows, she made her way to the stable and was met by four of her five hounds. "Where is Lucy?" she asked Carson and Jasper.

Both men removed their hats and kept their eyes averted, as if looking at her in her breeches might cause their souls to burst into flames. "Lucy and the wee ones are sunning in the side garden, my lady," Jasper said. "We nay had the heart to disturb them."

"Well done, gentlemen. They have earned an afternoon of sunning." Grace went to her horse, a fine bay thoroughbred, and gave it an affectionate rub. "Ready for a good, long run, Pegasus?"

The horse danced in place and bobbed its head as if champing at the bit to be on the way.

"Me too, old friend."

After Carson settled the short-legged, overly round Gastric into the customized seat attached to the back of the saddle, Grace launched herself up onto her mount.

Both Jasper and Carson ducked their heads, their faces reddening even more because she rode astride rather than sidesaddle. One would think veteran Broadmere servants would be accustomed to the unorthodox ways of the family after witnessing Mama and Papa's highly unique beliefs on child rearing and supporting their daughters' interests, which went far beyond what Society considered appropriate for females.

"Come along, Pete, Moses. You too, Ferdinand," she called to the bouncing herd of hounds as she and Pegasus quick-stepped out of the stable. She couldn't wait to race across the meadow and knew the horse and dogs felt the same. Leaning forward, she gave Pegasus his head, loosening the reins so he'd know his gallop had no boundaries. Gastric *woofed* his happiness from his post at the back of her saddle. The other dogs yipped and barked, loping along and keeping up admirably well.

The wind in her face and her animals' joyous freedom exhilarated Grace, making her laugh like a carefree fool. As they neared a ravine hidden by trees and tangled vines, she slowed Pegasus to a gentle meandering, knowing this particularly rough part of the land needed to be treated with respect and traversed with greater care. With some difficulty, she lowered Gastric to the ground, then returned to the saddle. "Good heavens, my sweet boy. We really must do something about your weight."

Gastric gave her a happy *woof*, then the dogs disappeared into the thick snarl of undergrowth. The lot of them loved nothing better than flushing a rabbit or fox out of hiding and giving chase. But they knew better than to cause the local fauna any harm. Grace had trained her hounds well. They knew their mistress would be most displeased if a creature suffered because of them. No one hunted on Broadmere lands—be they aristocrats or hounds. She refused to allow it, and Chance had yielded to her on that point long ago.

Relaxing in the saddle, she and Pegasus slowly wandered alongside the ravine as the hounds enjoyed their exploring.

"Oh, Connor, whatever shall we do?"

The tearful little voice coming from the depths of the bushes made Grace pull Pegasus to a quick stop.

"The vines have him," the child said, "and he is too tired to fight them any longer. We can't leave him. We just can't."

"No crying, Sissy," said a boy in a much calmer tone. "I will get him out. Galileo is standing watch."

Both children shrieked as Grace's dogs came upon them and sang out their find with the deafening bay of barks and howls.

Grace dismounted and pierced the air with a sharp whistle

that immediately silenced her pups and brought them to heel. "Hello," she called out, hoping she wasn't too late to save whoever was caught in the vines. For them to be unable to climb out of the ravine, they must be injured. "Who is there?"

Only the breeze rustling through the leaves and the quiet gurgling of the stream below answered.

"Whoever you are, I can help you," she said, trying to sound as safe and friendly as possible. "This is Broadmere land. I promise the duke is a most understanding man." The duke would never cross his sisters when it came to a pair of helpless children, possibly even more, found in dire straits upon his land. Poor mites. They were probably afraid he'd call the constable to take them away for trespassing or poaching. "Please let me help you. I mean you no harm. Truly."

Again, only the song of the wind, the crows' caws, and the bubbling stream answered.

Chapter Two

"GASTRIC, TAKE ME to them." Grace pointed at the overgrown ravine, then turned and nodded at the other three dogs. "You fine boys stand guard, yes? Set up a howl if anyone approaches."

The loyal brown and white foxhounds sat at attention, valiantly accepting her command.

Gastric wiggled his thick black-and-tan body forward, his somewhat shorter legs barely keeping his round belly off the ground. Grace had found this canine of questionable ancestry years ago, a starving little pup trying to maneuver the streets of London. While she loved all her dogs, sweet Gastric, with his floppy ears and endearing efforts to always keep up with the long-legged foxhounds, held a special place in her heart.

"I am coming to help you," Grace called out to the children and whomever they protected in the vines. "Do not be afraid. I promise I mean you no harm." Thankful for her boots and buckskins, she forged deeper into the wild cluster of saplings, butcher's broom, elder, and the almost impenetrable vines of woodbine that effectively hid the steep decline into the ravine. "And Gastric will not hurt you either." Although how anyone could ever be afraid of sweet Gastric was beyond her.

"Over here," said the child called Sissy. The little girl's timid voice touched Grace's heart. "We are sorry to be on Broadmere land."

After ducking and shoving through a particularly thick snarl of undergrowth, Grace came upon the young boy and girl crouching beside a half-grown terrier that was hopelessly ensnared in the strong, woody vines of honeysuckle. An extraordinarily large ginger cat stood guard at the poor little dog's head, hackles up, tail puffed and paw lifted and ready to strike Gastric's inquisitive nose.

Grace snapped her fingers. "Come, Gastric. Behind me, please. We mustn't frighten them." The jolly dog immediately obeyed, plopping down behind her as if ready to take advantage of the shade and enjoy a nap. Turning back to the children, she offered them a smile as she knelt in front of them. "My name is Grace, and I shall have your poor pup freed in no time." She eyed the cat that had flattened its ears and shifted its glare to her while continuing to vibrate with a warning growl. "Would you please tell your friend I only mean to help?"

The boy stood and gave her a formal bow. "I am Connor, and this is my sister, Susannah. I call her Sissy, and you can too if you really mean to help us." He pointed at the cat. "Galileo there is Hector's best friend and always protects him."

"As best friends always should," Grace said to the cat.

Poor, trussed-up Hector whined and frantically twitched, his little sides rapidly rising and falling as he panted with fear.

"It's all right, Hector." Grace extended her knuckles so the animals could sniff her hand. The cat gave her a leery look but no longer growled. Poor little Hector whined even louder. "I carry a penknife in my boot. It will make quick work of those vines. Do not be alarmed as I draw it out, all right?" she told the children.

Both of them nodded.

After cutting the small dog free, Grace noticed blood on Hector's front leg, and that he refused to put any weight on it when he stood. "Poor thing. The vines must have injured him. I carry balm and bandages in my saddlebag. Let's get him carried out, and I'll see to him."

Connor pushed his way between her and the dog. "I'll carry

him. It's my fault he got caught."

"Hector was after a rabbit," Sissy explained. "It is not Connor's fault. He thinks he has to take the blame for everything."

"It was an accident," Grace said. She stood and tucked her knife back into her boot. "Young dogs often get themselves into dire straits because they don't know any better."

"You talk like an adult," Connor said as he scooped up the dog and held it close.

Grace laughed. "I *am* an adult. Did you think me a child?"

"You are just not very big for a man," Sissy said. "And why would your parents name you Grace when you are a man?"

"Sissy!" Connor angled a fierce scowl at his sister.

"You never find out if you do not ask," Sissy argued. "He's dressed like a boy but says he is grown."

"I am a *she*," Grace said as they tromped their way back to level ground, where Pegasus and the other three dogs waited. The ginger cat sprang into the lead, growling and hissing at the trio of hounds to keep them at bay. "And these are my *adventuring* clothes. Riding habits tend to get in my way when I explore the countryside." She nodded at Sissy's dress. "Your mama will not be pleased about those stains and tears."

"Our mother doesn't care," Sissy said. "The governess told us we could be dead, and our mother wouldn't even bother to come back for our funerals."

"What a horrible thing to tell you." Grace clapped her mouth shut, her suspicions building. Two young children. On the edge of Broadmere property that adjoined the Wolfebourne estate. If these two were who she thought they were, the freedom of her adventuring clothes could well be over. "The Duke of Wolfebourne wouldn't happen to be your older brother, would he?"

Both children bowed their heads and remained silent, a silence that shouted she was correct. They halted in front of Grace's line of foxhounds, Connor hugging Hector to his chest, and Sissy now holding the cat.

"I am not asking so I can tell on you," Grace told them. "I am asking because I really do not like it when adults see me in my adventuring clothes. It makes my brother angry."

"Who is your brother?" Connor asked.

"The Duke of Broadmere."

"If you promise not to tell our brother we were on your land, we promise not to tell anyone about your adventuring clothes," Sissy offered with the grace and aplomb of an extremely experienced diplomat. Wiliness battled with pleading in her dark brown eyes.

"Agreed," Grace said as she fetched the bandages and balm from her saddlebag. She hoped the children kept to their word as faithfully as she intended to keep to hers. "Now, let's get Hector's leg seen about and then we'll get you home, shall we?"

As she knelt to take care of the frightened pup, she tipped her head homeward bound. "Gastric, Pete, Moses, Ferdinand—home."

All four dogs stared at her as if hoping she would change her mind.

"Home," she repeated in a more authoritative tone. "Now, please, or no soupbones."

The dogs took off, leaving poor Gastric at the back of the pack, struggling to keep up.

"They listen to you?" Connor asked in amazement.

"Of course they listen to me. They know I love them and would never ask the wrong thing of them." Grace patted the ground in front of her. "Place Hector here, please. And he will learn to listen to you too as long as you are kind, patient, and loving. Remember, he has to be given time to learn new things, just as you do. But if you reward him with love and sometimes a treat or two when he behaves as he should, he'll soon listen just like my pups."

"Your Gastric looks like he has had a lot of treats." Sissy idly scratched the much calmer Galileo's ears as she watched the dogs head across the meadow.

"Yes, well, my sweet Gastric loves to eat. I think it's because I found him on the streets of London, and he was half starved. Perhaps, deep down, he fears that someday he might starve again." Grace examined Hector's sore leg. "Thankfully, this is not bad at all. I think he is more afraid than anything."

"Can you bandage it anyway?" Connor asked. "I am sure that will make him feel much better and less afraid."

Grace tried not to smile. She normally didn't pay much mind or even tolerate children all that well, but she liked these two. "I would be happy to, and we shall put some balm on the scrape just to be certain, yes?"

Both children nodded as they knelt beside her, avidly watching her treatment of their sweet pup.

"What do you think, Galileo?" she asked the cat critically eyeing her and flipping his tail.

"It takes him a while to trust," Sissy said. "Our last two governesses were mean to him."

"A pox on them both," Grace said without thinking. She paused in her wrapping of Hector's foreleg. "I should not have said that, but I can't tolerate anyone being cruel to animals. Please add that to our agreement of mutual secrecy."

Both children grinned and bobbed their heads. Galileo even deigned to move a little closer.

"There now. All done." Grace scratched behind Hector's ears and the little white dog almost seemed to smile. "We shall be great friends, Hector." She held out her hand to Galileo. "Friends?"

The cat flicked an ear and blinked its great golden eyes as if to say he had yet to decide.

Grace understood completely. Once an animal had been mistreated, it was afraid to trust anyone.

"Thank you for helping us," Connor said. "And have no worry. We always keep our word."

"It was a pleasure meeting you," Grace told them, "and I always keep my word too."

"Hector refuses to walk," Sissy said. "It's a long way home to carry him all the way."

While Hector was a small dog, it would be quite the chore for them to tote him across the meadow and all the way back to Wolfebourne Lodge. Grace chewed on her bottom lip, battling with what she knew she *should* do and the need to protect the freedom of wearing her buckskins. The children could ride Pegasus while holding the little dog, but what would happen when she delivered them home and was spotted by one of the servants or, heaven forbid, someone of even higher ranking? But what if she got them *close* to home? She could deliver them well out of sight of anyone but close enough that carrying the little dog the rest of the way wouldn't be such an arduous task.

"I have an idea," she told them. "The two of you can ride my horse while holding Hector. I shall get you close enough to the lodge so you can carry him the rest of the way, but still far enough away so no one will see me. Do you think that might work to keep all of our secrets safe?"

"We will make it work," Connor said.

"But what about Galileo?" Sissy asked.

"Did Galileo not make it here on his own four feet…er…paws?" Grace eyed the cat, unsure what to do about him.

"Yes," the little girl said. "But he's tired now. Just look at him."

Galileo yawned.

"I am afraid I am not an expert on cats." Grace liked felines well enough. Especially after being around so many of them while visiting her married sisters. Blessing and Thorne's home was full of them, and Fortuity had four roaming her and Matthew's house. "Would Galileo stay put in Gastric's seat behind the saddle? I won't have him scratching Pegasus."

"Galileo likes horses." Sissy picked up the great ginger cat and held him up to Pegasus's nose. "Meet Pegasus, and be polite. He is our ride home because Hector can't walk with his sore leg."

Horse and cat touched noses and appeared to reach a peaceful accord.

"Will Galileo allow me to help him into the seat?" While the cat had ceased growling or hissing at her, Grace had not missed that he still gave her a wide berth.

Sissy nodded and held out the cat as if the question was silly.

"All right, Galileo. No scratching, if you please." Grace gingerly took hold of the cat and deposited it into Gastric's seat behind the saddle.

Galileo settled into the seat as if claiming it as his throne.

"Well done." Grace waved the children forward. "Let me help the two of you, and then I shall hand up Hector."

"I need to be in the front," Connor said. "I am the eldest."

"Only by a few minutes," Sissy said. "I should be in the front not only because I am a girl but because you need to hold Hector between the two of us to keep him safe."

"Your sister makes a sound argument," Grace told the boy.

"She always does," he said, sounding thoroughly disgruntled.

New to the role of peacemaker, Grace decided to do what her parents always did. "What shall it be, my friends? We are losing daylight, and the later you get home, the likelier it is you might receive a scolding from your governess or nanny or whoever looks after you. At your ages, I am not certain of your caretaker's title."

"A maid for now," Connor said. "Wolfe told our last governess to pack her things and get out after he heard of her telling Sissy she'd probably never be anything more than a dirty little lightskirt, just like our mother."

Grace clenched her teeth to keep from saying something entirely too harsh for the children's tender ears. "Thank goodness he turned out that evil woman," she said after several deep, calming breaths. "Both of you are as fine as fine can be, and I am honored to know you and call you my friends."

"Sissy can sit in front," Connor said with a worried glance in the direction of Wolfebourne land. "We do need to be getting back."

"Up you go, then." Grace seated him in the saddle first, put his sister in front of him, then handed Hector up. The pup curled into a tight ball, cowering in Connor's arms. "Will you be able to hold him like that, or do you think he would ride better if you supported him on the saddle?"

"I have him just right." Connor gave her a determined nod. "He's afraid and counting on me to protect him."

Grace forced a smile and swallowed hard, touched by the boy's devotion and understanding of his sweet little dog. She took hold of the reins and set out across the meadow at a fast yet steady stride to ensure Pegasus gave the children and their pets as smooth a ride as possible.

After a short while of companionable silence, Connor asked, "Are you married?"

"I am not." Grace prayed the rumors about the boy's elder brother looking for a wife weren't true. Connor's question worried her. What was the child up to? "Are *you* married, Connor?"

"Of course not, silly. I am but seven years old."

"Did your parents not promise you to anyone when you were born?" Sissy asked her.

"No. My parents wanted me to marry a man that I loved—not someone that somebody else chose for me." Grace inwardly flinched, wondering if she ought not to have said that. "My mother and father loved each other very much. They want my sisters and I to enjoy that same happiness."

"Are they gone?" Connor asked quietly, echoing a maturity well beyond his years.

"Yes," Grace said. "They are together in heaven, watching over me and my sisters and probably shaking their heads at my brother."

"So you have not found anyone you love yet?" Conner asked, steering the conversation once more.

"No. Not yet." She hoped this particular discourse would not prove to be a problem.

"Wolfe got promised to Lady Margaret when he was our age," Sissy said. "She was nothing more than a baby at the time. When she smiles, she looks as though she's about to bite you."

"Her mother is worse," Connor said. "We call her Lady Longface. She looks like a horse."

"No offense, Pegasus," Sissy said with a pat to the thoroughbred's neck. "You are quite the handsome fellow."

Grace bit the inside of her cheek to keep from laughing. This conversation reminded her so very much of the chats she and her sisters often had. Once she was certain she had her mirth under control, she asked, "If your brother *got promised* when he was your age, when did he marry?"

"He has not married her yet," Sissy said. "We are doing our best to make sure that doesn't happen."

"Sissy! You can't tell a secret plan and expect it to work." Connor groaned, bemoaning his sister's inadequacies. "Why could my twin not have been a brother instead of a sister?"

"Connor." Grace used the same tone that Papa had always used when determined to make Chance feel guilty over his treatment of his sisters. "You and Sissy balance each other. Always remember, everything happens for a reason. The two of you are as you are because you are destined for greatness. Would you spoil that by wishing your sister away?"

"Lady Margaret says I am destined for boarding school and Sissy is going to be sent abroad to learn how to paint or dance or something."

The more Grace learned about Lady Margaret, the less she liked her, and what sort of person was Wolfebourne to agree to send his siblings away when it was more than obvious they needed their elder brother's love and care? For heaven's sake, the children were only seven years old.

"I don't want to go away," Sissy said, the tears back in her voice. "Wolfe was always so nice whenever he came to visit us before Father died."

"Is he not nice now?" Grace knew she shouldn't ask, but she

had to know. She had already heard quite a bit about the children's lives that she didn't like. If there was more, she might have a word with Chance about confronting the Duke of Wolfebourne about his behavior. Papa had done that once at Mama's insistence after they had discovered a peer mistreating a child. It had sent ripples of shock through the *ton*, but Mama and Papa hadn't cared, and the little girl they had rescued from the cruel guardian's clutches, married now with children of her own, still sent letters singing Mama and Papa's praises.

Grace slowed her pace and glanced back at the children. "Is your brother not nice to you?"

"He is nice whenever he is with us," Sissy said. "But he says he knows nothing about being a father. Which I guess being our guardian makes him. I think he likes us still—just maybe not as much as before Father died and left us hanging around his neck. That is what our first governess told us."

Grace wished she could hunt down those heartless women and scratch out their eyes. How could they say such hurtful things to these two?

Movement just above the tops of the tall, swaying grasses farther across the meadow caught her attention, making her squint to sort out what it was. She prayed it was nothing more than a deer having a good stretch of its legs. They were on Wolfebourne property now, and this particular bit of land was an undulating length of dips and rises. The small hills and valleys, paired with the tall grass, repeatedly hid, then revealed, whatever was coming toward them. The source of the movement topped a hill again. It was not a deer.

"Drat." Grace adjusted her hat, making certain her hair was well tucked up inside it.

The rider headed their way was a man—a man the size of a freestanding continent—and he urged his equally enormous mount into a hard gallop as if the hounds of hell chased after them. The gleaming ebony shire stretched out its long legs, its nostrils flaring, its mane whipping in the wind.

"We are in trouble again, Connor," Sissy said with a resigned sigh.

"And brother looks even angrier than usual," Connor added with a low groan.

Grace resettled her footing and braced herself. So the beast of a man headed their way was none other than the Duke of Wolfebourne. Good heavens, had his ancestors descended from bears? She supposed he could be considered handsome in a dark, dangerous sort of way. She almost smiled, remembering one of her sister Fortuity's stories about the devil taking the form of a stunning man to successfully seduce the maidens. The duke's black hair was a tad overlong for the style of the day, and the streaks of gray glinting like silver at his temples surprised her. She wanted to ask the children how old he was, but he was nearly upon them.

"Sissy! Connor! Where the devil have you been?" He leapt from the saddle before his horse came to a full stop.

"Poor Hector hurt his leg," Sissy said.

"Gray helped us," Connor told his brother. "Bandaged his leg and everything."

As dark and glowering as a building storm, the duke bore down on Grace as if ready to break her in two. "I assume you are Gray?"

To protect Connor's well-intentioned lie, Grace pulled her cap lower over her eyes and did her best to adopt the accent and mannerisms of one of the stable lads back at their townhouse in London. "I helped the children's pup, if that be what you be asking. The wee one will be all right. Just a bit of a cut on his foreleg. Used some balm to take care of it." She tucked her hands behind her back. A stable lad would not have her long, feminine fingers, nor would his hands be clean and lack calluses.

"Where did you find them?" The man's dark eyes flashed with suspicion and the line of his square jaw hardened.

"Find them?" She tried to keep her head tilted so he couldn't see her face, making a show of shuffling her feet and glancing away.

"Yes. It is not a difficult question," he said with a low growl that reminded her of an animal caught in a snare. "Where did you come upon them?"

Grace tossed a nod and a vague flick of her hand at the land behind them. "Just over there a ways. Not far from here."

"So you admit to trespassing on my property?"

She bit her tongue to keep from giving this ridiculous man the comeuppance he deserved. "I heard them crying. Would you have me ignore a child what might be hurt?" *Drat!* She had forgotten to maintain the accent.

"Do you know who I am?"

Grace really didn't care who he was because her family was his equal—in her opinion, even better. But she couldn't let him know that or her buckskins would be in the dustbin, and Connor would be in even more trouble for lying.

She shrugged. "Can't say that I do."

"I am the Duke of Wolfebourne, owner of the land on which you are trespassing."

"But brother…" Connor said, but the duke silenced him with a glance.

Even though she would rather spit on his well-polished boots, Grace gave the surly man an elaborate bow. "Pleased to meet you, Your Grace."

"It is customary for servants to remove their hats when in the presence of their betters."

Well, fine. Dustbin or not. She had enjoyed enough of this insolent fool. *Presence of their betters.* Indeed. No one deserved to be talked down to in such a way, no matter their station in life.

Grace whipped off her hat and let her long blonde braid fall down her back as she charged forward. "It is also customary for a gentleman to treat his siblings with the love and care they deserve, Your Grace!"

Unable to control herself now that she had unleashed her demons, she thumped him in the center of his broad chest, a thrilling surge of victory rushing through her as he backed up a step. "Did you ever think they might like for you to embrace them in relief that you found them unharmed? Did you think to check on their poor little dog? Show your concern for him, for their sake? Did you ever think to help them down from the horse and praise them for watching over their animals rather than deserting them out of fear that you might be angry if they were late for tea?"

His disbelief and shock silenced him, granting her the satisfaction she sought and goading her onward. "No. Of course you did not, because you are a high and mighty duke who can't be bothered to care about his own brother and sister." She went to Pegasus, helped the children down, then handed Galileo to Sissy. "It was a pleasure meeting you both," she told them. After vaulting up into the saddle, she glared down at the duke still standing with his mouth ajar. "It was not a pleasure meeting you, Your Grace." She rounded the horse and headed toward home at a proud, steady trot meant to display that she never ran away from anything.

"Wait!" Wolfebourne's bellow echoed across the land like thunder.

Grace snorted. The fool had found his tongue. She reined in Pegasus and deigned to spare him a look. "What?"

"Who the devil *are* you?"

"I am Lady Grace Abarough, sister to the fifth Duke of Broadmere." She pointed at him. "And do not dare scold Connor for telling you my name was Gray. He and I had an agreement, and he was doing his best to abide by it. At least your brother has a sense of honor. I can't imagine where he learned it from, since you appear to have none."

"A sense of honor?" Wolfebourne charged toward her, his long-legged stride rapidly closing the distance between them. "You speak of honor, and yet you lie and pretend to be something you are not?"

He had a point, but she wasn't about to give it to him. "I speak of the honor of loyalty, love, and caring. Of chivalry and courage. Things Connor and Sissy know all about, but apparently your education sorely fell short when it came to such attributes."

"I will be speaking to your brother, my lady."

The duke's face had gone quite red with his fury, but Grace had to admit he wore the color well. It made her decide that if he had been a better-hearted man, she would indeed describe him as handsome. "I had no doubt that you would, Your Grace. After all, you have no honor and appear to be the spiteful, petty sort incapable of handling his own arguments. A pity you are so weak that you can't even deal directly with a woman—you have to strike back through another man!"

His ever-deepening shock made her laugh. She couldn't help it.

With a sweeping salute of her cap, she tipped her head to him again. "Good day to you, Your Grace. Happy tattling to my brother!"

— ❧ —

Chapter Three

ROMULUS "WOLFE" CRAIGSTON, the Duke of Wolfebourne, stared after the most infuriating…the most presumptuous… Damned if he could even come up with a suitable word to describe her. "Who the devil does that woman think she is?"

"She told you who she was," Connor said, "and when I get old enough, I intend to marry her. She is beyond compare."

Wolfe swung about but caught himself before stinging his little brother with an acerbic retort the child did not deserve. He pointed to the south, the direction of Wolfebourne Lodge. "Start walking. I am most displeased with the two of you—yet again. You could have been injured or kidnapped and no one would have been any the wiser. Where the bloody hell have you been, and how did you escape Miss Hannah this time?"

"Miss Hannah said we could play in the garden since we did our lessons so nice," Sissy said.

"This is not the garden, Sissy." He walked along beside them, leading his horse. "Connor?"

"What?" The lad trudged along, clutching his trembling pup to his chest.

Wolfe eyed his brother, taking in the boy's stubbornness and bravado. His sister was much the same. The children were indeed a pair of unrepentant little terrors, but they had been through so much, abandoned by their mother, and tormented by terrible nannies and governesses. Wolfe was at his wits' end with the precious siblings his father had left in his care. He had sorely failed the cast-aside mites he had always adored.

But they had certainly taken to the scandalous Lady Grace, and she had taken to them, defending them as if they were her own. Maybe the woman wasn't so infuriating after all. Wolfe allowed himself a sigh as heavy as his heart. "Mr. George can have a look at Hector's leg and ensure he heals properly. What happened to him?"

Connor sniffed and wiped his nose on his sleeve. "A rabbit tricked him and he got him all tangled up in a snarl of woodbine. If Grace hadn't come along and cut him free, I don't know what we would have done."

"*Lady* Grace," Wolfe corrected him. "She should be addressed as such."

"She told us we could call her Grace," Sissy said, "and I told her she could call me Sissy."

Wolfe deflated with a weary groan, too exhausted to argue. The fear that the children had come to some horrible end when they could not be found had raged through him and worn him down as if he were poorly forged metal against a grindstone. "I am sure she meant you could call her Grace in informal settings. If we happen to come upon her in the village or at gatherings, it is more respectful to address her as *Lady* Grace. It would make her more comfortable."

With a thoughtful nod, Connor gave his sister one of the looks the twins often shared. Wolfe had decided long ago it was their own secret language. "We should make her comfortable, Sissy. After all, she is going to be my wife." Connor turned back to Wolfe. "How long must I wait to marry?"

"You have many years before you should marry. Look at me. I am six and thirty, and I have yet to marry." Wolfe tousled the boy's ink-black hair that matched his own. Raven hair and sooty eyes marked all the Wolfebournes. "How many years until you are six and thirty?"

"Stop trying to trick me into doing sums," Connor retorted.

"Nine and twenty," Sissy supplied for him, always ready to help her twin.

Connor groaned, then frowned up at Wolfe. "Not everyone waits until they are as old as you to marry. How 'bout when I am ten?"

"Ten is not old enough," Sissy told him before Wolfe could answer. "You need to wait until you are taller than her. That way the two of you will look nice whenever you stand together."

"I could be taller than her by ten." Connor tipped a decisive nod. "Father said I would prolly be just like him and Wolfe—big and tall."

"Before we decide when you shall marry," Wolfe said before the conversation devolved any further, "there is the matter of your punishment for disobeying Miss Hannah and leaving the confines of the garden. The entire household turned the place upside down because we could not find you. We were all worried you had come to some sort of harm."

"No one worries about us," Connor said, portraying a disturbing lack of emotion that broke Wolfe's heart. Was that how the child truly felt?

"That's what makes it so easy to slip away," Sissy added, confirming Wolfe's fears.

He halted and knelt in front of the children, taking them each by the shoulder. "I worry about you. You are my only family. My brother and sister. I would be overwrought if anything were to happen to you." He stared into their dark eyes that mirrored his own, wishing he knew how to be a good father to them rather than a bumbling guardian that had, so far, failed them miserably. "I know I have chosen poorly when it comes to nannies and governesses—"

"Father chose the nannies poorly," Connor said, without a qualm about interrupting. "You just got tricked into bringing on the wrong governesses."

Wolfe narrowed his eyes at the child, waiting for the boy to realize he had been rude.

"You interrupted," Sissy whispered loudly with her hand cupped to her mouth, aiming the sound advice at her brother's ear. "Say sorry."

"Sorry." But the lad didn't sound as if he meant it.

"What am I going to do with you two?" Wolfe slowly shook his head, wishing the children knew how much he cared about them.

"Give us to Grace," Sissy said, sounding entirely too excited about that plan.

Connor gave him a solid nod. "Grace would take us. She likes us. You heard her say so—did you not?"

Wolfe let his hands drop from their shoulders but remained crouched at their level, even though the scarred knee he'd injured in the war ached like the dickens. "You think I do not like you?"

They both frowned at him, as if seeing him for the first time.

"You like us," Susannah finally said, "but we are a bovver to you. All the nannies and governesses said so, and so did Lady Longface. We heard her once when we hid behind the tea cart in the parlor, and she didn't know we was there."

Wolfe clenched his teeth to keep from laughing at his little sister's apt description of his fiancée's mother. Lady Euphemia Longmorten did indeed have the face of a mule. "Sissy—would you care to restate that in more polite terms?"

The child rolled her eyes. "Lady *Longmorten* said we was a bovver to you too."

While he had no doubt the spiteful woman had said such a thing, it would not be prudent to fuel the children's low opinion of his future mother-in-law.

He almost shuddered at the thought of *that.* Lady Long-morten was one of the many reasons he had yet to find the inclination to formalize the union his father had arranged when Wolfe was just a little older than Connor, and Lady Margaret, his affianced, was still a babe. At present, he would rather walk straight through the doors of hell than to the wedding altar.

"The two of you are not a bother to me," he said, "and we do not place store in the idle gossip of those who do not matter. The unacceptable nannies and governesses were all dismissed because of their dreadful behavior."

Connor gave him a sly grin. "You do not like her either, do you?"

"Whom?"

"Lady Longface."

"Connor."

The boy resettled his grip on Hector, who was now sleeping soundly in his arms with his muzzle propped on the lad's shoulder. "Fine. Lady Longmorten."

"She is an upstanding woman of Society." Wolfe almost choked on the words, but it was best that he not encourage the children's unruliness—no matter how accurate they might be.

"That does not mean you like her," Connor said. "Grace's mother is already in heaven. I won't have the problem of an old woman being rude to me when I marry Grace."

Wolfe rose to his feet before his knee grew so stiff that he couldn't walk. "How do you know Lady Grace's mother is already in heaven?" Although he vaguely remembered talk of the Broadmeres' losses. Apparently, the children had enjoyed quite the visit while Lady Grace was rescuing Hector.

"She told us when we asked her whether or not she was married, and how come she was wearing those clothes," Sissy said. "She said her papa always let her wear them as long as nobody saw her, and that her brother would be mad if he found out we had seen her. That is why we agreed not to tell as long as she didn't tell you—" The little girl clamped her mouth shut, and Conner groaned.

"As long as she did not tell me what?" Wolfe braced himself, wondering what else his siblings had done while adventuring with their dog and cat.

Sissy set Galileo on the ground, but rather than bound off, the cat sat in front of her as though guarding her. "As long as she did not tell you where she found us."

"So she lied to me about where you were?" Wolfe decided then and there that he would be having a stern conversation with Lady Grace rather than her brother. Especially since she had accused him of being too cowardly to deal with her directly. "Where were you? The truth, if you please."

"On Broadmere land," Connor said quietly. "It was my fault. I couldn't stop Hector from chasing after that rabbit."

"I see." Damned if Wolfe didn't owe the woman an apology for accusing her of trespassing when his own siblings had been the ones to ignore proper decorum. "Is there anything else I should know?"

"She said her parents never promised her to anyone when she was a baby because they wanted her to marry someone she loved," Sissy said. "She said her mama and papa loved each other very much and wanted the same for her. She said they watch over her from heaven."

"I love her," Connor said, "and I think she likes me well enough. Maybe she could love me too. I am going to marry her."

"Yes, Connor. You have made that abundantly clear." Wolfe stanched a groan and continued their plodding walk.

"I think we should go visit them," Sissy said. "They are our neighbors."

"But we can't talk about today during that visit." Connor gently nudged his sister as they walked side by side. "Then her brother would know we saw her in those clothes. We would have to act like we just met her and talk about something else." He looked up at Wolfe. "What could we talk about? People sound foolish when they always talk about the weather. It's either raining or not. Hot or cold. What difference does it make about the weather? And you are not going to tell her brother you saw her, are you? She helped us, and it would be rude to get her in trouble after she helped us."

"Yes, brother," Sissy chimed in, "quite rude and ungrateful."

Wolfe scrubbed a hand across his face and rubbed his tired eyes. Gads, these two would be the death of him. They had not even been punished for this latest adventure and were already plotting their next one. At least this time they had decided to include him. "I will not mention her manner of dress if and when I ever speak to her brother."

"If and when?" Connor stared at him in horror. "We have to visit them—or would you rather me and Sissy go alone, since Grace put you in your place?"

"Grace—Lady Grace—did not put me in my place. And you will not go anywhere without the proper supervision of either myself or someone from the household that I have assigned to watch over you. Is that understood?"

The children shared one of the secretive looks, then replied in unison, "Yes, brother."

Wolfe had no doubt they would plot a visit to the Broadmeres at their first opportunity and preferably engage in that visit without any supervision.

As they descended the last gently rolling hill, he pointed out the flurry of activity around Wolfebourne Lodge, the stables, the dovecote, and the other small buildings. "You see? Everyone is still searching for you."

"How did you know where to look?" Connor asked.

"I didn't. I intended to ride across every inch of the estate until I found you."

"Sorry," Connor said. This time the child sounded as if he meant it. "But I couldn't let Hector go off on his own. He would have never found his way back."

"And Galileo and I had to help," Sissy said. "He guarded us while we tried to get Hector loose before Grace—I mean *Lady Grace*—came along."

"There is Miss Hannah," Wolfe said, needing a stout drink and his comfortable chair in the quiet of the library before he sorted through this latest uproar any further. "Go to her. I shall decide your punishment and inform you of your fate before you have your dinner."

"We still get our dinner?" Connor brightened. "Good. 'Cause

I bet Miss Hannah will tell us we can't have our tea."

"You will have your tea. Tell her if she has any doubt about that to see me." Wolfe did not believe a child should be denied food or drink for poor behavior. He preferred they work off their punishment by cleaning stalls in the stable, scrubbing floors, or emptying chamber pots. That not only punished them but gave them an awareness of the unpleasantness servants dealt with every day. "Off with you now, and you may also inform her that Mr. George is to see to Hector's leg."

Connor tromped through the tangle of meadow grass until he stood in front of Wolfe and looked up at him. "Thank you, brother, and me and Sissy are sorry for running off and making everyone look for us. But you see now it was 'cause we had to help Hector and not 'cause we was just trying to be bad. You see that, right?"

Sissy moved to her twin's side, staring up at Wolfe with her big, imploring eyes that always twisted his gut and made him feel guilty about not being a better guardian. "We didn't mean to disobey Miss Hannah. It just sort of happened."

Before Wolfe could respond, Miss Hannah reached them. "Lord Connor! Lady Susannah! Shame on you both for giving me such a fright. I told you to stay in the garden. Did I not?" She dropped a quick curtsy to Wolfe and kept her gaze lowered. "To their beds without their tea and dinner, Your Grace?"

"No." Wolfe scrubbed a hand across his face again, at a complete loss when it came to being a proper guardian—especially when his siblings were so convinced that their existence mattered to no one but themselves. Lady Grace's admiration of the children's loyalty and courage regarding their animals came to mind as he noticed his little brother and sister holding their pets as if ready to defend them to the death. Such loyalty and courage were indeed admirable qualities. "They are to have their tea and their dinner, and also inform Mr. George to have a look at Hector's leg. It appears to be injured. Galileo will also be needing a saucer of cream. I am sure he is hungry after his adventure."

Her ruffled white cap askew, the young maid stared downward while wringing her hands. "Am I to be dismissed, then, Your Grace?"

Wolfe studied the woman the children seemed to tolerate better than any of the others who had attempted to manage them. She had never been cruel, nor had she ever taken it upon herself to fill their heads with hurtful opinions that would make them think themselves any more unwanted than they already felt they were. After so much trouble with the last governess, he had repeatedly asked Connor and Sissy about Miss Hannah's treatment of them. They always told him she was fair and reliable—she just never exhibited any emotions toward them. It was as if they were expensive trinkets she had been charged to guard and keep well dusted. At least, that was what Sissy had told him, and Connor had nodded his agreement.

"You are not to be dismissed," Wolfe told the nervous maid. "See to the children's tea and ensure Mr. George aids Hector, as I instructed."

Miss Hannah curtsied again. "Thank you, Your Grace. I will." Still unsmiling but not in an unkind way, she shooed the children toward the main house.

Wolfe had taken naught but a few steps farther before a stable lad met him and took possession of his mount. His horse, loyal Tenebrae, so titled with the Latin word for darkness because of the gleaming blackness of his coat, planted his enormous feet and refused to move until Wolfe nodded permission.

Buoyed by the horse's devotion, Wolfe's spirits fell as he turned toward the house and spied the tall, bony-faced Lady Longmorten headed his way. He had often wondered if the matron's disposition would improve if she ate more—or ate at all, for that matter. All he ever recalled her doing at meals was picking at her food and rearranging it on her plate. As far as he had noticed, she never actually consumed anything.

"Your Grace," she said with her usual shrillness that always triggered the same unpleasantness as metal scraping against stone. "I just passed Lady Susannah. The girl has completely ruined her gown. I am sure those rips can't be repaired. The embroidery along the hemline is frayed beyond all recognition, and that muslin shall never be white again with all those grass stains."

His ability to be civil had worn dangerously thin, so he drew in a deep breath through his nose, held it for a long moment, then whistled it out through his clenched teeth. "Lady Longmorten, it appears you are more concerned about my sister's wardrobe than her wellbeing. Might I inquire as to why?"

Mouth agape, the woman stared at him as if he were the devil himself—which lifted his spirits considerably. Perhaps he should practice curtness toward the dowager countess more often.

"My concern for the child is all encompassing," she finally said, her pale blue eyes snapping. "I could plainly see she was unharmed even though the same could not be said for her attire." She marched forward with the stomping grace of an angry bull about to charge. "Lady Susannah's future would be better served traveling abroad with my cousin, the one I spoke to you about. Lady Gransorrie would see to her proper training and return her to you as she should be."

"Both my sister and brother are exactly as they *should be*." Wolfe advanced on her, forcing her to retreat several steps. "While you and Lady Margaret are welcome guests, your advice is not. How I see fit to care for my only remaining family is no one's affair but my own. Is that understood, Lady Longmorten?"

The dowager jutted her long, angular chin even higher. "While my daughter is not yet your wife, Your Grace, she has been a promised member of your family since she was born. My advice is not ill-intentioned but rendered for the benefit of all. I feel certain Lady Susannah would come to thank me someday."

Wolfe forced a polite bow. "This conversation, along with my patience, has reached its end, Lady Longmorten. I shall see you and Lady Margaret at dinner—and not before, if either of you value your sensibilities."

He strode past her, allowing himself a faint smile when she fired an indignant huff after him. The insufferable woman should be thankful he had reined in the inclination to suggest that she and her daughter were more than welcome to take rooms at the local inn rather than remain guests at Wolfebourne Lodge. In fact, he would gladly pay for the length of their stay. The coin it would cost him would be a great deal less painful than their presence in his home.

Gads, he should have told her every bit of that. He berated himself for allowing that opportunity to slip through his fingers. The moment was past.

By the time he reached the library, his jaws ached from clenching his teeth, a habit that had become more prevalent the longer he found himself in the company of the two Longmorten women. He realized his father had initiated the childhood engagement because an astonishingly impressive dowry that included a great deal of land came along with Lady Margaret. But, gads alive, Wolfe wished his sire had allowed him to find his own wife. He couldn't help but wonder how Lady Margaret's father, an earl known to frequent the gaming hells, had managed to set aside such a sizeable amount for his only child and not gambled it away. But Wolfe's solicitor and banker had assured him the funds were there along with the deeds to the land.

And he didn't deny the dowry had its appeal, but unfortunately, Lady Margaret did not. The young woman was the spitting image of her mother and always looked ready to bite someone whenever she smiled. If she someday sprouted fangs, Wolfe would not be surprised in the least.

Currently, she exhibited a somewhat more pleasing demeanor than her mother, but it was feigned. The lady fawned all over him as if he had descended from the very gods themselves. But occasionally, her true nature reared its ugly, spiteful head, and she had to hurry to tamp it back down.

An involuntary shudder swept through him. He was well and truly trapped, since men were bound by their word, even though that word was his father's. Lady Margaret and her mother would not hesitate to sue him for breach of promise were he to break the engagement, and he refused to allow such damage not only to his reputation but to the Wolfebourne estate.

As soon as he stepped into his almost cavelike library, perfumed with the comforting scents of books, the finest pipe tobacco, and rich leather upholstery, his tension melted away, enabling him to breathe easy again. First and foremost, his priority was seeing to his brother and sister. With any luck, Lady Margaret and her mother would tire of waiting for wedding bells and break off the engagement themselves. After all, it was seen as more acceptable if the woman ended the agreement. He just wished they hadn't invited themselves to join him for a few weeks in the country. Hopefully, they would soon grow bored with that and either return to London or their own country estate, which was much farther—a great deal farther—to the southeast.

Just as he settled into the depths of his favorite chair, reveling in the welcoming creak and groan of its lush, leathery depths, a tap on the door delayed his first sip of whisky—his preferred drink to relax ever since the war. A second tap quickly followed the first, making him narrow his eyes at the offending portal of dark mahogany. Whomever it was had best have good reason for encroaching upon his lair. "Enter!"

The tall door creaked open, revealing Feebson, Wolfebourne Lodge's wiry little butler. "The Marquess of Strathyre is in the parlor, Your Grace. Are you receiving, since Lord Connor and Lady Susannah are safely recovered?"

The servant made the twins sound like rare jewels that had been lost and then found. Wolfe gave a wry snort. Perhaps that description was not so far off the mark. "Bring his lordship in here, Feebson. I am not inclined to move now that I am comfortable."

Feebson, who had always reminded Wolfe of a devoted rat terrier, tiny yet mighty, offered a concerned nod. "Shall I also inform Mrs. Havarerry to ready a warming poultice for your knee, Your Grace? One that could be applied directly after dinner, perhaps?"

A poultice for his knee would be the perfect excuse to avoid Lady Margaret's abuse of the pianoforte after dinner. "Thank you, Feebson, I would indeed find that remedy most welcome this evening."

"Very good, Your Grace. I shall return presently with Lord Strathyre." The man backed out of the room and softly closed the door.

Within moments, the door flew open again, and in strode Gregson "Strath" MacStrath, Marquess of Strathyre, and one of Wolfe's closest friends. "Knee paining ye again? Heard yer wee guard dog ordering a poultice from Mrs. Havarerry."

"You always did have the hearing of an owl." Wolfe pointed his whisky glass at the cabinet in the corner. "Help yourself. As I told Feebson, now that I am comfortable, I am not inclined to move."

"What have the bairns done now? Ye have that look about ye." The barrel-chested Scot swaggered over to the cabinet, poured himself a drink, then hoisted the bottle higher and waited.

Wolfe shook his head. As much as he would enjoy a second drink, it would be better for all concerned if he limited himself to savoring no more than one. "They slipped away from their maid—yet again. Trespassed onto Broadmere land, supposedly in chase of Connor's dog that was after a wily hare. Said hare proceeded to lead the dog into a snare of woodbine, and if not for the Duke of Broadmere's sharp-tongued sister, they would probably still be sitting in that thicket."

Strath settled into an equally sumptuous leather chair and leaned forward with his forearms propped on his knees. "Are ye saying the woman ran them off her brother's land? They're naught but children. What harm could they do?"

"She did not run them off their land. She rescued the pup and brought them home, placing not only Connor and Sissy on the back of her horse but the dog and that infernal cat too." Wolfe bit his tongue to keep from describing her scandalous clothing. After all, it was important to Connor that the lady not be outed to her brother or anyone else.

Strath grinned and waggled a bushy blond brow. "My Sarah will be inviting her over for tea when I tell her this tale. Which sister are we speaking of? 'Tis my understanding Broadmere Manor possesses a bevy of them. Although I think two are married now, with homes of their own."

"I doubt this one is married. She was…" Wolfe clenched his teeth again, frustrated at the inexplicable hope in his heart that Lady Grace was *not* married. Why the devil would he even wander down that path?

"She was *what?*" Mischief danced in Strath's eyes. "Ye said she was sharp-tongued. Did the lass get the better of ye, then?"

"No one gets the better of me," Wolfe said. "No one." But this woman had—in a way he couldn't get out of his mind. "But Lady Grace did win Connor's heart. He swears he is going to marry her."

Strath shook his head and held up his glass as if offering a toast. "Dinna do that to the lad. Look at the misery your father wrought on ye with such an arrangement."

"I would never put Connor through such misery. Although I doubt it would be in the case of Lady Grace."

"Really now?" Strath grinned. "Sounds as if she not only got the better of ye but caught yer eye as well."

Wolfe snorted but didn't acknowledge that remark with a response. He sipped his drink and held the rich liquid on his tongue before sending the burn down his gullet, along with his regret at not being free. His little brother had no idea how fortunate he was. Not only could Connor go his own way in life, he could choose the woman he wished to take along with him.

Chapter Four

"YOU DON'T FEEL the slightest bit guilty about leaving Merry and Felicity behind to deal with Seri's impossible state? Her planning of the annual Broadmere picnic borders on the irrational. You know that."

Grace couldn't resist giving her sister Joy a wicked smile. "Do you feel any guilt?"

Joy returned an equally mischievous grin. "Well, no. Now that you mention it. I do not possess the slightest twinge."

"It is a glorious day for a stroll to the village," Grace said. "Besides, Seri mentioned we needed to find a few extra trinkets for the nursery. We can take that worry from her long list of tasks yet to be done. After all, we can't have little Rorie and Quill thinking we've forgotten them in the flurry of the picnic festivities."

"Blessing and Fortuity have already accused us of overindulging our little niece and nephew." Joy twirled her bright yellow parasol that rested on her shoulder. "But with Rorie just over a year old and Quill barely two months of age, I find that accusation unfounded. Don't you?"

"Most definitely." Grace swung her parasol at her side, tapping the ground with its tip as though it were a cane. She hated the silly thing and adored the warmth of the sun on her face. Who cared if she got freckles? Sunshine made her feel alive.

"If you're not going to use your parasol, you had better pull your bonnet forward to shade your face," Joy said. "Seri nearly had an attack of apoplexy when you came in from your ride the other day with your face red as a beetroot."

Her face had been red as a beetroot because of her encounter with the Duke of Wolfebourne, but Grace wasn't about to share that bit of *on dit* with Joy. None of her sisters could keep a secret. But Joy, in particular, tended to use any delicate information as leverage to force her sisters to cover for her so she could enjoy the gaming tables during parties instead of looking for a husband, as Chance had ordered them all to do.

Grace tugged the brim of her cornflower-blue bonnet forward. It matched the embroidered flowers bordering the empire waist of her white muslin, the trim around her sleeves, and the wrists of her gloves. Her parasol and reticule were also the same shade as freshly bloomed cornflowers. Serendipity had informed her that the ensemble brought out the blue in her eyes and complemented her golden hair.

Grace snorted. What a load of stuff and nonsense. She looked the way she looked and no shade of blue or amount of frippery would change that.

"There. I am quite shaded now. Happy?"

"Don't be fractious with me." Joy ran her hand across the tops of the wild forget-me-nots blooming alongside the hard-packed dirt road. "These are so pretty. We should pick some on the way back for the entry hall vases."

"Are you forgetting dear Seri's orders as we walked out the door?"

"Ah, yes." Joy tucked her hand away from the flowers. *"Do not stain your gloves,"* she said, mimicking their eldest sister perfectly.

"It must be so tiring to be Serendipity." Grace almost felt sorry for her sister. She realized Serendipity's mother-henning came from a place of love and a deathbed promise to their mother. But sometimes the eldest sister carried it a bit too far. "She needs to realize that perfection is often not worth the cost."

"She will," Joy said. "Someday." As they reached the village, she perked like one of Grace's foxhounds. "Look there. It appears our neighbors decided to visit the shops today too, but they brought their carriage. I wonder if we'll catch sight of the duke's affianced. That is the Wolfebourne crest, isn't it? Maybe we shall finally set eyes on the Duke of Wolfebourne too. It is said he is quite the beast—both in size and temperament."

"Really?" Grace said after swallowing hard to ensure her voice remained steady. "I had not heard that about the man." Heaven help her if it was the duke and not his houseguests.

The insignia of a silver shield with a pair of wolves—one black, one red, facing each other with their noses pointed up to the heavens in what appeared to be a mutual howl—was most definitely the Wolfebourne crest.

Another gut-wrenching surge of irritation, dread, and inexplicable excitement flashed through Grace with a fury, threatening to render her speechless.

"You've gone all red in the face again," Joy told her. "Are you feeling unwell?"

"I am fine." Grace coughed as though she'd choked on something in the air and jutted her chin to a defensive angle. "Your face is pinking a bit too. I am sure it is nothing more than our brisk walk. London's stale air kept us from exerting ourselves properly. We must take more strolls to improve our endurance and health."

Joy narrowed her eyes. Rarely did anything slip past her. "Stay away from the card tables, sister. Your words say one thing, but your face says quite another."

Grace ignored her and increased their already spirited pace. "Shall we try Mettlestone's for baubles for the children? Their shop rarely disappoints."

"Even if we don't find anything that suits, it would be rude not to stop in and visit with Mr. Herbert and Mrs. Beatrice. We haven't seen them since last summer."

Grace quite agreed. All the sisters loved Mr. and Mrs. Mettlestone, better known as Mr. Herbert and Mrs. Beatrice. The shopkeepers were always such a joy.

As soon as the bell above the door merrily jangled at their entrance, a cheerful crow followed. "Mrs. Beatrice, come to the front! Lady Grace and Lady Joy are here!"

Grace gave Mr. Herbert a jaunty curtsy even though she knew that might make some frown. She didn't care. The dear old shopkeeper deserved every modicum of friendship and politeness. "Mr. Herbert! How are you, dear sir? Joy and I could not wait another day to come in for a visit."

The round little man's rosy cheeks plumped even more. Balding and possessing the sort of smile that made it impossible not to smile back at him, Mr. Herbert clapped his pudgy hands. "I am quite well, dear ladies, but not as well and lovely as the pair of you." He turned and peered over the tops of his wire-rimmed spectacles at the curtained-off doorway behind the counter. "Mrs. Beatrice! Come to the front, my darling! We have treasured guests." He turned back to them and lowered his voice. "Bless my dear wife's soul. I fear her ability to hear is becoming impaired, but please do not mention it."

Grace and Joy both shook their heads and pressed a finger to their lips. Mr. Herbert's confidence was safe with them.

An equally round, yet a tad shorter, and silvery-haired woman burst through the curtains of the doorway, paused a hairsbreadth of a moment, then gleefully clapped her hands. "Lady Grace! Lady Joy! I was hoping we would soon be blessed with a visit." She swatted her husband's shoulder. "Mr. Herbert! Why did you not tell me the ladies were here?"

He caught her hand and kissed it, then said with all seriousness, "Forgive me, my darling. I was so delighted to see the ladies that I simply forgot."

She forgave him with a loving smile and a touch of his cheek. "Not to worry, my dear one. Not to worry. The main thing is I know they are here now." As Mrs. Beatrice turned back to them, Grace held her breath to keep from laughing at Mr. Herbert wiping his brow with an exaggerated sweep of his hand and a comical wiggle of his head.

"And how is the rest of the family?" Mrs. Beatrice asked as she folded her hands atop the shelf of her plump middle.

"Of course, you knew Blessing and Fortuity are married now," Grace said, "but did Fortuity think to write and let you know about little Quill? He is just now two months old."

Mrs. Beatrice hurried over to a shelf and snatched down a book, beaming with happiness as she brought it forward. "Yes! When her latest novels arrived, she included a note that told us all about him, Master Quill Ravenglass. I adore that name." She hugged the book as if it were a babe. "And what about little Miss Aurora? Is she walking by now?"

"Almost," Joy said. "She loves to toddle around while holding on to your fingers."

"Any more banns to be read anytime soon?" Mr. Herbert asked with a waggle of his bushy brows. "By my count, there are still five sisters yet to marry."

"Much to Chance's disappointment—no." Grace glanced not once but twice out the large front shop window as a familiar figure, tall and dark, passed in front of it and approached the door. *Drat. Drat. Drat.* She was trapped more surely than poor Hector had been snarled in the woodbine. Heaven help her. The children were with him too.

The welcoming bell jangled, and the trio entered. The duke's broad shoulders filled the doorway, blocking any sunlight trying to enter with him. Or, at least, it seemed that way. Perhaps it was his black cutaway coat that made him appear so large, just as his buff pantaloons and tall, well-polished boots stressed his long legs. Young Connor wore identical dress, and little Sissy outshone them both in a soft pink confection with a matching bonnet.

Grace held her breath, praying the children wouldn't reveal they already knew her. She backed up a step without even realizing she did so.

Joy drew closer and whispered, "Is that—"

"Your Grace," Mrs. Beatrice said to the duke as she proffered the perfect curtsy. With a gracious wave of her hand, she motioned at Grace and Joy. "What auspicious timing—allow me to introduce you to Lady Grace and Lady Joy Abarough, sisters to the Duke of Broadmere and your neighbors to the north of your property."

Grace managed an awkward curtsy, noting that Joy did little better, since she appeared to be studying the man to report to the rest of their sisters once they returned home. Serendipity would be sorely put out that she had missed this meeting, as she prided herself on keeping up with the very latest *on dit*.

The duke removed his hat and returned a polite nod to them both. "A pleasure, ladies. Allow me to introduce you to Lord Connor and Lady Susannah, my brother and sister."

Impressive, Grace thought, somewhat amending her opinion of the odious duke. Perhaps he was not such an ogre after all. Few men would have bothered to introduce the children. She aimed a better curtsy at the young twins. "Lord Connor, Lady Susannah, it is a pleasure to meet you both."

Joy curtsied to them as well.

Connor squared his shoulders, marched forward, and took hold of Grace's gloved hand. "I am very happy to make your acquaintance, Lady Grace. Very happy indeed." The child held his gracious yet somber expression with admirable control, not giving away their prior meeting in any way.

Grace accepted his overture with a regal nod while stealing a glance at Sissy. The girl was just as well behaved. No one would ever guess about their adventurous first meeting. Upon returning her attention to the duke, Grace realized the recognition flashing in his dark eyes was not nearly as controlled. She immediately looked away, turning back to Mrs. Beatrice. "Do go ahead and take care of His Grace, since Joy and I are uncertain about what to get for Aurora and Quill."

"Yes, do," Joy said in a tone that alarmed Grace. Her sister had a nose for secrets, and she'd picked up on the scent. "We are more than happy to browse. You have so much from which to choose."

"We don't mind waiting," Connor said to Grace. "After all, you ladies were here first." He turned and shot a pointed look up at his brother. "Right, Wolfe?"

"Connor." The duke's tone spoke volumes, making Grace hold her breath to keep from laughing.

"No one need wait," Mr. Herbert announced. "Mrs. Beatrice can help the ladies, and I would be most pleased to assist you, Your Grace."

"Thank you, Mr. Mettlestone," the duke said, his discomfort with the entire situation unmistakable.

"Is something amiss, Your Grace?" Mrs. Beatrice toddled forward until she stood between him and Grace.

Grace turned away to grant the poor man a brief reprieve, making a show of examining a basket overflowing with hair ribbons.

"Sometimes, he is not always good at knowing what to say," Sissy announced to one and all. "But we are trying to help him overcome that."

"Susannah!" The duke retreated to the shop door, yanked it open, and pointed outside. "Into the carriage. Both of you. I shall join you once Mr. Mettlestone either confirms or denies your books have arrived. Any further outbursts, and we shall forgo our visit to the treat shop for ices. Understood?"

Grace's heart went out to the children as they trudged outside, their little shoulders sagging. "They meant no harm," she said before she could stop herself.

"Be that as it may…" The duke fixed her with the same scowl he'd gifted to her upon their first meeting, but this one seemed somehow softer, maybe even shaded with a little desperation. "They must learn that children are to be *seen*, not heard."

"I disagree." Grace rounded on him, moving a step closer. What was it about this man that made it impossible not to challenge him? "A child who is heard is a child who feels safe, secure, and loved."

He stared at her, the muscles flexing in his strong jaw. It was dusted with the seductive promise of a beard that would be just as dark as his hair if he ever went unshaven. His hard gaze poured over her, reaching into her soul and testing her worth. She would be lying if she said she didn't find it as thrilling as racing across an open meadow.

"Have you any children, Lady Grace?" he finally asked, his tone icy enough to cast a chill upon the warm summer's day.

"I do not, Your Grace. Have you?"

"I have my brother and sister—"

"Yet you imply that because *I* have no children of my own, only having siblings as you do, that any opinion I might possess on child rearing is sure to be inaccurate. Is that what you were about to say, Your Grace? I find that somewhat hypocritical."

The same lovely shade of ruddiness he had achieved a few days ago crept up his neck above the fine linen of his perfectly tied cravat. He opened his mouth, then snapped it shut, opened it yet again, then just as quickly closed it.

"You wished to say something else, Your Grace?" She knew she shouldn't taunt him, but doing so might just be worth the sacrifice of never wearing her adventuring clothes ever again. She just couldn't resist picking at him.

"Gracie!" Joy hissed from behind her. "Have pity on the poor man or Chance will give us no peace whatsoever. You know they always stick together," she added in a loud whisper.

"Lady Grace," Mr. Herbert said, hovering like an anxious butterfly while poor Mrs. Beatrice leaned in, straining to hear what everyone was saying. "Might I interest you in some of our new banners? I am sure Lady Serendipity would find them most lovely for picnic decorations."

Perhaps Grace had pushed the duke a little too hard. One look at Joy warned her that there would be a great deal of explaining to do during the walk home. *Lovely*. That would give her sister enough ammunition to extort whatever she wanted for the rest of the summer.

Grace offered the uncomfortably silent duke a conciliatory curtsy. "Good day, Your Grace." She turned to Joy. "Come, sister. Let us leave His Grace to complete his shopping in peace. We have days before Aurora and Quill arrive. Plenty of time to find suitable baubles to entertain them." She tossed a smile and a wave back at Mr. Herbert and Mrs. Beatrice. "Do send the banners to Serendipity. That will be one less worry for her. We shall return another day for Aurora and Quill's baubles. Good day, dear friends!" Then she swept outside and lifted her face to the wind, hoping it would cool her cheeks.

"Tell me immediately," Joy demanded as soon as she caught up with her. "Every bit of it. Now."

SHE HAD MADE him look the fool. Again. Wolfe stared at the shop door, rooted to the spot like an infernal rabbit too terrified to move. He turned and glared at Mr. and Mrs. Mettlestone, witnesses to his shame. "By damn, this is the last time I allow that woman to get the better of me."

Mr. Mettlestone appeared both apologetic and confused, as did his wife, even though the poor woman probably hadn't heard half of what had been said. "Beg pardon, Your Grace?"

"How long do the Broadmeres normally summer here? The entire parliamentary recess or merely a few weeks?"

The shopkeepers exchanged hesitant glances. "Before the fourth duke and his wife passed, they remained here in Binnocksbourne for the entirety of the recess, not returning to London until late fall," Mrs. Mettlestone said with a nervous shrug. "They so enjoyed the country. The lot of them did."

"And now?" Wolfe glanced out the shop window to ensure Connor and Sissy were still waiting in the carriage.

Mr. Mettlestone gave a quick shake of his head. "What with

the current duke anxious to marry all the sisters off, seems like their visits are sadly shorter each summer."

Mrs. Mettlestone waved both hands as if swatting at an onslaught of midges. "That is quite enough, Mr. Mettlestone. Gossip about true friends is poor behavior indeed." She forced a smile and a nod at the duke. "I fear your order has yet to come in, Your Grace. Surely the children's books will arrive by next week. Will there be anything else we can help you with today?"

Ignoring the obvious yet polite dismissal, Wolfe smiled. "Yes. What were the *baubles* Lady Grace mentioned she would be needing? For an Aurora and another person whose name I can't recall."

Mr. and Mrs. Mettlestone shared looks again, reminding Wolfe of how the twins communicated without speaking.

"Your Grace," Mr. Mettlestone began in an apologetic tone, "Lady Grace meant no harm. It comes from the way her parents indulged the sisters. They always speak their minds."

Mrs. Mettlestone hurried to bob her head in agreement. "Especially Lady Grace." She glanced back at the shop door and then all around as if they weren't the only ones in the place. "One might say she has always been a bit of a wild hoyden—but in a good way. Her heart is pure gold, and she would never bring dishonor down upon her family. She loves animals and the countryside better than any lady I have ever seen, and she always treats folks as fine as fine can be—no matter their station in life."

Wolfe refused to give way. "The baubles she was seeking, Mrs. Mettlestone?"

The pair of shopkeepers released a collective sigh.

"Trinkets for their niece Aurora and nephew Quill," Mrs. Mettlestone said. "The family always reunites for their annual picnic. This will be little Aurora's second, what with her being a year old and all. Precious Quill was just born this past April. It will be his first. In fact, I'd wager this will be his first outing since his christening and Lady Fortuity's churching."

Wolfe slowly prowled the circumference of the shop, critically examining each and every shelf while plotting his next move to put the audacious Lady Grace in her place and convince her he was not a man to be toyed with.

Running to her brother and tattling about her clothing in the meadow would be the action of a cowardly, powerless fool, and she knew it. But showering gifts upon her niece and nephew after her insulting behavior in the shop, and including a special gift just for her to remind her of her tenuous position due to her scandalous *adventuring* clothes, as Connor and Sissy had informed him they were called—now, *that* might be a well played move, indeed.

He pointed at a doll with a face embroidered with bright blue eyes and smiling red lips. Her hair was a cheerful yellow yarn plaited into braids on either side of her head. She was dressed in a muslin gown with a brilliant red ribbon tied around her waist. Her feet appeared to have been painted black to mimic shoes. "That one there, Mrs. Mettlestone. Suitable for a one-year-old? Sturdy enough so the child can enjoy it?"

The Mettlestones shared another of their meaningful looks, then Mrs. Mettlestone nodded as Mr. Mettlestone hurried to fetch the steps to reach the doll.

"And those toy soldiers." Wolfe wasn't sure what a babe in arms might enjoy, but the soldiers were colorful in their painted uniforms of red and gold, so they might catch the little one's attention.

"For Master Quill? Who is naught but a babe?" Mr. Mettlestone carefully handed the doll to Mrs. Mettlestone while keeping his focus locked on Wolfe.

"I can't very well send a gift to one without sending a gift to the other, now can I?" Wolfe dared the shopkeeper to argue.

"No, Your Grace. Of course not."

"And wrap a pair of buckskins in a fine length of dark blue silk," Wolfe added. A wickedly knowing smile came to him, and he fully embraced it. "Place them in a separate box all to themselves."

"A pair of buckskins?" Mr. Mettlestone repeated. "To be sent along with the doll and the soldiers?"

"Yes." Wolfe rubbed his hands together, envisioning the look on Lady Grace's face when that particular gift arrived along with the other two. "I want everything wrapped nicely in ribbons and bows, each in their own boxes, of course. Deliver them to Broadmere Manor with my felicitations for a happy summer holiday."

"How do we know what size buckskins to send?" Mrs. Mettlestone asked. "We shall have to get them from the tailor next door to send along with the toys. Do you wish a small pair for Master Quill for when he is old enough for breeches?"

"A bit larger than that. A pair that might fit a stable lad about this tall." Wolfe stretched out a hand to what he remembered as Lady Grace's exact height. "Slender, as well. After all, a stable lad is always quite fit."

And Lady Grace had indeed been quite fit in her buckskins. Never would he forget the shapeliness of her fine, round bottom as she had launched herself up into the saddle. The woman was the stuff of dreams—as well as nightmares. He cleared his throat and resettled his stance, forcing his thoughts back to the present, lest his body betray him with the arousal the memory invariably triggered.

"I would like the items delivered today, if at all possible."

"Of course, Your Grace." Mr. Mettlestone handed the toys to his wife. "We shall have them delivered before tea."

"Very good. I shall inform my man to come by and settle my account." As he reached the door, he paused. "And add the cost of the banners for Lady Grace's sister to my bill rather than the Broadmeres'. I insist."

"Yes, Your Grace." Mr. Mettlestone squinted over the tops of his spectacles and bowed. "Thank you for your kind patronage."

Wolfe touched the brim of his hat and exited, feeling a great deal better about the entire situation. What he wouldn't give to be an unseen observer when Lady Grace spied those buckskins.

He chuckled to himself.

"Your Grace! There you are."

The familiar voice made the hairs on his nape stand on end. With a heavy sigh, he turned and tipped a nod. "Lady Margaret. Lady Longmorten. Forgive me for missing you both at breakfast. The children and I had a prior commitment. I trust you had no issue with the instructions I left should you wish to leave the lodge. Did Mr. Kiddlington see to your needs?"

"Obviously." Lady Longmorten twitched with a haughty sniff and shot a side-eyed glance at the plain black carriage parked behind the one bearing the ducal seal. "We are here, are we not?"

"Now, Mother." Lady Margaret coyly batted her lashes and patted the light brown curls framing her face. "Do forgive her fractiousness, Your Grace. I fear Mother is not at her best today." She offered him an apologetic smile but sadly reminded him of a rabid dog baring its teeth. "You mentioned the children. Where are the little"—she wrinkled her nose as if smelling something foul—"the little mites?"

Wolfe clenched his teeth, taking umbrage at her tone. "In the carriage. They and I have a few remaining errands to complete before we return to the lodge."

"Mother and I would be most happy to join you."

A barely audible groan came from the carriage, making Wolfe clench his jaws even harder, this time to keep from laughing. Connor had obviously forgotten their discussion on how easily sound traveled.

"Good heavens." Lady Margaret recoiled, her disgust unmistakable. "Has one of them taken ill?"

"Quite possibly," Wolfe hurried to say, leaping on the opportunity to escape the women at least for a few more hours.

Lady Longmorten pressed a lacy handkerchief to her mouth. "We should carry on, Margaret. His Grace appears in fine fettle today. I am sure we will enjoy his company at tea *and* dinner. Will we not, Your Grace?"

"Of course, ladies." Wolfe forced a smile. There would be no escaping the duo now, no matter how much his knee or his need for peace might pain him. He touched the brim of his hat. "Until tea, then."

Both women curtsied and continued on their way.

As he climbed into the carriage, he released a low groan.

"Careful, brother," Sissy said in a loud whisper. "The ladies will hear."

"They heard you," he informed Connor.

"Sorry. It came out before I could stop it." The boy peeked out the window, then sagged back into the seat opposite Wolfe. "You are not going to make us come to tea with you, are you? Can we have it in the nursery like usual? We could eat dinner in the nursery too, if you wanted."

Wolfe resettled himself more comfortably before rapping on the ceiling for the driver to continue on to the treat shop. "You must come to dinner in the dining room as usual, but you may escape and have tea in the nursery as long as you both promise to better monitor what you say in the future. Just because you think it, does not mean it should be said. Try to sort out how it will be perceived and affect others before you speak."

"We made you look poorly back in the shop, didn't we?" Sissy scooted closer and rested her head against his shoulder. "I am sorry, brother. Please don't listen to Lady Longmorten and send us away."

Wolfe's heart twisted and dropped to the pit of his stomach. "I have no intention of sending either of you away, but I do need you both to do a better job of cooperating. Work with me rather than against me." Perhaps if he recruited them rather than continue to bend them to Society's mold, they would all be happier. The manner with which young Connor kept eyeing him gave him pause. "What are you plotting?"

The boy drew himself up as if insulted. "Just 'cause I was studying you, does not mean I am plotting. I was wondering something."

Even though Wolfe knew he shouldn't ask, he couldn't resist.

"And what were you wondering?"

"Why don't you send those women away and tell them not to come around anymore? It's plain to everyone that you don't like them. Prolly even plain to them."

"Plain to everyone?"

Sissy gave him a solemn nod. "Mrs. Havarerry. Feebson. Miss Hannah and all the rest of the maids. All of them said as much."

"And you know this how?" Wolfe resigned himself to the fact that perhaps he needed to pay more attention to what went on in his own household.

"You know servants gossip," Sissy said, then shook a finger at him. "But don't scold them. They feel bad for you. None of them like those two, either. At least, none of them other than Mrs. Havarerry. They think Lady Longmorten is the worstest of the pair. We heard them say they might could survive Lady Margaret as long as she don't turn as sour and mean as her mother."

Deflating with a resigned sigh, Wolfe bowed his head and pinched the bridge of his nose.

"Like I said," Connor continued, "why don't you send them off?"

"I explained to you about the betrothal," Wolfe said, hoping that would be the end of it.

"That's like a promise, right?" Connor patted his knees. "Sometimes promises get broke. I know it is bad when they do, but sometimes they still do."

"Yes, but if I were to break this promise, it would not only stain our name but very well likely cost us a great deal of money."

"Is that what a *breach of promise suit* means?" Sissy asked. "You have to pay them to get out of the promise Father made when you was little?"

"Where did you hear that?" Wolfe asked, staring at the two in amazement. They should be spies for the Crown, the way they ferreted out information.

"Never you mind," Connor hurried to say while shooting his sister a hard look. "How much would it cost to pay them to go away? It might be worth it."

While Wolfe tended to agree, he feared Lady Longmorten's avarice knew no boundaries. "It would be far better if Lady Margaret chose to sever our betrothal, both for her reputation and mine."

Sissy sadly shook her head. "We can't help you there. Lady Longmorten plans to be rid of us, so we won't be a bovver to her and Lady Margaret no more. She considers us deposable."

"Do you mean *disposable?*" Wolfe tightened his fists until his knuckles popped. "Did you overhear the woman say that?"

Sissy shook her head. "Didn't have to—she told us straight out."

"And she did say *disposable,*" Connor said with a nod at his sister. "She made Sissy cry that day."

Wolfe now found himself fully agreeing with Lady Grace regarding children feeling safe enough to speak their minds. He would not have his brother and sister mistreated. "Whenever anyone says or does anything unkind to either of you, you are to tell me immediately."

"That was the night of that party you let Lady Longmorten give at our house in London. Mrs. Havarerry said you was too busy, and we should try not to think about it." Sissy tipped a despondent shrug. "Sometimes it's hard to get to see you."

"Not anymore. I shall address that issue with Miss Hannah, Mrs. Havarerry, and Feebson as soon as we get back."

"Lady Grace might could help us," Connor said with a thoughtful nod. "She's wily enough to think of a way for us to be rid of those two. I'm thinking Lady Margaret might not mind leaving. Maybe that would make her happy. It's old Longface that's the problem."

"Connor—remember what I said about choosing your words more carefully?"

"Sorry." The boy pulled a face. "I thought it would be all right to speak my mind, since it was just us three."

"It is always all right for you to speak your mind when we are in private. However, if you become too comfortable with inappropriate words, you might forget and use them in public."

"Inappropriate words?" Connor wrinkled his nose.

"Rude words, Connor, for heaven's sake." Sissy shook her head. "Even though Lady Margaret's mother is a mean old woman, that does not make it all right for us to be rude and make up names about her." She smiled up at Wolfe. "Right?"

A weary sigh escaped him. "Correct, Sissy. Absolutely correct."

Chapter Five

"Extortion is a very ugly habit," Grace whispered to Joy as they pretended to listen to Serendipity's elaborate plan of attack for the annual picnic.

"Quite a necessary habit in this family," Joy replied. "And you very well know it."

"What are you two whispering about?" Serendipity swooped in closer, singling them out. With a petulant stomp of her foot, she pointed at them. "Not only did you shirk every responsibility by traipsing off to the village, you came home empty-handed after promising to find presents for little Rorie and Quill. I mean, really! And now you can't even show me the common courtesy of listening to all I have in mind."

"You deserted us," Felicity whispered to Grace as she offered a tray of petite sandwiches. She angled herself so their irritated eldest sister couldn't see her face and gave a long-suffering roll of her eyes. "Try these," she said, loud enough for all to hear. "They are my latest recipe. I thought to help Cook prepare them for the picnic. Seri does not like any of them."

"I simply told you those were not exactly what I had in mind," Serendipity said, then turned back to Grace and Joy. "Well? What do you have to say for yourselves?"

"Next time," Merry whispered from behind them, "take me with you."

"I heard that," Serendipity told her.

Merry gave an exasperated snort and sagged back into her seat as if trying to disappear.

"Forgive us, Seri," Grace said in a placating tone that almost choked her. "We got so caught up in visiting with Mr. Herbert and Mrs. Beatrice, whose hearing is becoming sadly impaired, I fear, but don't make mention of it, by the way—"

"You are babbling, Grace Elena Daisy Abarough." Serendipity glared at her. "You only babble when lying. Confess now and disarm Joy. You know she will use whatever you are hiding as a way to get whatever she wants."

"Seri!" Joy fired off an indignant huff. "You are so insulting."

"Yes—but am I incorrect?" Serendipity arched a brow to a lofty angle, then turned back to Grace. "Disarm her, Gracie. For your own sake as well as ours. The truth, if you please."

A knock on the door of the sisters' shared parlor provided a much-needed interruption. Grace wiggled in the uncomfortable chair that was sorely in need of thicker padding and new upholstery. Unfortunately, the sisters had yet to agree on a style or color for freshening the look of their private sitting room that linked their bedrooms and dressing room. Since each of them stubbornly clung to their favorite colors, the parlor remained decorated in the same faded yellow florals their mother had chosen well before Merry and Felicity were born, and the upholstery was almost threadbare.

"A delivery from Mettlestone's," Walters, their ancient butler, announced as soon as Serendipity opened the door.

"For whom?" She stepped back and swung the door open wider while pointing to the large, claw-footed mahogany table at the center of the room.

"A parcel for Miss Aurora, one for Master Quill, a bundle labeled *banners and ribbon for the picnic*, and a package tagged *a gift*." Walters waved the pair of footmen into the room, directing them to place the items on the table Serendipity had pointed out.

"Thank you, Walters," Serendipity said as she turned and narrowed her eyes at Grace and Joy. "That will be all." After the servants left the room, she tipped a curt nod at the parcels on the table. "Care to explain? What lie have you to tell about those, Gracie?"

Apparently, it was time to take a stand about Serendipity's picnic-planning madness, and since no one else was brave enough to do it, Grace took the mantle upon herself. "Enough of your bullying, Seri." She rose from her chair and squared off in front of her eldest sister. "We do our best to tolerate your impossible behavior when you are planning the family picnic each year, but you overstep every modicum of civil boundaries this time. We are not your enemies, nor are we your servants who must account for our every waking hour to ensure our actions meet with your approval until your infernal picnic is deemed a bloody success. Now, stop this foolishness at once!"

Serendipity went stock-still as if turned into a pillar of salt, her fists clenched to her middle.

Grace couldn't decide if her sister was about to burst into tears or fly into a rage and start throwing everything within reach. Serendipity was normally the voice of reason and often the peacemaker. At least, she always had been before Mama died. But, sadly, a new pecking order among the sisters had evolved after the death of their parents and Chance's ascension to the title. Not only had Serendipity promised Mama to watch over them until they all married, she had apparently vowed to be their taskmaster, their consciences, and their judge and jury. And Serendipity kept her vows with the tenacity of a Templar Knight.

"We love you, Seri," Grace said, gentling her tone, "but sometimes, you make loving you quite the chore."

Serendipity jutted her chin higher, but her fists slowly relaxed, and her hands gracefully dropped to her sides. "I see."

While Grace didn't usually worry about bruising anyone's feelings, she felt bad about hurting her eldest sister. After all, Serendipity was only doing her best to keep the promises she had made to their dear mama. "I should not have spoken so harshly, Seri. I know the picnic means a lot to you and is quite the ordeal.

Please forgive me."

The rest of the sisters remained silent. Not a single one of them moved to add their opinion. It was an unwritten rule among them when two openly battled. There would be no *pack behavior*, as Papa had called it—or at least they should attempt to observe that rule. The two at odds should work out their differences without the threat of the rest taking sides and collectively attacking the one. Mama and Papa had usually done the same, allowing the pair at odds to sort out their differences on their own unless one picked up a weapon that might do the other bodily harm. Their parents had once laughingly admitted they had adopted the rule of stepping in when a weapon was drawn to save poor Chance's life. As the only brother trying to survive a herd of seven sisters, he was terribly outnumbered.

Grace went to the parlor door, peeked out into the hall, then closed it once again and locked it. "Gather round, and I shall *confess*. However"—she swept a threatening look around the room—"one word about this to Chance, and I shall declare war upon each of you. Frogs in your beds. Knotted stockings in your drawers. Crickets in your chamber pots, and Gastric with a case of the winds in your wardrobes to *perfume* all your gowns. And that is just a hint of my arsenal. Understood?"

The four sisters nodded, easing in closer. Anticipation tingled through the room like an excited shiver.

"The reason Joy and I returned from Mettlestone's empty-handed is because the Duke of Wolfebourne and his young brother and sister interrupted our shopping." Grace waited for the obvious question. She didn't have to wait long.

"How did they interrupt your shopping?" Serendipity asked. "And is he as beastly as the rumors?"

"He is meek as a lamb around Gracie," Joy said with a wicked grin. "She attacked the poor man when he'd barely come through the door."

Serendipity turned to Grace with an open-mouthed stare, apparently struck mute by Joy's colorful description.

"I did not attack him." Grace gave Joy a somewhat gentle shove, then shook a finger at her. "This is my confession, if you please."

Still grinning, Joy threw up her hands and backed up a step. "By all means, proceed."

"As I said," Grace began, "I did not attack him. I merely corrected his opinion that children should be seen and not heard. His brother and sister are but seven years old and quite delightful, but the man appears unable to appreciate them."

"Unable to appreciate them *how?*" Serendipity folded her arms across her bosoms, adopting the same look of suspicion Mama had always assumed when listening to any of their confessions.

"They are more than a handful for him. Sharp and cunning as young foxes, but sweet as can be when treated as they should be. The duke has had issues with inadequate nannies and loathsome governesses, and his future mother-in-law is already attempting to ship off the children to the farthest destination she can find."

"And you discovered all this during your brief encounter in Mettlestone's?" Serendipity's silvery-blonde brow, the left one that always betrayed her emotions, angled higher. She knew there was a great deal more to the story without having to be told. "What have you done, Gracie?" she asked quietly.

"The other day, during my ride, I rescued the children's poor little dog and helped get them and their pets home."

Serendipity slowly closed her eyes and rubbed her forehead as though stricken with a terrible ache. "Oh, Gracie. Not the clothes."

"Little Hector was hopelessly snarled in the woodbine ravine. I couldn't very well leave them to their fates just so they wouldn't see me in my buckskins."

"And Hector is?" Merry asked.

"Connor's dog. Galileo is Sissy's cat. A huge feline who is quite protective of the children and the dog. It took some coaxing for Galileo to trust me. Sissy said one of the governesses had been mean to him, and that was why he has difficulties with new people."

"Oh, Gracie." Serendipity lowered herself into the chair beside the table bearing the gifts. "Did the children tell the duke about your clothing?"

"Well...that's somewhat of the point. They didn't have to." Grace took a deep breath, bracing herself for her sister's reaction. "He and I had a few words when he talked down to me because he thought me a servant and also accused me of trespassing."

"Oh, Gracie." Serendipity dropped her head into her hands. "Did you..."

"Of course I did. You know my temper."

"I think I should fetch more sandwiches," Felicity said, "and tell Mrs. Flackney we need tea and cakes."

"And maybe even some brandy," Merry added.

"At least there has been no sign he tattled to Chance," Joy said.

"But he may plan to," Serendipity said. She turned to Felicity. "When you go down for more sandwiches, check the basket on the entryway table. See if there are any messages from the Duke of Wolfebourne. I believe their crest has wolves on it."

"It does," Grace said. "We saw his coach when we reached the village."

"What if Walters already delivered the notes directly to Chance in the library?" Felicity fisted her hands so tightly that her knuckles went white.

Merry went to the door and waved for her to follow. "Between the two of us, we can distract him and see if anything is on his desk."

Felicity nodded, then hurried out behind her.

Serendipity eyed Grace as if plotting her demise.

"For heaven's sake, Seri, speak your mind. Your scowling silence is deafening." Grace poked Joy again. "And if you do not wipe that wicked smile off your face, I shall pinch you."

"Chance would be thrilled for you to marry a duke," Joy taunted her.

"The man is betrothed," Serendipity said. "Has been since he was a young boy. I believe her name is Lady Margaret. Daughter of an earl. Her father is dead, but it's my understanding that he provided quite well for his widow and only child."

"The duke is graying at the temples and doesn't look to be young," Grace said. "If he has been betrothed to her since he was a young boy, why haven't they married yet?"

Serendipity assumed the look that struck fear into all the sisters—the sly, plotting look, like a cat toying with its prey until ready to kill it. "It's my understanding the Duke of Wolfebourne is not in any hurry to visit the altar. Perhaps in hopes of Lady Margaret quietly breaking the engagement out of boredom and the wish to get on with her life."

"Can he not break it off?" Grace knew Serendipity would know. Her sister's ability to know the thoughts and whisperings of the *ton* as if they were her own never ceased to amaze her. "Is the man that chivalrous or simply a coward?" The duke had seemed quite awkward in the shop.

"If *he* breaks it off, Lady Margaret and her mother could sue him for breach of promise," Serendipity said. "While I do not believe Lady Margaret would be so inclined, her mother is known to be quite cold-blooded." She leaned forward and lowered her voice as if the walls might repeat her secrets. "I have heard it said Lady Margaret favors another, but her mother insists she marry the duke."

"Whom does she favor?" Grace whispered.

"*That* I have not been able to discover." Serendipity gave an irritated huff, then frowned at the parcels on the table. "While we wait for Felicity and Merry to report back, shall we inspect these parcels from the unknown sender? Surely the Mettlestones would never take it upon themselves to choose items for Rorie and Quill and send them on."

"I did ask them to deliver the banners for the picnic," Grace said. "Those should have been charged to our account. But I told them we would return another time and choose items for the little ones. Open the one that says *a gift*. Perhaps that will give us a clue."

Serendipity untied the twine and tore away the brown wrapping, revealing another layer, a length of gorgeous deep blue silk. "Lovely," she said in a leery tone. Ever so gingerly, she unwound the yardage of the fine material until the pair of buff-colored buckskins dropped into her lap. With a puckered moue, she lifted her head and locked eyes with Grace. "I believe these are probably meant for you, dear sister."

Grace stared at the damning breeches and swallowed hard, knowing the gift for exactly what it was—a declaration of war. "It is him. The Duke of Wolfebourne sent everything. Who else would dare send a pair of buckskins in that size to our home?"

"Who, indeed." Serendipity nodded at the parcels for the children. "But how would he know about Rorie and Quill?"

"We mentioned them in front of him," Joy said, "and I am quite certain the Mettlestones happily filled him in on all the rest."

Grace carefully unwrapped the parcel meant for Aurora and revealed the lovely cloth doll, perfect for a little one to cuddle and throw when tiny tempers flared. Her insides fluttered, and she swallowed hard, fighting to stanch any warming toward the man. "He chose well for our little niece." She unwrapped the other parcel and smiled at the brightly painted toy soldiers. "Quill is a bit young for these, but he should enjoy the colors."

Serendipity opened her mouth to speak but was interrupted when Felicity and Merry burst back into the room and slammed the door shut behind them.

"We intercepted a note to Chance," Merry said. "From the duke."

"He is coming to dinner tonight," Felicity said, her ample bosom heaving as she tried to catch her breath. "And he asked to bring Lady Margaret and Lady Longmorten."

"Well, he would," Grace said. "He couldn't very well accept a dinner invitation and leave them at the lodge, since they are staying with him." She turned to Serendipity. "Could he? And did you know anything about guests invited to dinner tonight?"

Serendipity chewed on the corner of her bottom lip while scowling at the toys on the table. "Chance may have mentioned something, but I've been so busy planning the picnic that I let whatever he says go in one ear and out the other without pausing in between." She shifted her attention to Felicity and Merry. "What did you do with the duke's response? Were you careful to leave it where Chance could find it and reply in time for tonight?"

Merry gave a smug nod. "Of course. It even looks as though the seal is still intact."

"How did you manage that?" Serendipity asked, then ducked her head and turned away. "Never mind. I do not wish to know."

"Who else might he have invited?" Joy asked. "You know Chance. He misses the brotherhood of the club whenever we are in the country."

"And heaven forbid he should pause in his matchmaking until we return to London." Grace rubbed at the hairs rising on the back of her neck, a sure sign that tonight could be disastrous.

Serendipity rose and went to the door. "I shall find out and report back." She arched a brow at Felicity and Merry. "Sandwiches? Tea? Brandy? We shall need fortification to survive whatever our silly brother has in mind—especially since the Duke of Wolfebourne could be a problem for our Gracie."

"They are on the way," Felicity replied curtly. "We heard Chance headed for the library and had to make our escape. Mrs. Flackney knows to send them up."

Grace busied herself with re-wrapping the gifts for Aurora and Quill. If she didn't do something, she would surely shatter into a thousand nervous little bits, and she simply refused to do that. "Gastric!" She needed her sweet dog. He would calm her.

A thud from the depths of the adjoining bedroom told her he had been lounging on one of the beds again, taking advantage of the household being busy with other things. She didn't mind if he slept on hers, and he always cuddled with her at night, but her sisters didn't share that same opinion and complained about dog hair on their bedclothes.

With a soft *woof*, he ambled into the parlor, his swaying, short-legged gait making Grace smile. He went straight to her and leaned against her leg, looking up at her with adoration in his eyes. No one would ever love her as unconditionally as Gastric.

"There is my good lad." She rubbed his head and scratched behind his ears, immediately feeling calmer.

"You like him." Joy meandered closer, a dangerous look in her eyes.

"I do not like him." Grace settled on the rug and pulled the dog into her lap. "I love him. Gastric makes everything bearable."

"Not Gastric," Joy said, "the duke. You like the duke."

Grace snorted. "I believe that is the most ridiculous thing I have ever heard you say."

"You do like him," Merry said. "Your cheeks have gone all pink, and you never blush."

"My color rises when I think of the man because I find him infuriating." Grace tried to think of anything but the darkly handsome duke and the exciting way his unkempt hair had whipped across his angry eyes when he and she had argued in the meadow.

"What would be wrong with your liking him?" Felicity asked as she settled into a nearby chair. "We promise not to tell Chance or Seri."

"Seri did say he belonged to another," Merry said.

"Another that he does not want," Joy added.

Grace hugged Gastric closer, burying her face in the softness of his floppy brown ears. She was not accustomed to being the center of attention, and she did not like it one tiny bit. Her dogs, horses, and the great outdoors mattered most in her world—not some infernal man who needed to learn how to better treat his siblings and find the gumption to break off an engagement if he found it unpalatable.

"My only unresolved issue with the Duke of Wolfebourne is

that he has seen me in my adventuring clothes, as have his brother and sister. I know I can trust them to keep my secret, but I am none too sure about him. Hopefully, I convinced him not to tattle to Chance by informing him that to do so would be cowardly." She found herself smiling without exactly knowing why. "That made his face go all ruddy that day."

"The same as it did in the shop?" Joy asked before giving a knowing nod to the other sisters. "That man is already darkly handsome. When his color rises, it enhances his looks quite nicely."

"Perhaps we should steer him in your direction?" Grace snapped, surprised by a sudden sense of possessiveness over her duke.

Her *duke?* Ridiculous! She had merely met him first. That was all. This was most certainly not a case of whoever saw him first got him. She scratched Gastric under the chin, smiling as the dog's eyes closed in sheer bliss and his back leg started thumping. "What say you, Gastric? Should Joy be the next on the chopping block? That would buy me more time."

"Absolutely not," Joy said. "You should have seen him," she told Merry and Felicity. "His eyes never left her the entire time we were in the shop."

Serendipity breezed back into the room, then held the parlor door open for the pair of footmen bearing trays of tea, brandy, sandwiches, and biscuits. "Thank you, George and Peter. I know Mrs. Flackney instructed you to pour, but I enjoy doing that myself. That will be all."

The young men nodded and hurried out.

Serendipity closed the door and leaned back against it. "We indeed have an onslaught of guests for dinner this evening." Counting off on her fingers, she continued, "The Duke of Wolfebourne, Lady Margaret, Lady Longmorten, the Marquess of Strathyre and his wife, Viscount Blytheston, and Sir Andrew Gransington."

"An odd number," Grace said, "Mrs. Flackney must be beside herself."

"Yes," Serendipity said. "She came to me with the seating issue. I told her to set an extra place, and we shall say someone we expected cried off on short notice."

"Will they not want a name?" Grace found these ridiculous games exhausting. It would be so much easier for her to claim to be ill and stay in her chambers with her dogs. "The pups and I would be happy to dine upstairs tonight."

"Oh, no you don't!" Joy, Felicity, and Merry said in unison. Joy shook a finger at her. "You are next on the chopping block. Not us."

"Must you phrase it that way?" Serendipity added a generous dollop of brandy to all their teacups.

"It is an apt description." Grace gently nudged Gastric out of her lap, rose from the floor, and joined the others around the table. She picked up her cup and lifted it in a toast. "An oath to stick together and protect one another from Chance's machinations this evening." She gave Serendipity a pointed glare. "Even you, Seri. Agreed?"

"Agreed," each of the sisters sang out.

"Heaven help me," Grace muttered to herself before taking a hearty sip that was entirely too lacking in brandy, considering the evening that lay ahead.

Chapter Six

GRACE PURPOSELY REMAINED seated in front of the mirror as her sisters exited the large dressing room they all shared. Maybe if she climbed into one of the wardrobes, they wouldn't find her until it was too late, and then they would have to carry on the dinner party without her. A loud snore rumbling at her feet reminded her that precious Gastric would surely betray her as he had often done when asked, *Where's Gracie?* The devoted hound thought it a wonderful game to sniff her out and bark until given the treat he felt he deserved for playing hide-and-seek so artfully.

"You are too quiet, my lady." Her maid added a finishing touch to Grace's curls and tucked a tall white feather into the beaded band that held her upswept hair in place. "Are you feeling poorly?"

Grace frowned at her reflection in the mirror. That feather reminded her of an irritated cat with its tail fluffed straight in the air. She snatched it off her head and tossed it onto the dressing table. "No feathers, please. Just stick some inconspicuous flowers or something in there. Or just leave the band as it is. It has beads. Is that not enough?"

"Of course, my lady. Forgive me."

Grace deflated with a heavy sigh. *Lovely.* Now she'd allowed her dread of going downstairs to make her cross with her poor maid, who had done nothing wrong. She turned on the cushioned stool and faced the older woman who always took the very best care of her. "Forgive *me*, Nellie. My temper is not of your doing. As always, you are a gem for tolerating me."

Nellie's broad smile made her feel a little better, but not much. The maid selected a delicate white spray of flowers crafted from silk and shimmering pearls. As she pinned them to the side of Grace's headband, she said, "Surely His Grace is not trying his hand at matchmaking out here in the country. Flora said old Froggie mentioned His Grace is already bored. Inviting folk in might help him feel better."

"My brother is at his most dangerous when bored." Grace eyed herself in the mirror, thankful that Nellie faithfully relayed the gossip among the servants. *Old Froggie* was Chance's longtime valet, whose real name was Frogsden.

"You are ready, my lady." The maid stepped back, clutching Grace's extra combs to her middle.

"That is a matter of opinion." Grace scowled at her reflection and heaved another sigh. There was no helping it. If she didn't go downstairs now, one or more of her sisters would soon be up to fetch her. "Thank you for preparing me for battle, Nellie."

"God be with you, my lady." The maid gave her a prayerful nod.

"Indeed." Grace held her head high as she left the room and descended the stairs as quietly as possible so as not to draw anyone's attention. If she'd had a brain, she would've taken the servants' stairs down to the kitchen, slipped into the hallway, and kept to the shadows. It wasn't that she was a coward. She simply wasn't in the mood for any of Chance's ridiculous games. Her only hope was to remain as unnoticed as possible.

"And there is my other sister," Chance said when she erred and stepped out of the shadows. His deep voice filled the hallway, strangling her hopes of slipping in without being seen.

Grace forced a smile but slowed her pace toward the guests assembled in the manor house's entryway. The area had been opened up by folding back several moveable walls to expand space into the parlor next to the massive dining room.

Chance went to her, looped her arm through his, and whispered, "Be nice, Gracie." Before she could respond, he tugged her toward a pale, nondescript man who looked as if he would rather be anywhere but Broadmere Manor. "Lord Blytheston, this is yet another of my lovely sisters, Lady Grace."

The viscount offered a cold but polite bow. "A pleasure, my lady."

Apparently not, Grace thought while dropping a curtsy. "My lord." The man's aloofness suited her just fine. He reminded her of a lizard, constantly flicking the tip of his tongue out past his lips as if in search of a juicy bug.

Chance squeezed her arm, a gentle reminder of his plea for good behavior as he guided her deeper into the crowd. "Lord and Lady Strathyre, please meet the final piece of the Broadmere familial puzzle, my sister, Lady Grace."

This pair didn't seem all that bad. Grace gave them a curtsy, noting how the marquess kept exchanging glances with the Duke of Wolfebourne. She would lay odds the two were chums. "Thank you for joining us tonight," she told the kindly pair, pleasing Chance immensely, judging from the brightness of his expression.

"'Twas our pleasure to be invited," Lady Strathyre said, revealing a soft Scottish accent. Her husband nodded his agreement with his wife's sentiment.

"Sir Andrew Gransington," Chance said as they moved to the next guest. "I would like you to meet another of my sisters, Lady Grace."

"A pleasure, my lady," said the tall, somber man, his voice quiet and somehow sad.

"The pleasure is mine, Sir Andrew." Grace noticed his attention kept slipping over to the Duke of Wolfebourne and his entourage. Was he part of the duke's guard or something? She also found it odd that Chance had saved introducing her to the duke's party last. According to the silly pecking order laws of the *ton*, as the highest-ranking guest, she should have been presented to the duke first rather than last. Surely Chance knew that. She knew for certain her sisters did because they were watching her—intently so. Suspicion sprouted deep within her. What game was at play here?

"Wolfebourne," Chance said as he tugged her over to the duke and the ladies beside him. "It is my understanding you and my sister are already acquainted—elsewise, I would have presented her to you first."

The duke offered her the slightest nod, watching her with the tenacity of a predator on the hunt. "Yes. We are acquainted. A pleasure to see you again, Lady Grace." He turned to the ladies on his left. "Allow me to present Lady Margaret and her mother, Lady Longmorten."

Grace bit the inside of her cheek to keep from reacting. Good heavens, but Connor and Sissy had been so right. Lady Longmorten not only had the long face of a mule but the large, slightly protruding front teeth as well. Her daughter was comelier, but the resemblance between the two was unmistakable.

Mama's voice resounded loudly in Grace's head: *A beautiful heart outshines all else. Do not become an ugly beast by entertaining ugly thoughts.* She offered the ladies her best curtsy. "Lady Margaret, Lady Longmorten, thank you for joining us this evening."

Lady Margaret responded with a strained smile that made the coldness in her eyes even icier. Lady Longmorten simply gave a haughty sniff and a curt nod. The ladies, or at least the mother, did not wish to be here. Grace felt it as plain as a slap on the wrist.

She turned her attention back to the duke. "While I am sure my sister already made mention of it, I would like to add my thanks for the thoughtful gifts you sent for little Aurora and Quill. I am sure they will love them."

Mischief flashed in his dark eyes and a slow, knowing smile tugged at his full lips. Good heavens, but the man was indeed handsome. Grace swallowed hard and struggled to calm her silly heart, which had taken to beating entirely too fast.

"It was my pleasure to send *all* the gifts, my lady." His voice was as deep and sultry as a lion's purr. "*Each* of them was chosen with the greatest of care, I assure you."

She clenched her teeth while forcing a polite smile, knowing he meant the buckskins. Wicked man. But she had to admit, it was well played. Perhaps he was a worthy adversary after all.

"Gifts?" Lady Margaret repeated with a nervous titter. Her mother narrowed her eyes in an incinerating glare focused on Wolfebourne.

"My sister and I had to rush out of Mettlestone's before we finished our shopping," Grace lied. Well, it wasn't exactly a lie. They had simply left before they bought any gifts. "I can only assume His Grace overheard how we wished to surprise our precious little niece and nephew with some new toys when they arrive next week. Then, this afternoon, the perfect dolly was delivered for Aurora, and even though Quill is naught but a babe in arms, I am sure he will be most entertained by the brightly painted toy soldiers."

"How nice," Lady Margaret said, but she didn't sound as though she thought it nice at all.

The poor lady was most unhappy, Grace decided. The rumor Serendipity had heard must be accurate. Perhaps Lady Margaret did love another. Or was she simply tired of waiting for Wolfebourne to take her to the altar?

"Yes," Grace agreed, almost as an afterthought. She was not good at meaningless chatter and was at a loss as to how to keep the conversation going without revealing too much of her history with the duke. She glanced around, looking for Chance, who had wandered off like a dog that had chewed through its lead. "It was a nice gesture, indeed." She looked over and widened her eyes at her sisters with their agreed-upon signal for *help me*.

Before they came to her rescue, Walters announced in a surprisingly loud voice, "The Earl of Middlebie."

"Bless my soul," said the hulking Scot, his voice booming through the room like cannon fire. He swaggered forward and clapped a hand on Chance's shoulder. "What a fine gathering, Broadmere. Thank ye for inviting me for a wee stay here in the English countryside."

Chance grinned like the wiliest hunter who had just set the perfect snare.

Grace shot a demanding look at Serendipity, who responded with a subtle shrug that shouted she had no idea Chance had invited Thornton Armstrong, the Earl of Middlebie, a boisterous Scot, to come to the manor for a stay of an undetermined length. The man was nice enough. Charming and gentlemanly too, even though he was always loud. But rumor had it that his propensity for poor investments and lavish spending had left him with little more than a crumbling castle in the Highlands and the kilt belted at his waist.

Grace fixed a hard look on her brother, determined that he *feel* her thoughts. She would not be bartered off to ease the financial woes of one of Chance's friends. The will said she would marry for love—not money.

Walters appeared at the doorway of the dining room and struck the small gong he held suspended from a golden ribbon. "Dinner is served."

Chance and Serendipity led the way, followed by the Duke of Wolfebourne and Lady Longmorten. The Marquess of Strathyre and his wife came next, and then the Earl of Middlebie and Lady Margaret. The Scot bathed the woman in laughter and endless chatter, and she appeared to enjoy it. The sour-faced viscount, Lord Blytheston, took his place beside Grace, and Sir Andrew fell in step beside Joy. Felicity and Merry ended the ridiculous ranked-by-peerage parade into the dining room.

The footmen hurried to fill the wine glasses and serve the soup. Grace didn't even attempt to repress a despondent sigh as she stared down at the creamy quagmire she had always hated. She couldn't refuse it. It simply wasn't done. *One must never refuse the first course,* her conscience reminded her in dear Mama's voice.

Felicity nudged her and whispered, "I convinced Cook to

change the recipe. It is much better. Try it, Gracie."

With the side of her spoon barely touching the thick broth, Grace risked a glance down the table and almost laughed. Wolfebourne was staring down at his soup with a similar expression of dislike. Then he lifted his head and their gazes met. Ever so slowly, he smiled, and she had to do the same. The pea soup was their shared enemy. At least they had that in common.

The servants brought in the second course, arranging the joint of mutton, chicken, roasted carrots, turnips, and parsnips in a pleasing array of platters. Pickled vegetables were also placed on each end of the table so the footmen could better fill the guests' plates.

Salmon pie, baked fish with wine and mushrooms, and potato pudding made up the third course. By that time, Grace had picked at all she could bear, but politely slid bits of food around on her plate since others were still enjoying their meal. Now and then, she slipped a tidbit to Gastric, who waited under the table to help her make it look as though she were eating. She couldn't hope to escape until after the dessert course, when the females would be excused to the smaller parlor while the men enjoyed their port and cigars in the library.

Grace noticed Lady Longmorten had eaten very little, if anything, as well. The woman had even given up on shoving the food in circles on her plate. She simply sat there with her hands in her lap, glaring at Wolfebourne and occasionally glancing down the table at her daughter. Even if Connor and Sissy hadn't told Grace of the woman's plan to be rid of them, Grace wouldn't like her. As Mama had always said, *Rarely can a mean-spirited person hide the blackness of their heart. They will always reveal their soulless ways.*

As the fritters, syllabub, cream puffs, jellies, and nuts were brought out, Grace breathed easier. Not much longer now until the women would be dismissed to the small parlor near the side garden. From there, she could slip outside and climb the trellis up to the second floor. She had done that so many times in the past that she could scale the wall with her eyes closed. If someone missed her after that, no one would bother to drag her back downstairs because, at least, she had made a showing when it mattered. Chance might get a little fractious with her, but she didn't care. She had behaved properly as long as she could.

When they were finally dismissed, she rose so quickly from the table that she nearly knocked her chair over backward. That earned her a hard look from Serendipity, which she answered with a roll of her eyes. They had all best be happy she had been the dutiful sister. She hated the societal and sometimes political maneuvering of balls, dinner parties, and tiresome soirees. A refreshing breeze cutting across a peaceful meadow sang to her soul and comforted her. Presenting herself like a fine, plump goose in the butcher window, all trussed up and ready for marriage, did not.

While Felicity talked recipes with Lady Strathyre, and Joy and Merry chatted about card games with Lady Margaret, Serendipity did her best to entertain Lady Longmorten.

Bless her soul, Grace thought as she looked on from her escape route beside the doors thrown open to the cool breeze coming in from the side garden. Serendipity would surely earn a special place in heaven for the patience and politeness she always displayed.

Grace was fairly certain her place in heaven would be shoveling out the stalls for the Almighty's animals. At least, she hoped so. If anyone understood her, it had to be the Creator.

She eased back another few steps as Serendipity leaned forward in an earnest attempt to draw the aloof Lady Longmorten into some semblance of conversation.

Then Grace slipped through the doors and was free. She scampered down the line of the wall, running her fingers along the roughness of the stucco and masonry, more relieved than anyone would ever understand. She almost laughed as she took hold of her old friend, the iron trellis, that had provided her an escape route to the countryside many times. Papa had once threatened to have it removed, but thankfully, he had relented when she gave in to a rare case of tears and begged him to let it stay. The only time she ever cried was when one of her beloved animals died. Papa knew that, and the sight of her reduced to such distress had stayed his hand.

Of course, it had been a few years since the last time she had climbed the old trellis. But she had no doubt she still remembered every foot- and handhold. She had nearly reached the second-floor windows when the ivy-covered iron framework reacted to her presence with a disturbing shudder. How many dangerously rusted joints did the leafy ivy hide? "Hold fast, old friend. I know I am a bit larger, but surely your strength can still bear me."

Metal gritted against stone with a sickening grind. She stretched but couldn't quite reach the ledge to the balcony of the bedroom she and her sisters shared. "Just a little more. Hold fast for a little longer. I am almost there."

And then the thing groaned and slowly wilted away from the wall, dangling her over the ground that was entirely too far down there to let herself drop.

She held on tight and bit back a scream. "A cool head always wins, Gracie," she said under her breath while gently swaying back and forth. As long as the iron continued its gradual bending away from the wall, she could drop to the ground as soon as she got close enough, and no one would be any the wiser.

But then it snapped and bounced her so brutally against the wall that she lost her grip. "Drat it all!"

"I have you, my lady."

She landed in the muscular arms of the Duke of Wolfebourne, elbowing him in the face rather hard.

"Bloody hell, woman!"

"Oh, dear heavens." The shadowy darkness hid his features, so she gently touched his face, checking him for injury. A warm, slick wetness met her fingertips. "Bless you, Your Grace, you are bleeding. I am so very sorry." She pulled a handkerchief from its usual place, snug between her breasts down behind her stays, and pressed it first to his nose and then his mouth. "Is it your lip or your nose?" she asked in a frantic whisper. "I can't tell. The moon has gone behind the clouds." Her heart pounded at a deafening rate, and her middle churned as if holding a thousand little birds madly batting their wings to be freed.

The night breeze blew the clouds aside as if trying to help. Moonlight flooded the small clearing beside the trellis, revealing she had indeed bloodied the poor man's nose. Without realizing it, she slid her fingers deeper into the silkiness of his hair and gently cradled his head while stanching the trickle of blood with her handkerchief. "I am so, so sorry," she said. "I hope I have not broken it. Can you breathe? Do you feel lightheaded?" Of course, that was a most silly question, because he still held her in his arms as if cuddling a cherished pet. That realization made her swallow hard. It would probably do them both a world of good if he would set her down. "Place me on my feet and let me tend to you. You have not answered a thing I have asked. Are you all right, Your Grace?"

Rather than lower her to the clearing, he hitched her higher against his chest. One of his dark brows ratcheted higher and, if she was not mistaken, sheer amusement flashed in his eyes. "I have not answered because I am unable to get a word in edgewise, my lady."

"Sorry." She forced herself to calm down and stop behaving like a mindless ninny. "I tend to babble when circumstances put me at a complete loss." *Or when I am lying,* but she didn't say that part out loud. There was no reason to arm the man with even more ammunition against her. Cringing, she dabbed at his nose again. "Thank you for catching me. Poor old trellis. I suppose I have worn it out over the years."

He strode over to the bench beneath the balcony, the one sheltered from the rest of the garden by a dense wall of shrubbery. Behaving as though it were the most natural thing in the world, he seated himself on it and settled her firmly on his lap. "Might I ask why you were climbing the trellis?" He tightened his arm around her when she tried to scramble off him and get to her feet.

"This is most inappropriate," she said as sternly as she could. It was difficult to speak with a pounding heart and a level of breathlessness the likes of which she had never known.

"Climbing a trellis is also most inappropriate," he replied, "as is a woman clad in buckskins and riding astride."

A hot surge of indignance flashed through her. "I might not be conventional or appropriate at all times, but I assure you I am no lightskirt. Release me at once, Your Grace."

Wolfebourne jerked his arms out from around her and held them aloft as if stretching his wingspan. "I meant no insult, Lady Grace. Forgive me."

Since they were once again in the shadows of the cloudy night, she *felt* more than saw his remorse. A hopelessness, an endearing sadness in his voice, immediately made her regret the sharpness of her words. She eased off him, but rather than rising to her feet as she should, she seated herself beside him. "I was climbing the trellis to escape this ridiculous dinner party my brother arranged because I am the next plump little Broadmere goose to be hung in the window."

"I beg your pardon?"

"My parents' will decreed that while Chance might inherit the title, he would not receive the fullness of his vast inheritance until all of us are happily married for love—not for societal or political alignment." She twitched a shrug. "Two of my sisters have married. Going by birth order, I am the next to be placed on the chopping block, because Seri promised Mama she would marry last so she could take care of the rest of us."

"I see."

She doubted that he did, but she would allow him to think so. After all, they both needed to be getting back inside. The rest of the guests would not necessarily miss her, but they would soon miss him. "How did you happen to be out here to catch me?"

"I abhor cigar smoke. The stuff chokes me." He shifted beside her with a heavy sigh as he sniffed and pressed her lacy handkerchief to his nose once more. "I love a good pipe tobacco, but sadly, the sweet aroma was overpowered by those bloody cigars."

Unable to resist, she leaned closer and sniffed him. The faint, acrid smell of burned wood came to her. "You smell like the fields when they burn off the stubble after the harvest."

"I assure you I shall bathe before retiring."

"I like a man who bathes," she said before thinking better of it. What the blazes was wrong with her? Something about him made her feel as if she had known him all her life and could tell him anything. That was a most dangerous development, since she already possessed a general laxness when it came to curbing her tongue.

"You like a man who bathes, do you?" The shadows hid his expression but failed to hide the amusement coloring his tone. Or was it amazement at her frankness?

"Yes." She shuddered. "Have you ever met the Marquess of Pellington? The man thinks bathing causes ill health." She couldn't restrain a quiet laugh. "The girls and I call him *Lord Smellington* because he reeks." Oh good heavens, why in the world would she say that? "Forgive me. That was most rude, and I should not have said it."

"Your secrets are safe with me, Lady Grace. You should know that by now."

His deep voice poured across her like the most intimate of caresses. It made her ache to be back in his lap, back in his arms. It made her wish—what?

She cleared her throat and scooted away, increasing the distance between them. "You should probably rejoin the guests, Your Grace."

"And what about you?"

"I have other secret routes up to my bedchamber. I shall not be rejoining the party."

"And what if I do not wish to rejoin the guests either?"

As much as she hated to remind him, she couldn't shake the

image of Lady Margaret and Lady Longmorten out of her mind. "You are betrothed, Your Grace, and we must not be found for I can't be the ruin of my family."

"Connor wishes to marry you," he said as if she had not spoken. "He swears he shall, in fact. You won his heart when you saved Hector and lauded Connor as a hero for not deserting his little dog."

That warmed her heart toward the duke even more, dangerously so. "Connor is a treasure. A true gentleman. I value his friendship as well as that of his sister's."

"And what of me, Lady Grace?" The clouds skittered away again, and moonlight flooded his face. He leaned closer and touched her cheek with a tenderness that made her shiver. His stare, the intensity of his gaze, made it impossible for her to move. "Lady Grace," he repeated, his quiet voice a rasping plea, "what of me?"

"What of you, Your Grace?" She allowed the heart-wrenching regret she felt to reach out to him. If only…

Mama once again whispered in her ear, *Beware the game of "if only," child, for it is fraught with danger.*

"You belong to another," she told him, "and I deserve someone free to belong to me alone."

"That you do, my lady." But he lowered his head and took her mouth, tenderly nuzzling her lips with a hungry groan that made her wonder if he thought her delicious. "But I cannot resist you," he whispered, his mouth brushing across hers as he spoke. "You are unlike any woman I have ever known." Then he kissed her again, longer, deeper. He tasted of port, of forbidden excitement, and a regret she refused to bear.

She broke the dangerous connection, stumbled to her feet, and backed away. "Good evening, Your Grace. Return to Lady Margaret, for it is with her that you belong. Not me. Not ever me, as long as you are promised to her. As I said, I deserve better and will never settle for less."

He stood, his looming height barely diminished with his

bowed head. "Forgive my abhorrent behavior, Lady Grace. I assure you, it will not happen again." Then he turned and disappeared into the shadows with the same silence of the clouds blotting out the silvery moon's light once more.

Grace touched her lips. They tingled and throbbed and longed to be kissed again—by Wolfebourne. Or Wolfe, as she had heard Connor call him. The name fit the man well: a lone wolf slipping into the darkness.

Laughter from the intimate ladies' parlor in the distance startled her into motion. Serendipity must not find her. She caught up her skirts and dashed to the old servants' entrance hidden behind the lush rose garden Papa had planted the year Mama died.

Teeth clenched so tightly her jaws ached, she vowed to behave as though tonight had never happened. She would completely forget about it, wash it from her mind. As she pushed inside and climbed the servants' stairs to the second floor, she prayed for the strength to keep that vow to herself.

Chapter Seven

WHAT THE DEVIL *is wrong with me?* Wolfe exited the side garden, shoved through the hedging, and returned to the wide terrace outside the library's open doors. As he stepped inside to the cigar haze and the men's quiet, rumbling conversations, he realized he still clutched the lovely Lady Grace's handkerchief in his hand. He hurried to tuck it deep inside his jacket's innermost pocket, then patted the garment in place, ensuring no bulge betrayed the precious memento he intended to keep. It didn't matter that it was stained with his blood. It smelled of her. Even with his poor beak throbbing from the glancing blow of her elbow, the alluring scent had made its way to him—the soft, tempting sweetness of lilacs and a deliciously entrancing young woman. It had immediately both soothed and inflamed him.

"There you are, Wolfebourne," Broadmere called out from across the room. "My apologies for the lingering smoke. Even with the doors and windows open wide, the place never airs well. Must be all the bookshelves. Are you better settled now? Would a brandy help?"

Wolfe was not settled at all, but it had nothing to do with the lingering cigar smoke. However, he couldn't very well tell the young Duke of Broadmere that Lady Grace possessed the sweetest mouth this side of heaven. "I am much better now, thank you. But I do believe it is time to gather the ladies and bid everyone goodnight. I enjoyed this evening very much and thank you for your hospitality. Perhaps you would consider joining me for a hunt sometime?"

Broadmere stiffened and rolled his shoulders, appearing as uncomfortable as if Wolfe had suggested something as treacherous as treason. "Thank you for the invitation, but I dare not accept out of fear for my life."

"Fear for your life?" Sir Andrew asked before Wolfe could.

"Wolfe's not that bad of a shot." Strath grinned and lifted his glass in a mock toast.

"Old Broady's sisters would draw and quarter him." The Earl of Middlebie chuckled, then feigned a horrified expression. "Fiery lasses, the lot of them. Especially Lady Grace when it comes to hunting. And her sisters would unite to protect her, I grant ye that. Even her Papa bent to her will and forbade hunting on Broadmere lands. 'Tis a wonder the lady even eats meat."

"If you ever bothered to observe her at the table, Middlebie," Broadmere said, "you would see that meat never touches her plate. All the servants know better, and if they don't, they soon learn." He turned back to Wolfe. "Thank you for the invitation, but I do not relish sleeping with my eyes open to ensure Gracie doesn't do something horrid to me while I sleep."

The enlightening conversation made Wolfe remember a gentle nudge and inquisitive snuffling against his leg under the table during dinner. He hadn't thought much about it at the time. He'd been too amused by the fact that he and Lady Grace shared a mutual hatred for pea soup. "Did one of her dogs dine with us this evening? Under the table, perhaps?"

Broadmere dragged a hand across his eyes and groaned. "Forgive me. That was probably Gastric. Sometimes he slips past the servants and sneaks into the dining room. Usually, he stays at Gracie's feet and avoids all others. She found him as a pup wandering the streets of London and brought him home. I am surprised he made it to your end of the table, because she constantly slips him tidbits. Please accept my apologies. I will speak to her—again—about securing him in her room during dinner parties."

Wolfe couldn't help but grin. The more he learned about the enigmatic Lady Grace, the more he liked her. "Leave it be, Broadmere. No harm done." He winked. "And I would not wish the lady upset with me because I complained about her hound."

An immediate interest lit in the duke's eyes, like a spark from the strike of a flint. "I would not wish the lady upset with you either. By the way, are the banns soon to be read in Binnocksbourne, since Lady Margaret and her mother have joined you here in the countryside?"

"Forgive me, but I find myself in need of air." Sir Andrew abruptly stood and hurried outside into the night.

Wolfe stared after the man of which he knew very little. The knight had always traveled with Lady Margaret and Lady Longmorten. He had been somewhat of a personal guard or equerry to them even before the Earl of Longmorten had died.

"Oh dear." Broadmere frowned, his gaze following Sir Andrew. "I do hope nothing was *off* with the meal. Is anyone else feeling unwell?"

Middlebie rose, refilled his glass, and lit another cigar. "The meal was fine." He turned to Strath. "Course, we Scots possess the constitution of Highland goats, aye?"

"Aye, we do." Strath stood, set his glass aside, and gave Wolfe a subtle, narrow-eyed look. "But perhaps it *is* time to gather the ladies and be on our way."

"What a shame," Broadmere said. "My sisters will be so disappointed. I am sure Merry planned to regale us with a few lively tunes on the pianoforte."

"Another time, perhaps." Wolfe tipped an almost indiscernible nod to Strath. His friend wished to talk about *something*. Wolfe couldn't imagine what that something might be.

As Broadmere and Middlebie made their way out of the library, Wolfe purposely lagged to speak with his friend. "What is it, man?"

"Who hit ye?"

"Why would you ask such a thing?" Wolfe glanced back at the open door leading out to the garden. Sir Andrew had yet to reappear. Of course, knowing the man and his odd and sometimes rude ways, he had probably gone round to the carriages to idle away the remainder of the evening. Even though he was a well-respected knight and a war hero, he did not seem to mix well or hold his own at gatherings.

Wolfe turned back to Strath, who had remained silent, his smug expression speaking volumes. "Well?"

"The others failed to notice, but I've not hit the spirits as hard as they. Yer nose is unnaturally red, and I daresay the night air is not cold enough to turn it to such a shade." Strath spared him another critical once-over, then flicked at a spot on his cravat. "Blood. From that red nose of yers, I'd wager. Again, I ask—who hit ye?"

"Now is neither the time nor the place to have this conversation." Wolfe nodded at the women trickling into the hallway.

"Ye think those women of yers will fail to notice the state ye're in?" Strath emitted a quiet snort. "I doubt Lady Margaret will comment, but I grant ye, old Lady Longmorten will bend yer ears until they glow as red yer nose." He poked Wolfe in the shoulder. "Dinna move. In fact, back into the library with ye. I have a plan to save yer arse and yer ears."

They had saved each other's lives innumerable times during the war, and only a little less often during peacetime. Wolfe trusted Strath implicitly, so he did as the man suggested.

It wasn't long before Strath reappeared. "Come. We need to leave through yon doors to the garden. My Sarah is seeing yer women and that odd Sir Alexander home in my carriage because ye and I have a business proposition to discuss. Then ye will be good enough to deliver me home in yer coach."

Strath's diplomacy and ability to convince a person that they really wished to do something they usually wouldn't agree to never ceased to amaze Wolfe. "How the bloody hell did you manage that?"

"Scottish charm. Now, on wi' ye afore Broadmere and his sisters get suspicious and come out of the parlor. I told them ye'd had to rush outside again. He fears the salmon in the pie must have turned, because he ate none of that and neither did Middlebie or myself. But we must go now because some of his sisters surely must have eaten it and will know it was fine."

Wolfe hurried back across the room and out into the fresh night air, filling his lungs to expel the stench of the cigars. Strath caught up with him as they made their way around the back of the large manor house and headed for the circular drive out front, where Wolfe's carriage waited.

"Now, as I asked before," Strath said as they strode through the darkness, "who punched ye?"

"Lady Grace."

"Lady Grace? What the devil did ye do to her?"

"I caught her as she fell from the trellis she had climbed, and she did not punch me. As she dropped into my arms, her elbow caught me in the nose." Wolfe flexed his fingers, remembering the feel of her warm, soft weight against his chest. She had fit him perfectly, and left him more than a little certain she would fit him perfectly in any other position as well.

Strath caught hold of his arm and yanked him to a stop. "Ye caught the woman as she fell from a trellis? Was she attempting to escape ye by climbing the wall?"

Mildly insulted, Wolfe glared at his friend. "She did not know I was in the garden. She was attempting to escape the party, which she found extremely loathsome, since her brother is trying to marry her off to satisfy the requirements of his parents' will."

Strath huffed. "So the rumors are true, then? The lad must see his seven sisters wed afore he gets his fortune. Word has it his father possessed a golden touch, and the family is richer than Croesus."

"But according to Lady Grace, the sisters must marry for love—not for power or politics." Wolfe couldn't imagine such a union. His father had never truly loved any of his wives. He had been fond of them—at least for a while—but they had been more like items he collected to keep him amused. "Is such a thing truly possible? A marriage built on love?"

Strath snorted. "Dinna speak like that in front of my Sarah or she'll box yer ears for ye. Of course a love match is possible, ye silly arse. I love my Sarah, and she loves me."

"You can leave off with your condescending manner," Wolfe told him. "Have you forgotten I was one of your witnesses at your *arranged* marriage you were none too certain about at the time?"

"Aye, well." Strath tugged him onward toward the carriage. "I had forgotten, actually, because Sarah and I were fortunate enough to be well matched and fall in love." He rolled his shoulders and made a face as if trying to swallow something horrible. "Yet I fear ye will not be so blessed if and when ye marry Lady Margaret. Her and that mother of hers..." He shuddered. "And ye ken the daughter is much like the mother when she nay realizes anyone is watching? Why do ye not break it off? I understand it would nay be easy or pleasant—but dammit, man, ye are miserable. Break it off."

"Her mother would unleash a breach of promise suit the likes of which the *ton* has never seen. You know that." It was Wolfe's turn to shudder. "And I can tell Lady Margaret will one day become her mother. Maybe even worse. Why do you think I've avoided the altar as long as I have? It is my hope she will break the engagement." A subtle wave of guilt washed across him. "I am sure Lady Margaret will make a fine wife for someone—just not me."

"Ye canna carry on as ye have, man. 'Tis not fair nor good for either of ye. What are ye now? Seven and thirty and without an heir?"

"Six and thirty, you bloody devil, and you well know it."

"And ye canna dally with Broadmere's sister. Ye *know* that— aye?"

"I know." Wolfe stopped walking toward the carriage and

turned into the cool night breeze, lifting his face to it in the hopes of clearing his head. Lady Grace both infuriated and entranced him. The woman must be descended from a long line of seductresses, because he found himself unable to shake her from his thoughts. She was a thorny rose that had pricked him and gotten into his blood.

Strath stood there in the darkness watching him. "Gads, man. Has she already bewitched ye?"

Wolfe huffed a humorless laugh. "Not only me. Connor intends to marry her."

"Aye, ye mentioned that the other day."

Thoughts of that first meeting with the enchanting Lady Grace made Wolfe smile as he stared off into the darkness, seeing her once again garbed in those scandalous clothes, her lovely face flushed with righteous fire. "Connor proclaimed her *beyond compare* after she saved his pup and gave him and Susannah a ride home on her very fine thoroughbred."

"Beyond compare, eh? From where I'm standing, it looks as if ye feel the same."

"Quite possibly." Wolfe expelled the deep breath that he felt he'd held since first setting eyes on Lady Grace. "I've never met a woman like her, Strath. She's always in my thoughts. Always on my mind."

Strath nudged him onward toward the carriage. "Appears to me it's time ye did *something*—even if ye fear that something is wrong. Ye have a woman ye dinna want, and canna have the woman ye wished ye had. 'Tis not fair to either of them, unless…"

"Unless?"

"Unless Lady Grace would rather spit on yer grave as to look at ye when it comes to accepting your attention." Strath shook his head. "If ye want her, 'tis time ye cleaned yer house, made things right, then went after her. She'll not remain unattached forever, ye ken? That is something ye need to think about as well."

"Where the bloody hell do you get all this wisdom about

affairs of the heart?"

Strath winked before stepping up into the carriage. "My love-ly wife. Where else?"

"Then ask your lovely wise wife how I might disentangle myself from my current predicament with Lady Margaret."

Strath dipped a curt nod. "Consider it done. My wee Sarah has always loved a challenge."

GRACE SHOULDERED OPEN the door the servants had used long ago, before Papa had the second floor redesigned for the expanding family. It was partially hidden behind a wardrobe in the sisters' shared dressing room, but the large piece of furniture was angled so the door could still be used due to Papa's concerns about house fires trapping those he held dear.

"Merciful heavens!" Nellie jumped and launched her armload of freshly folded clothes into the air.

"Oh, Nellie. Forgive me." Grace scrambled to help the poor maid gather the stockings and shifts tossed about the room. "I forgot you might be in here sorting things for bedtime."

"Oh, my lady, did the evening not go well?" With a sympathetic tilt of her head, Nellie quietly clicked her tongue like she always did when disappointed for Grace.

"*Not go well* does not begin to cover it." But Grace knew better than to share all that had happened with the Duke of Wolfebourne. She had long suspected the servants were Serendipity's ears. While Nellie was as devoted as she was efficient, the maid would not hesitate to share anything and everything at the downstairs kitchen table. "Are you aware that Chance invited the Earl of Middlebie for an extended visit?"

Nellie unhooked a shift from where it had snagged on the corner of the mirror, shook it out, and refolded it. "I was not, my lady, else I would have told you. Is anyone else staying? I've not been downstairs yet this evening."

"No one, as far as I know." Grace spotted a tear in the hem of her gown. She must have caught her skirt on the trellis when it snapped. "Drat! Can you repair this? Seri will have nine kinds of fits if she discovers I have ruined yet another silk, and this shade of pink is so difficult to find. Madame Couire said so when we chose it."

The maid knelt and examined the damage closer, then winced. "The dressmaker in the village might be able to add a bit of lace as trim to hide it. If I try to mend that rip, I fear the material will pucker." She gave Grace a look of gentle accusation. "The trellis again?"

That reminded Grace of the mess she'd made of that. "Of course the trellis again, and would you mind getting word to Fred or Jasper that I would be ever so grateful if they could see to it before anyone is the wiser?"

Nellie winced again. "Before anyone is the wiser about what, my lady?"

"About the fact that it appears to have torn away from the wall and snapped in two. I prefer that Mr. Warren not discover it, because he will insist on mentioning it to Chance." Mr. Warren was the estate overseer doing his best to foster the same genuine interest for the country estate in Chance that Papa had always possessed, but Grace feared that was a lost cause. Chance loved London and the excitement it offered.

At Nellie's open-mouthed shock, she held up a hand. "I was not injured. It slowly sagged away from the wall and enabled me to land safely." Which was not a lie. She had landed safely in Wolfebourne's arms—of course, the *safe* part was debatable at this point, especially since her heart still beat so fast that she was somewhat breathless. She extended her arms. "See? Not a scratch."

Nellie stared at her in earnest. "Forgive me for being so bold, my lady, but your dearly departed mama—God rest her soul— would be most displeased."

"I am in no mood for lectures, thank you. I get quite enough from Seri." Grace didn't appreciate being scolded by her older-than-usual lady's maid who had been chosen for her because she was deemed too much of a handful for a maid closer to her own age. She especially didn't like being scolded when she knew the maid was correct. She turned and gave Nellie her back. "Please undo my hooks and buttons, then I can handle the rest. You may retire and enjoy what little there is left of the evening."

"Yes, my lady." Nellie's regret about speaking her mind was unmistakable in her tone.

"I am not angry." Grace bowed her head and rubbed her temples. "I am simply tired and wish to be alone before the herd comes upstairs."

"Of course, my lady."

Lovely. Grace blew out a frustrated sigh. For the next few days, Nellie would *my lady* her to death, and there would be no further updates on tidbits of gossip from the servants' table. She supposed that served her right for getting churlish with poor old Nellie, but this evening had rattled her to her core. She clenched her teeth and waited for the maid to finish and leave the dressing room before she sagged down onto the stool in front of the dressing table.

"How could you let him get the upper hand?" she asked her reflection in the mirror. "Allow him to kiss you not once, but twice?" She dropped her head into her folded arms, trying to escape this mess of her own making. But the kisses had been so very nice. She swallowed hard, trying to dislodge the knot of emotions making her throat ache. The Duke of Wolfebourne, *Wolfe*, was not for her. He belonged to another. Society placed him and Lady Margaret within a hairsbreadth of the classification of husband and wife.

A gentle nudge against her leg paired with a snuffling woof made her lift her head. "Oh, Gastric. What am I to do?"

The sweet hound whined and thumped his tail while snuggling closer.

Slipping off the stool and onto the floor, she hugged him into her lap and rested her cheek against his velvety head. "I let him kiss me, Gastric. I am such a fool."

"You did what?" Joy stood in the doorway of the short hallway that interconnected the bedrooms. "Who kissed you?"

"Lower your voice," Grace snapped, defensive desperation nearly choking her. "Who else has already come up from the circus below?"

"I am the only one for now, but it won't be long." Joy hurried over and plopped onto the floor with her. "Who kissed you?"

"Are you truly that thick?"

Joy smirked. "Well, I thought I would give you the benefit of the doubt. I certainly hoped it was the Duke of Wolfebourne and not the lizard-like Blytheston or that cold, pasty Sir Andrew. I knew it wasn't Middlebie because we would have heard the man crowing about it—besides, he seemed more than a little attentive to Lady Margaret this evening." She went serious and stole a glance at the open doorway. "Speaking of Lady Margaret—what about her?" Her eyes flared wide as her thoughts vividly played across her face. How in the world Joy ever won at cards was a mystery to Grace, because her sister's expressions always betrayed her emotions. "Has Wolfebourne revealed himself to be an insensitive rake?"

"When I reminded him that he belonged to another, he seemed genuinely remorseful." Grace worried with Gastric's long, floppy ears, wishing for wisdom about this impossible situation. "And I do believe it was an accident—the kiss, I mean, not his remorse. He saved me from a nasty fall when the trellis broke."

"For heaven's sake, how are you going to keep Chance or Seri from finding out about that? Seri will check it, you know. She saw you slip out into the garden, but that horrid Lady Long-morten finally deigned to join the conversation, so Seri couldn't escape to go after you."

"Nellie is seeing to that for me. I asked her to get one of the lads to clean up my mess before anyone finds it." Grace angled an ear toward the open door. She swore a floorboard had creaked, as if someone approaching had mis-stepped. Most of them knew which spots on the floor groaned the loudest and gave their stealth away. "Did you hear that?"

Joy narrowed her eyes at the door. "Merry. Felicity. Come along. We know you are there."

The sisters appeared, both looking sheepish.

"I told you not to step there," Merry said to Felicity, accusation dripping from every word.

"It was not me." Felicity gave an indignant snort. "You did it."

"I did it," Serendipity said from behind them, making all of them jump and clutch at their hearts. She homed in on Grace, marching forward like an enraged archangel ready to vanquish evil. "Explain yourself."

"I find such an unfounded attitude quite offensive," Grace shot back, determined to bluff her way through this.

"Unfounded?" Serendipity arched a brow while slowly circling the dressing room that had become uncomfortably crowded. "I saw the trellis just as Fred and Jasper arrived to clear away your evidence, and just now overheard bits of your conversation. I repeat, dear sister, explain yourself. Fully, if you please."

Grace cleared her throat and attempted a demureness she in no way felt. "What exactly did you overhear? Eavesdropping is rude, you know. Mama always said so."

"Mama also told you to stay off the trellis, remember? Something about it being meant for roses and not a means of escape for a young girl who should know better?" Hands on her hips, Serendipity stared down at Grace, then pointed at the door. "Everyone into the sitting room. This area is entirely too small for a proper discussion into whatever you have done this time that could bring all our reputations down around our ears."

Pushing herself up from the floor, Grace shot a meaningful

yet subtle look at Joy, silently imploring her to keep mum. "Come, Gastric." She clicked her fingers at her devoted hound, who immediately fell in step beside her. Sensing more than seeing her sisters follow along, she toyed with the idea of confessing fully, as she had done before about her first meeting with the duke, or trying to dance around the facts so that no one but Joy knew what had happened. But was Joy the only one who knew? How much had the others overheard?

Serendipity seemed suspiciously horrified, and Merry and Felicity appeared to be enraptured. Knowing those two, they wanted every detail about the kiss. Joy would be disappointed by a full confession because, once again, she would be disarmed and wouldn't have any secrets to use in the future.

"Up on the settee, Gastric. I need your protection." Grace patted the cushion beside her, and after three valiant, short-legged hops, the dog launched his weightiness up onto the sofa and settled down beside her. She gave Serendipity a regal nod. "Proceed with the interrogation, sister."

Serendipity's delicate features hardened, and her eyes narrowed. She folded her arms across her chest and ambled back and forth in front of Grace, never once breaking eye contact. "What happened in the garden?"

"What makes you think anything happened in the garden?"

Serendipity tipped her head in the direction of the other three sisters. "Joy is jiggling her foot. A sure sign she knows something she believes no one else knows. Merry's cheeks have gone too red, and Felicity has chewed on her bottom lip so much, it has noticeably plumped." She closed the distance between them and gave Grace a curt nod. "Your hem is torn. You are clinging to Gastric even more than usual, and I *saw* you slip out into the garden. Upon mentioning that to Chance, he informed me that the Duke of Wolfebourne also briefly stepped outside for some air, claiming the cigar smoke troubled him. He said the man was absent from the library for quite some time. Whether your trip outside and the duke's have anything in common remains to be seen, but from what little I overheard, I strongly believe that it does."

"There was no cigar smoke in the ladies' parlor. That is not why I left." Grace knew full well that Serendipity held the advantage in this conversation. Try as she might, she simply could not think of a plausible way to explain all that her sister had not only overheard but believed she already knew. "I left the parlor because I had enjoyed the dinner party for as long as I could stand it. You know my penchant for the trellis. Unfortunately, due to its age, this time it broke, and that route was no longer viable."

Serendipity stared at her with such fierce intensity that Grace couldn't help but squirm. She finally threw up her hands. "I swear you should work for the Crown interrogating prisoners," she told her sister. "Wolfebourne caught me as I fell. His Grace saved me from possible injury."

Serendipity still didn't speak, just narrowed her eyes further.

"What?" Grace demanded. "Have you trained tiny birds to hide in the dressing room and eavesdrop on us, then fly back to you and repeat everything we have said?"

"I distinctly overheard the words *kiss* and *rake*."

"You must have the hearing of an owl." Grace stifled a groan. She was well and truly snared. "Wolfebourne and I found ourselves overcome by my nearly perilous fall from the trellis and the moonlight. He kissed me, and I informed him that while I might be unconventional, I am not a lightskirt, and since he belonged to another, he should go back inside and leave me alone."

"And he said?"

"He apologized for his abominable behavior."

With her arms still primly folded across her chest, Serendipity slowly paced back and forth in front of Grace as if determined to examine her from every angle. "You smiled at each other at dinner. During the first course."

"I smiled because the man seemed to loathe pea soup as

much as I do. I can't possibly fathom why he smiled back at me. Probably just to be polite." Good heavens, how on earth had Serendipity noticed such a fleeting moment? Unless she had purposely been watching. "How did I become such an object of interest when, as the eldest and the hostess, you should have focused your attention on our guests?"

"Because of your initial encounter with the Duke of Wolfebourne, and his throwing down of the gauntlet—or should I say *buckskins?*" Serendipity lunged in so close that Gastric rumbled with a rare growl, warning that while he was a good-natured sort, he would not hesitate to protect his mistress. Serendipity frowned down at him. "Oh, stop, Gastric. You know I would never harm our Gracie."

The hound positioned himself more firmly between Grace and her sister, determined to shield her no matter what Serendipity said.

"Do you love him?" Serendipity asked quietly.

"Love him?" Grace hugged Gastric closer. "Who?"

All the sisters groaned and shook their heads.

"Now who is thick?" Joy asked, impatiently tapping her toe so quickly that her skirts shook.

"I just met the man. How could I possibly love him?" And yet a disturbing rush of heat swept across Grace, and those infernal birds in her middle started batting their wings again. But that wasn't love—that was because she had very much enjoyed his kisses. "I do not love him. Besides, even if I did happen to harbor any feelings for him, what good would it do? He is betrothed to Lady Margaret."

"Oh, Gracie." Serendipity sank into a nearby chair and propped her head in her hand.

Joy, Merry, and Felicity all stared at Grace with the same sympathetic looks they always gave her whenever one of her beloved animals passed.

"What?" Grace asked so sharply that Gastric perked his ears and *woofed.*

"You may not love him yet," Merry said, "but the seeds are sown and sprouting. Remember what Mama said about relationships being like a garden?"

A soft knock on the sitting room door made them all turn and stare at it.

"Lady Serendipity?" Mrs. Flackney, the housekeeper, quietly called as she barely opened it a crack. "Forgive the intrusion at this late hour, but I have a note for Lady Grace. Nellie mentioned she might already be abed, but I saw the light under this door and heard voices, so I thought I would ask."

The fluttering wings in Grace's middle churned harder, threatening to expel her supper. She drew in a deep breath and scolded herself for such silly behavior. It was probably a written apology from the duke—no more, no less. "Do bring it in, Mrs. Flackney," she told the kindly matron who had minded their household for ages. "I am still awake, but I fear Gastric has me pinned."

The housekeeper hurried into the room, handed her the note, then nodded and left just as quickly as she had entered, softly closing the door behind her.

Grace unfolded the small slip of paper that appeared to have been torn from the corner of something else. It was written in graphite, smudged, and the script was messy, as if done in haste. As Grace made out the words, an ominous chill touched her to the bone.

"Gracie? You have gone dangerously pale. What does it say?" With Gastric much calmer and no longer a threat, Serendipity scooted in beside Grace and wrapped an arm around her shoulders. Joy, Merry, and Felicity drew in close as well.

"*He belongs to another and will only be the ruination of you and your family,*" Grace whispered before choking on the malice behind the words. She clutched a fist to her chest, coughing and wheezing to draw in air.

Joy rushed to the bellpull, yanked it hard, then hurried to the door. "I can't wait till they come up. I'll be back with Mrs.

Flackney shortly. She can tell us who sent that threat."

Grace nodded and waved her on, then crumpled and gave in to something she rarely did—tears.

Chapter Eight

CLAD IN AN annoying walking dress that snagged on every bramble and blade of grass, Grace plodded along the old fence line that kept the cows from straying into the crops and grazing them down to nothing but stubble. Gastric stayed beside her while her other hounds trotted up ahead, noses to the ground, snuffling for something exciting to chase. As she meandered along, she snapped off the tops of the tallest grasses and imagined shoving them up Lady Longmorten's nose—the author of the odious threat to stain not only Grace's standing amongst the *ton* but her sisters' reputations as well. For if one Abarough sister fell, they all fell. Even Chance would be somewhat marked by any gossip about his sisters.

The sad thing was, nothing the horrendous woman had said in her hastily scribbled note was untrue.

"And there's the rub, Gastric," Grace informed the sweet dog hopping alongside her.

His only response was a happy *woof.*

Oh, to be a carefree canine. She looked to the south, wondering what the unhappy Duke of Wolfebourne was doing at this very moment. For he was unhappy with his life. Pure melancholy shouted from him. Such a shame. When he smiled, his charm and strong good looks became almost overpowering. She hitched in a deep breath and walked faster. *If only…*

The steady thud of hoofbeats at a hard gallop made her turn

and shield her eyes from the sun. It was Jasper. On her horse. Something must be terribly wrong. "Come to me, lads!" she called to the dogs, then caught up her skirts and ran to meet the groom.

Jasper halted Pegasus and leapt from the saddle. "His Grace wants you back at the house, my lady."

"What is wrong? What has happened?"

The lad shook his head. "All in the household are well so far as I know, but His Grace said to fetch you back quick as a minute."

Irritated beyond belief, Grace yanked at her skirts. "Dressed as I am, I can't ride. Since this appears to be one of my brother's whims, I shall return at my own pace." She kissed her horse's nose. "We shall ride later, Pegasus. I promise." With a nod at Jasper, she stepped aside. "Inform His Grace I will get there when I get there."

Ducking his head, the young man struggled not to smile. "Yes, my lady. Shall I keep Pegasus ready for your ride?"

"No, since I am unsure as to what His Grace wants."

"Yes, my lady." Jasper retook the saddle and turned the horse toward home, glancing back once to ensure she followed.

She snorted a bitter laugh. The groom knew her too well.

"Come along, my boys," she told the dogs. "We have been summoned." She set off at a purposeful but not strenuous pace. While she normally took great pleasure in annoying Chance, struggling with the complications that had come with the Duke of Wolfebourne had wearied her into a shocking state of compliance, and she was at a loss as to what to do about it. She supposed all she could do was put the man out of her mind, but that was much easier said than done.

"I am better than this," she told Gastric as he swaggered along beside her, his long ears swinging in time with every step. "When have you ever known me to be this silly over a man—a quarrelsome, judgmental, opinionated, and *completely unavaila-ble* man? This is utterly ridiculous, Gastric."

Gastric sneezed several times and pawed at his muzzle.

"Hold fast, old friend. We are nearly out of the tallest grass. I know how it tickles your nose." As she looked up from her devoted companion, she caught sight of a carriage bearing the all-too-familiar ducal seal of a pair of wolves with their noses lifted in what appeared to be a long, mournful howl. It was parked in the circular drive in front of the manor house.

"Oh, Gastric." She allowed herself a groan. "What does he want now?" Or worse yet, maybe it was Lady Margaret or Lady Longmorten—or both. They would surely have use of the duke's carriage. After all, not only were they guests at Wolfebourne Lodge but also very nearly attached to the duke by marriage. "Come, my lads." She signaled the dogs to tighten their ranks and follow as she changed course and headed for the servant's entrance into the kitchens. She refused to enter the house without knowing what awaited her. Forewarned was forearmed.

The scullery maids looked up as she and her dogs entered. Busy preparing vegetables for the evening meal, they curtsied where they stood beside the worktable. The one on the end nearest to the ovens said, "Welcome, my lady. Cook! Lady Grace and her pups be here."

A stout, older woman with silvery-white hair that always did its best to escape the confines of her ruffled cap toddled out of the pantry, hugging a large crock in each arm. "The lads done had their soupbones, my lady, and Lucy and her pups done had their milk-soaked bread. Mr. Carson took it out to them some time ago."

"Thank you, Cook, but that is not why I am here. You always feed my precious ones well." Grace directed her dogs to take to their blankets along the wall beside the pantry, then edged over to the doorway that led to the dining room. She pushed it open the barest crack and peeped out. "What do you know about our guests?" she asked in a loud whisper.

Cook placed the crocks on the worktable with a heavy thump, then wiped her work-reddened hands on the apron lashed around her ample waist. "Old Walters fetched tea and cakes for four—His Grace, Lady Serendipity, and the Duke of Wolfebourne. He said nothing about who be the fourth, though."

Grace knew the identity of the fourth. It was her. What in heaven's name had happened now? Her heart fluttered into her throat, making her swallow hard. Had the duke ended his engagement to Lady Margaret? Was he here to…

No. Stop. Grace fisted her hands and forced herself to stop her ridiculous spiraling into the dangerous game of *what if.*

If the duke had broken his engagement off, then Lady Longmorten would have already shown up at the manor with her teeth bared and her claws unsheathed. Grace knew that as surely as she knew her own reflection in the mirror. The engagement was still intact. Gossip like that traveled like a raging fire burning across dry fields. Every servant in the Lake District would have reported such an astonishing event to their masters.

"Did you happen to send any brandy with the tea?" she asked Cook.

The kindly old woman sadly shook her head. "You be the fourth, then?"

"I be the fourth."

Cook nodded. "I figured so after—" She clamped her mouth shut and turned back to the worktable. "Be there anything else, my lady? Shall I give the pups extra scraps?"

Lovely. The servants knew everything. Grace had feared as much. "Yes, Cook. Please give the pups extra scraps and do not forget about sweet Lucy and her babies. They need more treats too."

"It shall be done, my lady." Cook looked up from the crock she was unsealing. "God be with you, Lady Grace. We all wish everything to go well for you."

"Thank you." Grace had no doubt the devoted servants only wanted the best for her. She just didn't like being at the center of their gossip. Rather than dwell on the matter, she pushed through the doors and made her way to the main parlor, where she felt sure the pair of dukes, her brother and Wolfebourne, were holding court. As she entered, she locked eyes with Chance and completely ignored Wolfebourne. "You summoned me, brother?"

"Gracie!" Chance glared at her, then pointedly tipped a nod at the duke. "Where are your manners? We have a guest."

She spared the man an aloof curtsy but kept her gaze on the floor. "Your Grace."

"Lady Grace."

The sorrow in his deep voice washed across her and made her lift her head and look him in the eye. She swallowed hard at the pain she saw there. But this pain and worry was not because of her. The poor man was beside himself in misery. Alarm seized her heart. "Connor and Sissy—are they all right?"

"I cannot find them," he said, his voice raw and raspy. "I prayed they had come here—to you."

Panic threatened to choke her. "I was in the field with the dogs, walking the fence line. I have not seen them." She shared a desperate look with Serendipity. "I can't abide the hindrance of these skirts while I help His Grace search for the children. Pegasus and I can cover a great deal of ground if I change."

Serendipity gave a resigned nod, but Chance jumped to his feet. "No, Gracie! I forbid it."

"You have no right to forbid me anything," she told him. "I am of age." She granted Wolfebourne a gentle look that he more than deserved. "And he has already seen me in my buckskins but was gallant enough to guard my secret and protect my reputation. Connor and Sissy are my friends. I intend to find them and see them safe."

"You can't ride alone with him," Serendipity said, more than concern echoing in her tone. "Enough boundaries have been crossed."

"Then come with us. You or Chance or any of the others." Grace turned toward the door. "Whether chaperoned or not, I am going." She looked to Wolfebourne. "You can use one of our horses to save time." She turned to Chance. "Tell Jasper to get Pegasus ready. I shall be back down momentarily."

"Gracie—please." Her brother closed the distance between them and took hold of her hands. He opened his mouth to say more, but she silenced him with a hard look she knew he would understand.

"They are children, Chance, only seven years old, and there is so much out there that could harm them. Is the Abarough name, the Broadmere title, more important than the life of a child?" She stared him down, knowing he believed in the right answer even though it pained him to admit it.

He exploded with a loud snort and stepped back from her. "Fine. Do what you must, Gracie. We will pick up the pieces and mend whatever needs mending once the children are safe."

Without another word, she caught up her skirts and ran upstairs. "Nellie!" she shouted as she burst into the sitting room, crossed it, and ran down the short hallway to the dressing room. "Nellie, I need your help. Quickly."

"My lady?" Nellie emerged from the bedroom with her hands clasped to her chest. "What has happened?"

"I need to change into my buckskins. Quick as a minute. Children have gone missing, and I must find them."

"Children gone missing?" Nellie rushed to undo the buttons and hooks of Grace's gown. "What on earth happened, my lady? Whose children?"

"I am unsure of the details." Hopping on one foot, Grace loosened the laces of her walking boot, then kicked it off.

"Here, now. Let me tend to that, afore you fall and harm yourself." Nellie knelt and helped her remove the other one.

"They are only seven years old," Grace said, "a boy and girl. The Duke of Wolfebourne's young brother and sister." She fought with the laces of her stays so she could shed it and remove her shift. "They are full of mischief. I just hope they have not come to harm because of it."

Nellie hissed like a boiling kettle. "There is talk, my lady.

Those poor little mites may not have caused their own mishap. Might be, they had some help in whatever's become of them."

Grace froze with her buckskins halfway up over her hips. "What are you saying?"

The maid sadly shook her head as if that explained everything.

"Words, Nellie. I need words." Grace yanked her clothes in place and fastened the falls.

"Lady Margaret and her mother planned to be rid of those children long ago. They blame those innocents for the duke taking so long to get to the altar. Lady Longmorten has especially been trying to shift those little ones away for a while now."

"The children told me those women wanted to send them off, but surely His Grace would never allow that. Are they not his only family?" Grace chose her words carefully, not wanting to add any fuel to the gossip already swirling around her and the duke. It was bad enough that everyone seemed to know they had been in the garden together—in a most compromising and unchaperoned way. But it was her greatest hope that no one but her sisters knew about the kisses. "I'd never let anyone send Chance or any of the girls away. Family is…well, everything!"

Nellie helped her step into her trusty riding boots, then helped her with her braces and handed over her tattered hat and jacket. "Not everyone cherishes family the way yours does, my lady. Your mama and papa raised the lot of you to love and protect each other. Many are not so blessed. My lady—your hair!"

"I can't wear my cap with it fluffed and pinned the way it is," Grace said as she tore out the astonishing number of pins and let her thick braid fall down her back. "You can fix it when I return."

"Yes, my lady." Nellie gave a heavy sigh as she gathered the hairpins and returned them to the container on the dressing table.

Grace shrugged on her jacket and pulled on her cap. "Come now, Nellie, you know you wouldn't have me any other way. Your life would be entirely too boring."

"That be true, my lady. God be with you, and I hope you find those poor little mites." Concern filled the maid's eyes. "A shame they couldn't be brought here, where they would be safe."

It was as though the maid had read her mind. Grace nodded as she headed out the door. "I agree."

She bounded down the stairs, slowing at the sight of Serendipity not only already dressed in her riding habit but cradling a gun in the crook of her arm. Her sister was gifted with remarkable aim, but was a gun truly needed? "Does Wolfebourne believe foul play is afoot? And how did you dress without my seeing you? I was in the dressing room."

"Bess helped me dress in the bedroom, and Wolfebourne said nothing about foul play, but I suspect it." Serendipity glanced up and down the hallway, then hurried Grace forward with a wave of her hand. "Come. I will share what I know on the way to the stables."

"I already know the ladies in the Wolfebourne household wish to be rid of the little ones," Grace said. "But last I heard, they were only attempting to send them away. Not harm them. They planned to ship them off to boarding schools or studies abroad—which is ridiculous. They are entirely too young to be torn away from their brother." Grace snapped her fingers as they passed through the kitchen and exited the house. Her hounds responded with excited barks and loped ahead, their noses already to the ground.

"Gastric too?" Serendipity gave the short-legged dog a pained look. "He can't keep up, Gracie."

"He rides with me in the saddle carrier Tom made for him. When we stop and search the ravine, he has the best nose of them all and has met Connor and Sissy." Grace lengthened her stride, anxious to get to it. "Now, tell me what you know about what may have happened to the children."

"Word has it that Lady Longmorten's patience has reached its limit. Since the duke refuses to set his siblings aside and get on with a new life with her daughter, she intends to be rid of them in any way possible." Serendipity struggled to keep up, the long skirts of her riding habit sweeping the ground behind her. "I believe this is the first time I ever envied you your buckskins."

"Why in heaven's name would the servants not step in and warn the duke? How could they let anything happen to Connor and Sissy? If that woman hurt those children…" Grace trembled with rage the likes of which she had never felt before. "I will shoot her myself, and then clear his house of every servant who chose to remain quiet rather than defend those dears."

Serendipity hushed her as they reached the horses already saddled and ready in front of the stable.

"Who do you intend to shoot, my lady?" Wolfebourne asked. "And what do I need to know about my house and my servants?" The man took her breath away as he approached her, moving with the mesmerizing grace of a lethal predator. He was broad shouldered, dark, and dangerous. Her pounding heart and fluttering middle made her swallow hard. What she wouldn't give for this man to be free of his ties. "Lady Grace?" he said, staring down at her, his gaze searing her soul.

"Lady Longmorten wants to be rid of Connor and Sissy, and your cold-hearted servants appear to be disinclined to protect them and come to you about that woman's treacherous ways."

"And you know of this how?" he asked through clenched teeth.

She turned to her sister. "Tell him."

"I can't reveal my sources, Your Grace." Serendipity jutted her chin higher. "But they are reliable, I assure you. Lady Longmorten intends to take matters into her own hands so that your marriage to her daughter will not be delayed any longer."

He launched himself up into the saddle of the borrowed horse. "You will not be required to shoot that woman, Lady Grace. If what your sister says is true, I will dispatch Lady Longmorten and my servants myself."

"I understand." Grace mounted Pegasus, then nodded to Jasper to place Gastric into his seat behind her. "I say we go to the ravine first. That was where I first met your brother and sister. If they ran away, as we all hope they did, they might hide there. Did you check to see if Hector or Galileo have gone missing too?"

Wolfebourne bowed his head, then bared his teeth and rumbled with a frustrated growl. "I am a bloody fool. I never thought to check."

Grace sidled her horse closer to his and, without thinking, reached over and touched his arm. "You are not a fool. Merely frantic to find them. Do you happen to have anything of theirs that would give my lads a good scent? Their noses are quite good, even though they never hunt."

He stared down at her hand on his arm, as if memorizing the feel of it. "I have nothing of theirs with me," he said quietly. "Should we ride to the lodge and fetch something?"

"No. Not yet." Grace whistled for the dogs, waved them in the direction she wished them to go, then gave Pegasus his head. They barreled across the meadow to the ravine. As a child, whenever she ran away to get Chance and Serendipity in trouble for *losing* her, she had always gone there. It was the perfect place for a child to hide, what with the overgrown gullies and washed-out holes in the embankments that the wayward stream carved into the land. She prayed the children had merely run off and were safe. If they had, when she found them, she would give them a stern tongue lashing, but only after she had hugged them so tightly it made them squeak. They simply had to be safe. She couldn't bear it if they weren't.

As they neared the overgrown patch of land, her worry for Connor and Sissy increased. The dogs had yet to signal the scent of anything out of the ordinary. Heads down and tails in the air, they trotted along, giving no excited barks or yips to tell her they had found something they wanted her to see.

"I am going down there." She swung down from the saddle and reached up for Gastric.

"Let me help with him," Wolfebourne said. "It is the least I can do." He unbuckled the straps that kept the dog from leaping out and harming himself during a ride. "Come along, old man. I need your help more than you can imagine."

Gastric wiggled with excitement, his entire back end wagging along with his tail.

"I shall ride alongside the ravine, then take to higher ground and study the area from there," Serendipity told them, before giving Grace a sad smile. "That was how we always found you. Whistle sharply if you find them. I shall do the same." Then she turned her horse and ambled away, her focus locked on the tangle of overgrowth walling off the jagged tunnel the stream had cut through the land.

"I thought she came along to protect your reputation?" Wolfebourne asked, watching her ride away.

"Seri knows our focus is the children." Grace crouched and went nose to nose with Gastric. "Remember our friends from the other day, sweet boy? Not the cat or the dog but the boy and the girl? Find them, my precious. I know you can do it."

Gastric emitted a soft woof, licked the end of her nose, then disappeared into the tall grasses.

"You truly believe he understood you?"

"Animals understand far more than you realize." She wouldn't add that she understood them much better than she understood people. "How long have your brother and sister been gone? When was the last time you saw them?"

"At breakfast." He plodded along beside her, ripping aside vines so the rough land wouldn't grab hold of their feet and twist their ankles. He halted and stared downward, seeming trapped in his own personal hell.

She gently touched his arm, wishing she could promise him everything would be all right. "Your Grace?"

He jerked as if he had forgotten she was there. "Wolfe. Please call me Wolfe."

His dark eyes reminded her of polished onyx or the blackest jet beads. But it wasn't their shade that made her catch her breath—it was the loneliness and pleading for help and under-standing that deepened their richness.

She swallowed hard and tried to manage a reassuring smile. "Wolfe"—she loved the way his name *felt* when she said it— "what happened at breakfast? It seemed like you remembered something there for a moment."

"Lady Margaret and her mother *strongly* implied that a summer wedding would be just the thing." He scowled at the embankment as they slowly made their way deeper into the gully. "They even mentioned stopping by to see the vicar so the banns could be started as early as this Sunday." He yanked at a tangle of woodbine and ripped them out of the way. "Then Lady Longmorten suggested a special license to avoid having to wait any longer—and when she said it, she smiled directly at the twins, daring them to challenge her."

Grace couldn't imagine Connor or Sissy taking that well or failing to share their objections about the marriage. "Was there a terrible row, or did they simply run away and leave the room?"

Wolfe snorted a bitter laugh. "Connor informed me of his deep disappointment in me if I went ahead with the marriage to Lady Margaret, and that it would prove beyond a shadow of a doubt that he was the only intelligent son our father had sired. Sissy agreed with him, and also warned I would not only be miserable but that marrying Lady Margaret would make me die sooner rather than later because unhappy people do not live as long as those who are satisfied and joyful."

"My goodness." Grace bit the inside of her cheek to keep from smiling. "Such wisdom for ones so young—and how did your fiancée and future mother-in-law react?"

"Lady Margaret called them wicked little beasts, and Lady Longmorten informed me I had not only failed to discipline them properly but should have stripped them of any familial connections and named them the insolent little bastards they truly were long ago."

Rage swept through Grace, making her turn from a crack in the embankment that was large enough to hide a child. "Tell me you threw them out and told that vile pair never to return."

"They and their things are headed for the Binnocksbourne Inn as we speak. Unfortunately, during my robust conversation with the ladies, Connor and Sissy slipped away."

"How much of your *robust* conversation did they overhear?" Grace couldn't imagine the twins running away if they knew their brother had disinvited the houseguests and ordered them to move to the inn. "They were aware you sided with them. Yes?"

His shoulders slumped. "I fear they may have left while I foolishly attempted to be polite and logical with my guests." He slowly lifted his gaze. "What if they believe I did not *choose* them? If anything happens—"

"Stop this instant. You must not talk like that." Grace maneuvered back from a deep, washed-out fissure, caught her toe in the vines, and stumbled into his arms.

He held her there, willingly trapped by his embrace and desperation. "They are all I have, Grace...if I may call you Grace."

"Yes...of course. And they are not all you have. You have my...friendship." She allowed herself the momentary thrill of resting her hands on his hard, muscular chest, then inwardly shook herself and reluctantly stepped back. The urgency to find the children pressed her to put distance between them, even though her selfish wish was to remain in his arms. "Come. We have Connor and Sissy to find."

A deep, loud, mournful baying farther down the stream echoed back to them. It was joined by a series of excited yips and barks that vibrated through the meadow.

Grace's heart leapt. "Gastric has found something—he's calling us and the other dogs. As happy as he sounds, it must be the children. He rarely gets that excited about a hare or field mouse."

"Thank God Almighty. I pray it truly is them." Wolfe caught her by the hand as if it were the most natural thing to do, tugging her along as he took the lead toward the sound of the dogs. "What if they try to slip away or hide?"

"My dogs will think it a wonderful game and give chase. If it's Connor and Sissy they've found, we'll not lose them again."

"I pray you are right." Wolfe caught her up in his arms again just as she slipped on some wet stones. "Take care, my Grace."

"*My Grace?*" She tried to play off his awkward endearment as a jest, giving him a means of escape.

He held her there for the longest moment, staring into her eyes as if willing her to hear his innermost thoughts. "Yes. *My Grace*—if I have my way about it." Then he set her back on her feet and held her hand just as tightly as before, and they took off again.

If he had his way about it. Hopeful giddiness bubbled through her, making her catch her breath. *My Grace,* he had said—and oh dear heavens, the way he had said it. But now was not the time to dwell on what the future might hold. They had to find Connor and Sissy. Only then would her excitement be complete.

Chapter Nine

"THOSE SLY LITTLE imps," Grace said as they scrambled across the rocky yet more even ground alongside the stream. "I wager they've hidden in the deepest part of the gully, where the stonemasons and gardeners get the gravel and boulders for the estate." She skipped faster, taking the lead while still tugging Wolfe along by the hand.

She amazed him. He had never known a woman with the grace and speed of a deer, the tenacity of a hound on the scent, and the cunning of a wily huntsman. More importantly, she showed a genuine affection for his brother and sister, as if they were her own. He agreed wholeheartedly with his little brother—Lady Grace was beyond compare.

"Thank you for helping," he said as they jogged along, "and thank your wonderful dogs too. I shall buy them every soupbone in Binnocksbourne. All of you have made this day so much easier to bear." This precious woman had no idea how much he appreciated her in every sense of the word.

"Connor and Sissy are my friends." She scrambled across a slippery span of rocks with the agility of a river otter. "I couldn't imagine not helping ensure they are safe."

And that was just one of the many differences between Grace and the difficult family to which his well-meaning father had leg-shackled him. The scene at breakfast had as much as decided Wolfe that no matter the cost, the engagement to Lady Margaret had to end. He refused to submit his younger siblings to the machinations of the cold-hearted women any longer. Once the Longmortens were gone, his only issue would be gaining Connor's forgiveness for pursuing Lady Grace, since Connor had already declared his love for her. Wolfe prayed Grace would give him a chance to prove he wasn't the aloof, beastly duke she must surely think him to be.

As they crossed the rugged ground, helping each other whenever they stumbled, the vastness of the Broadmere estate impressed him. "How the devil did those two cover so much ground?"

"They are children, and from what little you told me, I imagine they were very angry. We must climb out of the ravine here because it narrows too much up ahead at the stream's level. We can descend again a bit farther down the way." Grace let go of his hand and climbed the much steeper embankment on all fours, granting him a most pleasing view of her shapely behind. "Think back to when you were that age," she called back to him. "Whenever you became angry, were you not filled with boundless energy to fight your foes?"

"I was in boarding school at their age, and if I caused a tenth of the mischief that those two wreak, the headmaster would have beaten me bloody."

Grace halted so fast, he nearly collided with her. She turned and stared at him, her expression a heartwarming mix of rage and compassion. "That is despicable. Promise you will never send Connor to such a place. Promise me, this very instant."

"I will never send Connor to such a place," he said, vowing so much more to her but afraid to say it aloud. Now was not the time. "Nor will I send Sissy away. I swear that as well."

Gastric bayed again, louder and more frantic. The other hounds joined in, adding a racket of sharp, high-pitched yips.

"They sound different now." Wolfe helped Grace scale the remainder of the embankment, and they turned toward the sound. "Why is the pitch of their barking so different?" The worry in her eyes concerned him.

"They want us to hurry. Something is wrong." She shoved through the remaining snarl of vines and grasses walling off the ravine, then took off at a hard run, loping across the meadow's grassy hillocks. She split the air with a sharp whistle, and soon, both horses joined them. "Stay close, Pegasus, and keep Barberry close as well." She pointed at a break in the overgrowth. "There. We can get to the rock gully through there."

"Connor!" Wolfe powered the bellow with all his worries and fears. "Sissy!"

"Brother!" Sissy's tearful whimper made them maneuver the steep wall of the gorge even faster. "Connor and Galileo are buried in a hole. I can't dig them out."

"Dear God, do not let it be so." Wolfe barreled down the last of the incline and charged across the rocky ground. Sissy cowered against the opposite wall of the small quarry. Connor's dog, Hector, frantically pawed at a pile of fist-sized stones. Terror clenched icy fingers around Wolfe's heart at the sight of a pale, little hand barely reaching out of the darkness of a small hole where the rocks rested against the embankment. Connor was indeed buried—but at least he was alive.

Grace reached for the little girl, giving the child a reassuring smile. "Come to me, Sissy. Your brother will have Connor and Galileo rescued before you know it."

Sissy dove into Grace's arms, clutching her as she sobbed against her shoulder. "I told him to let me get Galileo out of the cave, but he said it was too dangerous."

"He was protecting you," Grace said, patting the overwrought child. "That is what brothers do. Now, we must be brave while Wolfe digs him out."

"Can you please still hold me?" the little girl asked with a pitiful sniff.

"Of course I can still hold you." Grace hugged the child closer and gave Wolfe a look that assured him she would watch over Sissy while he did his best to free his brother.

He took hold of Connor's hand, thankful that it was warm with life. "Are you hurt?"

A sullen *no* echoed out of the hole. "I'm just mad at Galileo. He jumped out and left me behind."

"Perhaps he felt you would follow him and then you would both be safe. Is that a possibility?" Wolfe knew the boy loved the cat as much as his sister did.

"Maybe if I'd left with him instead of staying behind to pry loose a pretty rock for Grace—I mean—Lady Grace so's she would let me and Sissy stay with her, maybe then I'd not be in this sorry state. So, I guess maybe I can't blame him for leaving out of here when the rocks started to fall."

"Lady Grace would have allowed you to stay with her as long as you had my permission. She would not have demanded payment of any kind." Wolfe glanced back at Grace.

She rolled her eyes and mouthed, *Of course.*

Then it occurred to Wolfe that Sissy had said Galileo was trapped with Connor. An ominous dread filled him. Had the cat tried to escape too late and been buried beneath the rockslide? He started to ask Connor to check again for Galileo but feared it would alarm the boy. He glanced once more at Sissy, still clinging to Grace, and decided they could sort it once Connor was safe. If poor old Galileo had used all of his nine lives, Wolfe would get them another cat.

"I'm going to enlarge this opening and pull you out," he said. "If anything starts shifting, tell me immediately. Understand?"

"What the bloody hell is that supposed to mean?"

Connor's indignance and coarse language made Wolfe smile. At least the lad still had plenty of fight left in him. "Language, young man. There are ladies present."

"Sorry." A loud sniffling echoed out of the hole. "Shifting is what got me trapped. I don't care too much for that word no more."

"I know, brother, but stay strong." Wolfe scooped away the smaller rocks by the handfuls and grappled the larger ones one at a time. "I believe the hole is large enough now. Give me your hands. I am going to pull you out."

"Hurry, Wolfe—something is in here with me. I heard it growl farther back in the darkness."

Wolfe prayed it was that damn cat. He braced his footing, reached down into the hole, and locked hold of Connor's wrists. "Close your eyes and duck your head." He gave a mighty pull, yanking the boy up through the opening and into his arms. "Thank God Almighty. I have you, Connor. I have you."

"Galileo!" Sissy cried. "Come here, sweet kitty."

The huge orange cat streaked down the pile of rubble and leapt into Sissy's embrace.

"I thought he jumped out," Connor said. "He must've turned back when I covered my face 'cause of all the dirt in the air." He pried free of Wolfe and joined his sister, petting the cat while rubbing Hector's head as the little dog excitedly bounced around him. "He could have squeezed out that small hole any time he wanted, but he stayed with me. Thank you, Galileo. Sorry for what I said about your deserting me."

"Such a misunderstanding is very understandable." Grace pulled the boy into a tight hug and squeezed him until his little cheeks went red with embarrassment. She wrapped an arm around Sissy and tugged her into the frantic embrace as well. "Shame on you both for putting such a fright into us. Shame! Shame! Do you not realize we could never bear it if anything happened to either of you?"

For the first time in his life, Wolfe envied his brother and sister. What he wouldn't give to find himself in Grace's tight embrace, bearing a scolding because she cared so much about him.

"Does that mean you love us?" Sissy asked, her voice slightly muffled since she had her face buried in Grace's shoulder.

Grace gently set them away, then knelt and gave them each a stern scowl. "Of course I love you. You are my friends."

"Friends?" Connor scowled at her. "But I want to marry you.

You need to love me better than just a friend."

Wolfe couldn't resist giving Grace a sly grin when she glanced his way. He folded his arms across his chest, interested in hearing what the lady would say to that.

"Connor." Grace took the boy's hands in hers. "I can't marry you, but I will love you as a dear friend and cherish our friendship for all the days of my life. I promise you that."

Connor's scowl darkened and his bottom lip pooched out farther. "Why can you not marry me? Give me one good reason. Our ages do not matter. Father had wives that were a whole lot younger than him. We would just be the other way round, with you being the old one and me being the young one."

Wolfe was impressed with his brother's reasoning. He tipped his head and winked at Grace. It was her turn to respond.

She narrowed her eyes at him the slightest bit, thrilling him to no end. With a barely perceptible roll of her shoulders, she turned back to Connor. "By the time you reach the marriageable age of one and twenty, I will be a very old five and thirty—much too ancient to marry."

Connor eyed her for a long moment. "Wolfe is six and thirty, and Lady Margaret still plans to marry him. You should have heard her and her mother at breakfast today." He pointed at his former rocky prison. "Me and Sissy would rather live in that hole than stay with Wolfe 'cause she is sure to get worse once she is the duchess for real."

"Your brother needs you now more than ever. You must be brave and stay at his side." Grace gave the lad such a shaming look that even Wolfe felt a wave of guilt.

Sissy sidled closer to her brother. "We still love him, but we can't protect him from those mean women. We are naught but children, and they intend to send us away." She nodded at Wolfe. "He's heard them say so. All we can do is aggravate them until they get their way and get rid of us."

"No one is sending anyone away." Wolfe had heard enough. "And Connor, you should cherish the loving friendship Lady

Grace so generously offered. A true friend, one you can trust with your life, is as rare as a priceless diamond."

"But I want to marry her," Connor said.

"Connor." Grace took hold of the lad's hands once again. "I love you as a friend, but not as a man I wish to marry, so I fear I must refuse you. Some day you will understand. I promise."

"But I will never meet another woman like you." Connor tugged on her hands, his dark eyes glistening with unshed tears.

"I should hope not," Grace said, obviously attempting to lighten the moment. "And my brother would tell you to consider yourself fortunate on that count, because I embarrass him at every opportunity."

The boy turned to Wolfe with a dark look that warned trouble was brewing. "*You* marry her, then."

Wolfe almost choked on his own air. Not brave enough to witness Grace's reaction, he kept his focus locked on his little brother. "What?"

"You heard me," the boy said. "You marry Lady Grace. She can't refuse you because you are too young."

"Your brother can't marry me," Grace said, sounding mournful enough to give Wolfe some hope. "He is betrothed to Lady Margaret." She motioned for the children to move along, trying to herd them like a pair of wayward lambs. "Come, now. Let's get you back to Broadmere for tea and cakes in the kitchen. You can give Gastric and the other dogs their treats, then play with Lucy's puppies before it's time for you to return home."

"Can Hector and Galileo come along too?" Sissy asked.

"Of course," Grace said. "We can't very well leave them here, now can we?"

Connor shook his head and planted his feet. "I ain't going anywhere until you promise to marry my brother, since you refuse to have me."

"I can't promise to marry your brother," Grace said in an even tone that revealed the slightest strain of her attempt to maintain control.

"Why not?" Wolfe asked her. He captured her blue-eyed gaze and intended to hold it until she agreed. If his little brother was courageous enough to speak his own mind, he should be as well. "After this terrible morning, I have decided to end the engagement to Lady Margaret—no matter the cost. That betrothal will no longer be an impediment or a grounds for your refusal of me."

She stared at him, her mouth slightly ajar.

Connor tugged on his sleeve. "I think she would've been more impressed had you gone down on one knee. Father did that with that last woman he was going to marry, and after Lady Whatever-Her-Name-Was said *yes*, old Feebson helped him get back up again. Course, you do have that bad knee from the war, so maybe that would be bad form too. You might get stuck like Father did. But you could still say something nice to get her to say yes." The boy nudged him, trying to push him closer to Grace.

"Me and Connor could help you up," Sissy told him. She turned an angelic smile on Grace. "Will you tell him *yes* if he gets down on one knee and asks you really nice? He prolly still won't say anything all soft and pretty like Prince Charming says to his lady love, but you could pretend Wolfe was all gallant and such, just like in the storybooks."

Wolfe groaned and hung his head.

Grace snorted, her shoulders trembling with poorly stifled laughter.

Determined to prove them all wrong *and* take control of the situation, Wolfe moved to stand in front of her and took her hand. "My siblings are correct. If I kneel, my knee will either lock or give out. Neither choice is good whenever that happens." He pressed a tender kiss to her knuckles and tugged her a step closer. "Grace—*my* Grace, I think you hopelessly trapped my cold, jaded heart on our very first meeting. No woman ever put me in my place before or so thoroughly convinced me that place was at her side." He resettled his footing, grinning when she caught hold of his arm as if to stop him from kneeling. "You see? You do care for me—or at least for my knee. Might I dare hope you care half as much for my heart that you have awakened?" He had never realized how blue her eyes were until that very moment. A man could spend a lifetime in those eyes of hers. He touched her cheek, then slid his fingers into the silky wildness of her hair. "Say yes, Grace. Please? It will take a little while for the issue with Lady Margaret to be sorted, but at least say yes for now so I might have the hope of *us* to give me strength."

She wet her lips, making him ache to taste them once again if two seven-year-old chaperones were not watching with such avid interest. Her eyes narrowed the slightest bit, as if sighting in a target. "You should not speak of such things until free to do so, Your Grace," she finally said in a breathless whisper she apparently hoped would stay between them.

Your Grace. A heavy sigh left him. She had addressed him as *Your Grace.* Even as thick-skulled as he was, he recognized it as the gentle reprimand that it was. He had insulted her by speaking out of turn and should not have done so. Damn his lack of patience when it came to something he wanted, and heaven help him, but he wanted her.

He let his hands drop to his sides, bowed his head, and took a step back. "Forgive me, my lady. You are correct. I spoke out of turn and was quite thoughtless."

"What did she say?" Connor moved closer, as did Sissy. He peered up at Wolfe, then turned to Grace. "What did you tell him, Lady Grace? Did you tell him *no?*"

Grace eyed them both, then reached out and straightened Sissy's ebony curls and tousled Connor's black thatch of hair. "I told him now was not the appropriate time to ask, since he is still bound to another."

"But he said he's done with Lady Margaret," Sissy said.

Connor bobbed his head in agreement. "And when my brother says he's done with something, he means it. You should see his temper when he's had enough. He's—"

"Connor, you are not helping!" Wolfe scrubbed a hand across his face, then raked his fingers through his hair. Grace had turned away with her head bowed. "Grace…Lady Grace…I am…" Gads, he was such a fool, and enough was enough. He refused to lose this precious woman. He took hold of her shoulders, turned her to face him, and gently tilted her face up to his.

Merriment filled her eyes, and her face had gone red from holding in her laughter.

Relief flooded through him, along with the urge to kiss the wily minx senseless. "You think this humorous, my lady?"

She hissed with mirth, then covered her mouth to stop it. After delicately clearing her throat, she tried to assume a solemn expression. "Indeed, I do, Your Grace."

"I need you to agree to marry me, woman. I know it is not the proper time to ask, but I have never been a proper man, and dare I say, since you are a most unconventional—yet quite pure and upright—lady, you should do me the courtesy of giving me a solid *yes* at this very moment."

Both her fair brows rose in mock astonishment. "Should I now?"

"Indeed, you should."

She tipped a graceful nod. "I will marry you when you are free of your entanglements. *However*"—she lifted a finger, pointed at him, then aimed it at Connor and Sissy—"we must not speak of this around anyone. Especially the servants. It would be most unsavory for this to be tattled across the countryside. Understood?"

Thrilled beyond measure, he hugged her close and kissed the finger she still held in the air as if it were a weapon. "Agreed. It will be our secret until the proper time to share it." He gave the twins a stern look. "Mine and Lady Grace's reputations depend on you two not speaking about this to anyone. It must be our closely guarded secret until all the legalities and ties with the Longmorten family have been seen to. Do you both understand the seriousness of this matter? Can I trust you to protect this wonderful news and keep it away from those who would use it to try to destroy our good names?"

The children nodded, then dove in and hugged Grace. "You are going to be ours!" Sissy crowed.

"This is almost as good as me marrying you!" Connor shouted.

Grace laughed and wrapped an arm around them while still hugging close to Wolfe. For the first time in his life, he felt complete. *This* was right and good and as things should be.

While he hated for the wondrous moment to end, it was time they returned and assumed their roles of secrecy. "We should get back now," he said with a heavy sigh. "Many are worried about you two," he told the children.

"If anyone is worried about us," Sissy said, "it's only Lady Grace's household. I'd wager Lady Margaret and her mum are dancing a jig 'cause we're gone."

Grace patted his chest, then stepped away and steered the children toward the easiest incline to exit the gorge. "Come, now. Sissy, you and Galileo may ride with me and Gastric. Connor, fetch Hector and help him. You and he can ride with Wolfe." She flinched. "Oh dear. I need to let Serendipity know we found them." She placed her fingers against her mouth and split the air with a deafening whistle. "There. She should turn this way now and see Pegasus and Barberry."

"Can you teach me how to whistle like that?" Connor asked, his voice filled with awe.

"Only if you promise not to tell my brother," she said. "Chance hates it when I do that. It is not exactly a ladylike accomplishment."

Wolfe laughed as he picked up poor, short-legged Gastric and carried him up the embankment while the other hounds bounded past them. "Let me help you, old fellow. After all, I owe you a great deal." He smiled at Grace as he shifted the wiggly dog in his arms. "I owe him everything."

When she gifted him with a shy, adoring smile, a rush of emotions flooded his senses. Yes, indeed. This rocky gully fenced in by brambles and woodbine was paradise on earth.

Chapter Ten

"SINCE MERRY HAS taken the children out to play with Lucy's puppies," Serendipity said with a pointed nod first at Cook and then Walters, "I believe my sisters and I would be more comfortable taking our tea in the parlor."

Walters bowed. "Right away, my lady."

"Thank you." She caught Grace by the elbow and steered her out of the kitchen at an impressive speed. Felicity and Joy scurried along behind them.

"Seri!" Grace yanked free and marched faster, her boots clumping across the polished wood floors in a most unladylike manner. "Calm yourself. The children are found, and as soon as we have our tea, I shall change into more appropriate clothing."

Serendipity slid the double doors of the parlor shut with a quiet bang but remained in front of them as though standing guard. Joy and Felicity hurried to take their seats with the excitement of attending a long-awaited play. "Why did Wolfebourne insist upon a closed-door meeting with Chance?" Serendipity asked.

Grace meandered deeper into the parlor, plucking out the sticks and leaves caught in her long blonde braid. She wasn't entirely pleased with that development herself. When she and Wolfe had agreed upon secrecy, she had assumed it also meant from her siblings, and yet the man had practically made a beeline to her brother as soon as they arrived back home. "How would I have any idea about His Grace's intentions? Perhaps he wished to apologize for the children's unruliness and the interruption of our schedules with such a disturbing game of hide-and-seek." She inwardly patted herself on the back. What a good lie. It sounded convincing even to her.

"I smell a porky pie," Joy said in the irritating singsong voice from their childhood. "Look at her, Seri. She is trying not to look any of us in the eye."

"Leave her alone." Felicity tapped her foot in Joy's direction, a subtle warning that a swift kick came next. "Is it not obvious? She can't possibly tell us she loves a man who is betrothed to another—even though we would never judge her as Society would."

Grace glared at her sister, silently willing her to close her mouth, go away, or both.

"I saw the looks between the two of you," Serendipity told Grace, keeping her voice lowered. "What happened out there? Was his behavior unseemly after I rode away? Did you threaten to go to Chance so he could demand satisfaction for you?"

"We had no idea if the twins were alive or injured, and yet you suggest we were so debased that we paused the search long enough to fall into each other's arms? I take umbrage at that, sister. You should be ashamed to even suggest such a thing. We spent our time on the hunt—nothing more. Thanks to my dogs, we made it to Connor while he was still alive, even though he was trapped in a rockslide and would surely have perished if not found. I can't even bear to think of the horror had Wolfe been unable to dig him out."

"Wolfe?" Serendipity seized on the intimate address, forgetting to whisper it.

Drat and bloody hell. Grace jutted her chin higher. She had been doing so well before that little slip. "We agreed to suspend the use of formal address during the search in the name of simplicity."

Her sisters snorted in unison, then dared to laugh.

"We did," Grace insisted. This battle was all but lost, but she refused to give up. "It's much easier to use names than constantly *Your Gracing* or *my ladying* each other."

"I see." Serendipity looked ready to crow her victory from the rooftops.

"I see too," Joy said with a smugness that decided Grace to secure a bucket of frogs for all of their beds.

"So, how does he plan to end his engagement?" Felicity asked. "You know that could get messy and will likely take some time. Lady Longmorten does not strike me as a mother who will calmly accept the duke setting aside her daughter."

Grace plopped down on the blue velvet settee beside the hearth and refused to answer. Since the trio knew so much, let them sort it for themselves. She fixed her gaze on a tiny spider spinning its web in the corner of the ceiling. Interesting. Mrs. Flackney must be losing her touch at instilling fear in the newest batch of maids hired from the village.

A soft tap on the double doors preceded Walters sliding them open and supervising the new footman wheeling in the tea cart. "Over there, Gerald," the ancient butler said to the young man carefully pushing the cart. "That will be all." As soon as the footman left the room, Walters turned to Serendipity. "Shall I pour, my lady?"

"No thank you, Walters. I shall see to it. You may go now."

The butler bowed, exited the room, and slid the doors shut once again. All three sisters turned to Grace, behaving as if she owed them an answer. Which she did not. She returned her attention to the industrious spider in the corner. "By the way," she said without moving her focus from the web weaver, "I would like to invite the twins to stay here for a few days, since Nellie was adamant they are not safe at Wolfebourne Lodge." That should shift her sisters to a different subject. All of them liked the children.

"I don't believe them safe there either," Serendipity said. "Even though I'm sure His Grace will address the dangers to them. His rage was quite plain when he overheard us discussing the threats to his siblings."

"The Longmorten women have already moved to the inn, but his servants showed an exorbitant lack of worry and care for the twins. That alone makes me fear for their safety." Grace crossed her legs at the knee and bounced her foot because it always annoyed Serendipity when she did so.

"Do sit properly, Gracie, and be still. Good heavens." Serendipity poured their tea and served them. "If you want a cake or biscuit, help yourselves." She sat beside Grace on the settee. "Have you discussed the children staying here with His Grace?"

"No." Grace wasn't entirely certain how to broach that subject to him, either. "I've as yet to think of a way to go about it without his thinking I believe him incapable of protecting them."

"Incapable of protecting whom?" Wolfe asked from the doorway. Chance stood beside him, looking entirely too pleased with himself.

Grace inwardly groaned. Their oath to keep their plans a secret had been well and truly breached. Her brother was now privy to her agreeing to marry Wolfe as soon as he was free. They might as well shout it from the rooftops at this rate.

"We must tell Walters to stop having the footmen oil those sliding doors," Grace told Serendipity. The wretched things once squeaked and warned if someone was about to cross the threshold, but not any longer.

"Grace?" Wolfe arched a dark brow, pinning her with an intense look. "Who is incapable of protecting whom?"

In for a penny, in for a pound. "Remember what you overheard Seri and me discussing at the beginning of our wild search?"

"Yes." The fury in his face lent quite a deeper meaning to that simple response.

Floundering in the depths of his dark-eyed gaze, Grace swallowed hard. "If the Longmorten women were willing to go to any lengths to rid your household of Connor and Sissy, why did your servants not warn you?" She braced herself for his reaction.

"Indeed."

The deadliness of his icy tone made her shiver. While she would never betray her maid's confidence, he deserved more information. "Servants always know more about a household than the master himself." Before he could speak, she rushed to continue, "I thought Connor and Sissy might stay here for a visit to help with the puppies. Lucy's little ones will soon be old enough for new homes. Your brother and sister can help me choose their new owners wisely."

Wolfe's eyes narrowed. "Since those in my employ need their loyalties investigated because they failed to warn me of the dangers to my brother and sister?"

"Yes." She prayed he realized she was in no way saying he was a poor protector of the children. It was simply a matter of giving him the opportunity to get his house in order.

"That could work to your advantage," Chance said, helping himself to a biscuit from the tea cart. "Your solicitor could use that information as your reason for dissolving the engagement. Those servants could be witnesses in your favor were things to get...*difficult*."

"Rather than fire the lot of them with no references, you feel I should try for a confession?" Wolfe asked Grace. The way he looked at her, spoke as if no one else was in the room, made it a struggle to form a logical thought, let alone speak.

He moved closer and held out his hand. Without hesitation, she took it and allowed him to help her to her feet. "I value your insight. I know you would do anything to keep Connor and Sissy safe. What are your thoughts? I am so furious that I wouldn't think twice about burning the lodge down around those murderous servants' ears with them inside."

"Let the twins stay here for a few days—at least until after the picnic." She wished she hadn't left her tea on the table. Her mouth had gone dry as dust. "And perhaps you should wait until after the picnic to speak with Lady Margaret. That will give her mother time to calm a bit after being ousted from Wolfebourne

Lodge. It could make things easier."

"Speak to Lady Margaret?" He stared at her as if he'd not thought of doing such a thing.

His response not only amazed Grace but caused her to wonder if he had changed his mind. "You can't merely send her a note or allow your solicitor to notify her. You are a better man than that. Or have you changed your mind?"

"I have not changed my mind." He stared down at her hand, idly rubbing his thumb back and forth across her bare knuckles in a most intimate manner. "I fear you think me a much better man than what I am, my lady. I *had* planned on allowing my solicitor to handle everything, since the engagement was forged by such persons when I was but Connor's age."

"It might go better than anticipated if you granted Lady Margaret the courtesy of telling her yourself." While Grace had noticed the woman was an unpleasant sort, that in no way meant Wolfe should be unpleasant as well. "Be as curt as you wish to her mother. I imagine she is the one behind the plot to rid you of your siblings."

"I'm not so certain about that," Joy said. "From our brief visit with Lady Margaret the other evening, I drew a few conclusions about her. Do not underestimate her, sister. She learned much at her mother's knee. They possess identical streaks of cruelty."

"Joy is an excellent judge of character," Felicity said as she offered Wolfe a cup of tea and a shy smile. She leaned in with a confidential tip of her head. "Never play Commerce with her. She rarely loses."

Grace gave in to a heavy sigh and looked up at him. "What happened to keeping our intentions a secret?"

"Honor and respect for you demanded that I speak with your brother." He kissed her hand, then turned to her sisters. "But we should keep this as quiet as possible. I do not wish the Broadmere name sullied because I did not see fit to handle the unpleasantness of my situation before now."

A conversation from a few days ago came back to Grace with

surprising clarity. "Seri?"

"Yes?"

"Did you not say you heard Lady Margaret favored another?"

The way Serendipity's smile started out faint, then slowly grew, lifted Grace's heart.

"Why, yes, I did hear that." Serendipity delicately balanced her saucer in her palm while lifting her teacup for a sip. She aimed the slightest nod at Wolfe. "Were you aware of that rumor, Your Grace?"

Wolfe's interest immediately perked. "I was not. Whom does she favor? That could simplify things immensely."

"I have yet to discover the identity of her secret admirer, but I've also heard her mother expressly forbids it. She wishes her daughter to become a duchess." Serendipity narrowed her eyes, her smile turning wicked as she shifted her attention to Joy. "Lady Margaret seemed most interested in your techniques for winning at games of chance. If she grew to trust you…"

Joy proudly tossed her head, making her blonde locks bounce as she preened like the proudest of peahens. "You would owe me so very much for this favor," she told Grace, her grin as impertinent as usual.

Grace gave her sister an impertinent grin of her own. "I will proudly dance at your wedding, since you will be next on the chopping block. You do realize Chance will now aim the Earl of Middlebie and Viscount Blytheston at you?"

Joy's saucy smile disappeared.

"Chopping block?" Wolfe asked, looking from sister to sister to brother.

"Family jest," Chance said, with a pointed glare at Grace. "And a poor one at that."

"Are we in agreement, then?" Grace asked Wolfe. "Connor and Sissy will stay here until after the picnic, and perhaps longer, if the situation warrants it?"

"Connor and Sissy may stay here until I have interrogated my household and adjusted it where necessary. I expected more loyalty from well-treated servants. If I can't trust them to come to me when those I care about are endangered, I do not want them anywhere around me or mine."

"The children will be safe here," Grace promised.

"And we shall try our best not to teach them too many bad habits," Joy said.

"Do they enjoy cooking?" Felicity asked.

"Lawn games will be just the thing," Serendipity said. "And I'm certain we have several horses docile enough for Connor and Sissy to enjoy a few riding lessons."

Wolfe edged a step away from the sisters, taking refuge beside Grace. "Your hospitality is overwhelming, ladies." He bowed. "And much appreciated."

"Wait until you meet my other two sisters," Chance warned. "You have no idea the comfort I find in another male joining the ranks."

"We are not so bad," Grace told her brother. "We've allowed you to live this long."

Chance motioned for Wolfe to join him. "Come. To the library for something stronger than tea. Trust me. You will need it." He cast a sweeping glance around the room at his sisters. "That will give these four time to plan their attack of Lady Margaret at the picnic."

Wolfe turned back to Grace. "Attack?"

"Subtle attack." She offered a reassuring smile to her poor, reserved husband-to-be.

Husband-to-be. Really and truly? Yes. This gorgeous, grumpy, aloof man was perfectly hers. At least, once he was free he would be.

Her spirits dipped the slightest bit. Was she utterly reprehensible for being so bold, for going against Society's measure of what was proper and telling a man who was promised to another that she would gladly be his? She hoped Mama in heaven had briefly looked away and wasn't watching—at least until everything was sorted and proper.

HANDS CLASPED TO the small of his back, Wolfe slowly walked back and forth in front of the servants he'd summoned to the wide entry hall, studying each of them closely. How could they turn a blind eye to alarming threats against his young brother and sister? Why had they not come to him?

Some of them nervously shifted in place. All of them stared straight ahead as if waiting to be shot. The thought had occurred to him.

"I wish to speak with each of you," he said after tormenting them with a long, purposeful silence. "Privately. In the library. I shall start with you, Miss Hannah. The rest of you shall remain here and wait your turn."

He gave them a curt nod, then strode down the hallway, not bothering to wait for the young maid he had assigned to watch over his precious brother and sister. She would follow or find herself unemployed without benefit of a recommendation letter. Once seated behind his desk, he allowed her to stand in front of it for another uncomfortably long pause before nodding at the chair beside her. "Be seated."

Hands clasped in her lap and her head bowed, the girl hesitantly perched on the edge of the cushion.

"When you leave this room, you will not speak of anything said in here or you will be immediately dismissed without reference. Is that understood?"

"Yes, Your Grace." She added an almost imperceptible nod.

"Tell me what you know about the plans Lady Margaret and Lady Longmorten had for Master Connor and Miss Susannah."

The maid raised her head and blinked at him as if stricken with something in her eyes. "Plans, Your Grace?"

He nodded, refusing to speak in order to give the girl enough rope to hang herself.

She gave a cowering shrug. "I know they wished Master

Connor sent to boarding school and Miss Susannah sent to travel with Lady Longmorten's cousin, but I fear I can't remember that cousin's name."

"And what else?"

She angled an ear toward him. "What else, Your Grace?"

"Yes."

The maid's befuddlement worked in her favor, granting her an air of innocence. "Forgive me, Your Grace, but I'm not certain of anything else you might be asking about. Lady Margaret did tell me once to make sure I never brought the children around her." She cowered lower, adding a respectful nod. "I tried my best to keep them out of the same room or the same garden as her. The only time I know they got into the same room with her was at meals. Was I supposed to keep them in the nursery? It was my understanding you wished them to join you at mealtimes. Was I wrong, Your Grace?"

"I did wish them to join me at mealtimes, Miss Hannah." Wolfe leaned back in his chair, propping his elbows on the leather armrests and steepling his fingers in front of him. "What if harm were to come to Master Connor and Miss Susannah?"

The girl looked satisfactorily horrified. "Oh, Your Grace—" She choked on the words and clutched a fist to her chest. "Are they...are they gone?"

"You may go, Miss Hannah. Return to whatever duties Mrs. Havarerry has assigned to you, since the children are no longer here. Send in Feebson."

The maid rose and managed a quick curtsy, then ran from the room, swiping at the tears spilling down her cheeks.

At least she appeared to be innocent and would have had the closest access to the twins. And neither Connor nor Sissy had ever complained about the maid's behavior toward them. She might have been firm and lacked emotion, but they never mentioned her being mean-spirited or cruel.

A soft tapping pulled him from his internal assessment of Miss Hannah. "Your Grace?" Feebson quietly said through the partially opened door.

"Come in, Feebson." Wolfe very much doubted the butler to be the culprit but didn't wish to be careless and fail to identify the traitor who believed wrongdoing toward his brother and sister could be ignored. In fact, it bore remembering that Feebson was the one who had reported their last governess for disparaging Sissy. The tiny old man had appeared quite incensed when the woman told the child she would be nothing more than a lightskirt, just like her mother. Wolfe nodded at the same chair he'd had Miss Hannah use.

"Forgive me, Your Grace, but I would rather stand if you can see to allow it." Feebson stood ramrod straight, unsmiling as always, but a shimmer of emotion, a sadness, filled his eyes. "Mrs. Havarerry excused Miss Hannah for the next hour or so, what with her being so overwrought. The girl refused to speak of what you told her, though. She said she wasn't allowed." The stoic little man bowed his head. "Aught it be something to do with Lord Connor and Lady Susannah?"

"I am afraid so, Feebson." Wolfe studied the butler who had served his father for many years before serving him. He took note of his raspy, sorrowful tone.

The older man nodded while keeping his gaze locked on the floor. "I feared as much, Your Grace. When you came home without the children, I knew it had to be something terrible."

"There are those who would celebrate something terrible happening to my brother and sister," Wolfe said, baiting the servant to gauge his reaction.

"Then a pox on them for their cruel hearts!" Feebson clamped his mouth shut and shook his head. "Forgive me, Your Grace, but I can't abide anyone wishing something bad on those two. Those children have not had an easy way of it." He gave a more formal bow. "Begging your pardon again, Your Grace."

Feebson was not the traitor, and Wolfe was glad of it. "Repeat nothing said in this room, Feebson. You may go and send in Mrs. Havarerry."

The butler nodded and shuffled out, carrying himself as if the weight of the world rested on his thin shoulders.

The longer it took Mrs. Havarerry to respond to her summons, the more Wolfe methodically reviewed the housekeeper he had never quite liked. Her only redeeming feature, other than running the household with the efficiency of a combat veteran, was her ability to make soothing poultices for his bad knee. He recalled she was also the one who had refused to allow Sissy and Connor to speak with him on the night of Lady Longmorten's London party, when that insufferable woman had informed Sissy that the twins were disposable. He tightened his fists so hard, every knuckle popped. Granted, he had been very busy that evening, but he had always made it quite clear that the twins had access to him no matter the circumstances or the hour. Perhaps Mrs. Havarerry was the betrayer he sought.

After another few, very long moments, he pushed up from his chair and went to the door. How dare the woman make him wait? "Mrs. Havarerry!" he bellowed down the hallway. "Report to the library at once."

Instead, Feebson appeared at the end of the hall, hurrying his way. "Mrs. Havarerry is gone, Your Grace."

"What the devil do you mean, *gone*?"

"Left the premises, Your Grace. Sam and Mathias said she lit out of here as if her petticoat was on fire." The butler tipped a nod. "Begging your pardon. The maids said the same. Said she left without taking a thing with her. Soon as I went into the library to talk with you, out the door she went. Headed toward the village."

"To the Longmortens at the inn, no doubt. I imagine she assumes they will ensure her of employment when she conveys to them that the children did not return home when I did."

Feebson slowly shook his head. "I must be getting old, Your Grace, seeing as how I don't understand how one has anything to do with the other."

"It has come to my attention that the Longmortens wanted

the children gone by any means necessary—be it legal or nefarious."

The butler's jaw dropped. "Hurt the children?"

"That is not to leave this room. Do you understand me?"

"Yes, Your Grace." Feebson drew a shaking hand across his eyes. "Those poor mites. And Mrs. Havarerry was part of it?"

"By not informing me of the Longmortens' inclinations? Yes. I demand loyalty from my household. Anyone not reporting threats or dangers to those I care about might as well strike the killing blow themselves, for I consider their hands just as bloody."

His entire person trembling, Feebson bowed his head and whispered, "Would I have known, Your Grace, I swear I would have done whatever it took to save them. I am so very sorry."

Still leery about his siblings' safety, Wolfe chose not to come forth and actually tell the man that Connor and Sissy were safe and well. Mrs. Havarerry might not have been the only member of the household who had drawn closer to the potential mistresses of Wolfebourne Lodge by assisting them with whatever they wished. "Your loyalty is duly noted and appreciated, Feebson. Thank you."

"Will there be anything else, Your Grace?" the butler asked, his manner dejected and his voice cracking with emotion. "Shall I send for the constable?"

"Not yet, and do be good enough to send in the footmen one at a time, thank you."

Wolfe watched the man go, wrestling with his conscience about allowing the faithful servant to believe Connor and Sissy were gone forever. It couldn't be helped. Until he had spoken with every individual who had ever come into contact with his little brother and sister and felt certain they were loyal and trustworthy, the twins' whereabouts and the condition of their health could not be shared. He had but a short time to complete this investigation, seeing as how the infamous Broadmere picnic was in a few days. Then all would see Connor and Sissy and know them to be hale and hearty—and the fun and games would truly begin.

Chapter Eleven

"Never shout at them." Grace loosened the puppy's determined grip on Sissy's hemline by gently prying open its little jaws, then offering it a thick square of scrap leather to chew in its place. "Give them a firm *no*, then once you disengage them, distract them with something else to teethe on and praise them when they take it. Puppies learn a great deal from your tone and how you behave. You must always be kind and consistent. If you do that, you'll not only win their trust and loyalty, but their love."

"Won't Lucy be sad when you give her babies away?" Sissy scooped up the runt of the litter and cuddled the wiggly bundle of white and brindle close. "Won't *you* be sad to see them go?" Her cat Galileo flattened his ears, jealousy filling his golden-eyed glare locked on the puppy.

Grace wouldn't lie to the child who already knew her too well. "I will be sad to see them go, and I imagine Lucy will miss them too. That's why I need you and Connor to help me find good homes for them—homes we can visit."

"We should keep them all," Connor said with a decisive nod as his dog Hector herded the puppies in a somewhat contained grouping on the grassy area beneath the old oak in the back garden. "Think on it. When you marry Wolfe and bring your dogs with you, this lot could stay here. That way both houses would have a fine kennel of dogs."

"Connor!" Grace glanced around to ensure they were truly alone. "Mind your words, please? Remember our intentions to keep everything quiet until the proper time?"

"But everyone here already knows." He dangled a knotted rag in front of one of the pups. It immediately latched on to it for a rousing game of tug-of-war. "Even the servants know. Sissy and I heard Cook and Mrs. Flackney talking about it just yesterday, plain as could be."

Grace didn't doubt that a bit. Secrets were a rare thing in the Broadmere household. "And what did they say?"

Connor grinned. "That my brother will have his hands full, but he'll be the happiest man in the world once he gets used to how you do things."

Grace wasn't sure whether she should be insulted or pleased. "Regardless of what you heard, we must still guard our words. If the Earl of Middlebie gets wind of the news, he is sure to share it with the world. He is a well-meaning man but a worse gossip than a gaggle of old women."

"Merry says that's because he's a Scot," Sissy said. "She also thinks he can't hear too good, and that may be why he talks so loud."

"Merry could be right. We must bear that in mind whenever we speak to his lordship." Grace strolled away from them to the bench against the outer wall of the kitchen. She settled down on it and lifted her face to the gentle warmth of the sun. Freckles could just be damned.

"They are here!" Felicity called out from the kitchen window. "The babies are here!"

"Babies?" Connor looked up from his game of tug and wrinkled his nose. "What babies?"

Grace hopped up from the bench and waved the children toward the door. "My niece and nephew. Rorie and Quill. Come meet them and their parents."

"Will they like us?" Sissy asked, hanging back beside the tree.

"Of course they will like you, and you can help us keep up

with Rorie. She's just now started walking." Grace realized the children had been shunned by so many, they were now leery of strangers. "Bring Hector and Galileo. Blessing and Fortuity adore cats and will also be very impressed with Hector's ability to herd Gastric. No one has ever been able to steer him as effectively as Hector does."

Connor and Sissy eyed her as if weighing whether the invitation was a trap. Their hesitation hurt her heart and made her even more determined to protect them from the world's mean-spiritedness.

She went and took them by the hand, easing them across the garden toward the house. "Blessing and Fortuity are my older sisters. They're between me and Serendipity in age. Blessing loves astronomy, and Fortuity writes books. You will like them, and they will like you. I promise."

She tugged them along, through the kitchen that was already astir about the arrival of the rest of the Broadmere family, then down the hall and into the larger of the two parlors.

"Gracie!" Fortuity rushed over and caught her in a warm hug, then stepped back and smiled down at Connor and Sissy. "Seri was just telling us about our special guests here." She curtsied to the children. "I'm Lady Ravenglass and very happy to meet you. You may call me Lady Fortuity if that's easier for you."

Sissy returned her curtsy and politely said, "I am Lady Susannah Craigston, but you can call me Sissy. Lady Grace told us you write books. Do you make up stories about princes and princesses?"

Fortuity nodded. "Sometimes I do." She pointed at the baby fussing in Serendipity's arms. "Lately, though, my strong-willed son Quill has kept me too busy for stories."

Connor stood taller and straightened his shoulders. "I am Lord Connor Craigston, and Lady Grace would have accepted my offer of marriage instead of my brother's if I had been old enough. You can call me Connor."

Fortuity nodded and gave him an even deeper curtsy. "I am

honored to meet you, Connor, and look forward to meeting your brother." Eyes dancing with mirth, she wrinkled her nose at Grace.

Grace clenched her teeth to keep from scolding Serendipity or whichever of her sisters had already spilled the secret within moments of the rest of the family's arrival. She forced a smile and narrowed her eyes at Fortuity, warning her to behave. "And where is Blessing, little Rorie, and my two brothers-in-law?"

"We are here," Blessing said, entering with a jubilant toddler bouncing on her hip. She combed her fingers through the child's silvery-white curls, making the little one chuckle and clap her hands. "She is faster than you think. Never take your eyes off her. Remember how Merry used to be? Rorie is even faster." Blessing handed the child off to Joy, then swept across the room and hugged Grace. "Congratulations, Gracie!"

"See?" Connor said. "I told you everyone already knows."

Choosing to ignore both their comments, Grace rested a hand on each twin's shoulder. "Allow me to introduce you to Lady Susannah Craigston and Lord Connor Craigston. Children, this is my sister, Lady Blessing Knightwood, and over there is her daughter Aurora."

Blessing curtsied to them both. "I am very happy to meet you. You can help us keep up with Rorie. That's Aurora's nickname, and much easier to shout whenever you're trying to catch her."

"Where are her leading strings?" Sissy asked. "Her nurse should have pinned them to the back of her clothes first thing this morning."

Blessing wrinkled her nose. "While I know many mothers and nursemaids insist upon them, I consider them too dangerous. What if little Rorie were to get caught in them and tangled? Besides, with all the cats in my house, leading strings could prove more trouble than what they are worth."

"You sound like Grace…I mean…Lady Grace," Connor said. "She does things different too, and her way makes a lot more sense than the way everyone else does it. I was going to marry her, because she is beyond compare. But she told me I was too young. So I let her marry my brother instead."

"Connor," Grace said in a warning tone she prayed the boy would heed.

"What?" He nodded at Blessing. "She needed to know too, since I already told Lady Fortuity. I got to be fair."

"Indeed you do," Blessing said with a solemn expression and laughter in her eyes.

"And my brothers-in-law?" Grace asked, determined to take control of the conversation.

"In the library," Serendipity said. "Chance was most excited for more males to arrive, since he and Middlebie find themselves outnumbered."

"Middlebie?" Blessing and Fortuity repeated in unison.

"The Earl of Middlebie. Chance's Scottish chum from university. The loud one. Remember?" Grace couldn't remember if Chance had thrown Middlebie at Blessing and Fortuity as a possible husband, but she was certain he had. Dearest brother never missed an opportunity to leg-shackle them. After all, the sooner they all married, the sooner he inherited the entirety of the family's coffers.

Blessing slowly shook her head. "I can't place the name with a face, but I am sure I'll remember once I see the man, since Chance paraded us in front of every marriageable male he could find. I assume our darling brother invited him here for the summer?"

"Well, he might as well send him on." Connor puffed out his small chest. "My brother and I claimed Lady Grace first."

"Connor…shh!" Sissy nudged him. "If we don't behave nice, how can we 'spect them to behave nice to us?"

"I wasn't being not nice. I was just saying—"

Sissy silenced him with a finger in his face. "Hush it. Now."

With the babbling toddler balanced on her hip, Joy held out a hand to the little girl. "Sissy, would you like to come along and see how Rorie likes the puppies?"

"I better come along too," Connor said before his sister could answer. "They get pretty lively. We don't want them to scratch her and make her cry."

"What a thoughtful young gentleman," Blessing said, before bending to kiss Connor's cheek. "Thank you for watching over Rorie. I know you will keep her safe."

As the children left with Joy, Fortuity collected baby Quill from Serendipity. "Time for this one to see his nursemaid for a nap so we can all chat. Joy won't mind our talking without her, since we aren't discussing games of chance." She paused in the doorway and gave Grace a stern look. "Do not start until I get back. I want to hear everything from the beginning for clarity."

Grace was tempted to run after Joy and the twins. She found it difficult to talk about the entire situation because years of Mama's training quietly scolded her for not only showing interest in an engaged man, but actually agreeing to marry him once he was free. That simply was not done. Granted, Lady Margaret seemed as interested in Wolfe as a man would be in attending a needlepoint club's weekly tea, but Grace's conscience, molded by Mama's sense of right and wrong, still refused to condone her actions. Wolfe belonged to another woman. Grace didn't particularly like Lady Margaret, but that didn't grant her license to do whatever she wished. She might be unconventional, but she wasn't a selfish, back-biting little chit.

"Oh my," Blessing said to her, "and what is that morose look all about?"

"We are supposed to wait for Tutie, remember?" Grace went to the table spread with an elaborate tea and poured herself a cup while trying to think of a means of escape. Never before had she ever had to worry about being the center of attention. With her birth order somewhat in the middle of the brood, she had always been able to slip away and spend time with her beloved animals rather than remain and perform on cue as if she couldn't imagine being anywhere else. It suddenly occurred to her that if she married Wolfe, she would be a duchess and expected to do just that.

She inwardly groaned. *Heaven forbid.* There was no question she longed to be with him. No man had ever made her heart drum so rapidly just by walking into a room. But the duchess part—that was something else entirely.

She stirred her tea, rhythmically clicking the spoon against the sides of the cup as if counting off the minutes until Fortuity returned to the room. Maybe being the Duchess of Wolfebourne wouldn't be all that bad. She wouldn't classify Wolfe as reclusive, but he did seem to keep to himself. Of course, this was the Lake District—the Broadmere family picnic as much as kicked off the summer festivities around Binnocksbourne, and everyone else's events followed. Was he really the sort that enjoyed attending every soiree? Dear heavens, she hoped not. Whatever had she promised herself into without discussing such important things with the man?

"Grace?"

The richness of his deep voice surrounded her. She turned so quickly that she nearly spilled her tea. "Good heavens, you startled me. What are you doing here?"

He arched a dark brow. "It's good to see you as well, my lady. I thought to visit with Connor and Sissy—and you, unless your diary for today is otherwise filled."

Just as she was about to deliver a scathing reply, she noticed they were alone in the room. "Where are my sisters?"

"While your thoughts trapped you in your teacup, Lady Serendipity introduced me to Ladies Blessing and Fortuity, and when you failed to respond to any of them repeatedly clearing their throats, they excused themselves to the garden after my sworn oath to abstain from any ungentlemanly behavior."

He took her cup from her and set it aside. "What is it, Grace?" he asked softly. "What have I done to displease you? Where is that light in your eyes that always makes me feel so welcome?"

She stared up at him, her selfish heart pounding faster. This wonderful man made her feel as awkward and uncertain as a newborn calf. "You have not displeased me. *I* have displeased me." She tried to turn away, but he stopped her.

"Pray tell me you haven't decided to set me aside before we are even together?" He kissed her hand and leaned in closer, trapping her in his dark-eyed gaze. "What is it, Grace? Tell me what is wrong."

"Mama would scold me for allowing myself to love a man who is engaged to another," she blurted, cringing at the whininess of her tone. "I abhor balls, dinner parties, and elaborate teas that are more like battles for territories and finding broodmares for heirs rather than social gatherings—and yet here I have agreed to marry an unavailable man, who, if he can extricate himself from his situation, will make me his duchess and expect me to plan and give such balls, dinner parties, and elaborate teas in his name so he might do well politically." She sucked in a deep breath, gasping like a winded racehorse.

"I see." He tenderly kept her hands in his, calmly watching her. "Is that everything, or were there any additional rabid thoughts I need to be made aware of?"

"I am not like this."

"Like what?"

"A bacon-brained, babbling ninny." She yanked her hands out of his and turned away, unable to believe the person she had become. It was all his fault because he had somehow made her care for him. She whirled back around, ready to explain her case further, and became infuriated by his expression. The man looked entirely too pleased with himself. "And what, pray tell, are you smiling about?"

"You said you loved me."

"I did not."

"Indeed you did, my lady." He ambled closer. An errant shock of his dark hair fell across his forehead in a most rakish way. "I can't express how happy that makes me, because I can't imagine myself loving anyone other than you."

"But you shouldn't." Did he not understand her moral co-nundrum here?

"Why? Because my father ordered his solicitors to draw up some ridiculous agreement between a seven-year-old and a newborn to expand our family's unentailed lands and bank accounts?" He caught her hands in his yet again. "I should have ended the engagement long ago but didn't because I feared the cost." He tugged her close and wrapped her in his arms. "I no longer care what it costs, because you, my lady, are a priceless treasure I cannot live without. I will have you as my wife, my life mate, or I will have no one at all."

"Oh my."

He gave her the softest smile, a smile that made her heart swell and tears threaten to embarrass her. "Is that a good *oh my* or a poor one?"

"No one has ever said anything like that to me before."

"I should hope not, else I would have to duel them and put them out of their misery."

"You understand I am not a lightskirt?" He had to know that just because she had promised to marry an unavailable man, she was not immoral. "I know I am unconventional, but I would never be anyone's mistress or casual romp. My...*intimacies*...are only for my husband."

"I am very pleased to hear it." He tenderly cupped her cheek. "Even though I had already surmised as much." He grazed his thumb ever so lightly across her bottom lip. "When I kissed you in the moonlight, you tasted like a rare, untouched wine." He leaned in, drawing his mouth closer. "A wine I long to taste again and again."

Mesmerized, she tipped her face up and wet her lips. "Did you not promise my sisters you would behave?"

"I am behaving," he whispered, then brushed his mouth to hers. "I am behaving like a man in love." He paused and drew back the slightest bit, waiting until she opened her eyes. "Is that all right, my precious lady?"

"Yes—as long as that means you are going to kiss me."

FAR BE IT from Wolfe to ever refuse a lady, especially the lady who possessed his heart. He tried not to groan aloud as he indulged in the kiss but failed. Grace was indeed a rare, untouched wine of which he would never get enough.

"Ahem!"

Grace shifted against him, broke their exquisite connection, then eased out of his arms with a heavy sigh. Her smile bolstered him, somewhat softening his disappointment at the interruption. "Yes, Seri?" she said to her sister, who stood in the doorway.

"Oh, so you heard me this time?" Serendipity swept closer and aimed a scathing look at Wolfe. "You should find that insulting, Your Grace. Earlier, her teacup kept her from hearing me, but just now, your attentions did not."

"I credit her heightened awareness to a woman's ingrained need to guard her reputation." He offered Grace's sister a polite bow. "It was but a moment ago she informed me she was a proper lady, and that I best remember it."

"Indeed." Serendipity shifted her glare back and forth between them. "The two of you looked as if you forgot it." She drew herself up as if sorely put upon. "I thought you should know that Lady Margaret, her mother, and Sir Andrew have responded that they will indeed attend our picnic."

"Does the man go everywhere with them?" Grace asked Wolfe.

"Yes. Always has. The old earl assigned him to accompany them anywhere they went." Remembering why he had come to Broadmere Manor in the first place, in addition to visiting his siblings and enjoying Grace's company, he tipped a nod toward the hallway. "I discovered my housekeeper, Mrs. Havarerry, was very much aware of the Longmortens' determination to rid me of my brother and sister. But before I could dismiss the woman, she deserted her post. According to my butler and footmen, she was last seen running toward the village. I can only assume she joined Lady Longmorten and her daughter at the inn. Who knows what she reported to them? Do you know which of your servants she would have confided in? It concerns me that not only word about the twins' whereabouts might become public knowledge before the picnic but also my intentions about breaking the engagement."

"Nellie is the one who told me about the danger." Grace turned to Serendipity. The sisters appeared to communicate without saying a word. "But she's not left the manor since we arrived. Her information had to have come from the downstairs table."

"The downstairs table?" Wolfe had no idea what that meant, but it sounded ominous.

"The servants' dinner table in the room off the kitchen," Serendipity said. "They gather there when they have a spare moment from their duties. We always call it the downstairs table because, in Town, their area is the lowest level of the town-house." She turned back to Grace. "I can't think of a single one of them who might have a connection to Wolfebourne Lodge's housekeeper."

"Gerald is our newest footman," Grace said. "I don't recall the names of the two new maids. All three were brought on from the village." She turned back to Wolfe. "Did your Mrs. Havarerry have connections in the village?"

"She is *from* the village. The housekeeper before her was dismissed for recommending a governess with a penchant for belittling the children." He strode to the doorway and glanced up and down the hall. "If your footman and maids know Mrs. Havarerry, our situation could be exposed." Endangering Grace's reputation and her family name would be unforgivable. "Perhaps the twins should come home with me today."

"But you promised them they could stay until after the picnic." Grace stubbornly jutted her chin higher, tempting him to pull her back into his arms and kiss her again, even though her sister was standing right there. "You can't break your promise," she said. "Especially not when we don't even know if any damage has been done. If none of our servants have been to the village since the twins arrived, then Mrs. Havarerry should be none the wiser."

Serendipity yanked on the bellpull. "Walters will know and can be trusted implicitly."

Uneasiness churned in Wolfe's gut. He had already summoned his solicitor, but the man had yet to arrive and had no inkling about the assignment he was about to be given. Complications that could either prevent or delay—no, not prevent, never prevent. Grace would be his wife if he had to whisk her away to Gretna Green and live in Scotland until the gossips of Polite Society found someone else to destroy. Of course, Broadmere wouldn't appreciate that choice, and neither would Grace's sisters. It was Wolfe's sincerest hope that such drastic measures could be avoided, but he would do whatever was required to ensure a glorious happily-ever-after for Grace, himself, and his brother and sister.

Walters appeared in the doorway and waited with an expectant look.

Serendipity waved the man forward and motioned for him to close the doors behind him.

The butler twitched a bushy gray brow, but that was his only betrayal of emotion as he quietly slid the double doors shut, then faced them with his hands calmly folded in front of him.

"Gerald and the new maids," Serendipity said, "have they visited the village since we hired them?"

Walters blinked several times as if struggling to stay awake. "Visited the village, my lady? On errands for the household?"

"Errands or leisure time."

"They have not been with us long enough to receive a day off. None of the three are due their day until next month and have been assigned no errands to the best of my knowledge. Mrs. Flackney and Cook sent young Jasper to the butcher, greengrocer, and mercantile for supplies the day after we arrived, but he returned straight away. No other member of the staff has been to the village since." The elderly butler hitched forward and tipped his head as if fearing what she was about to tell him. "Is there a problem I should address with the newest servants?"

"Spiders," Grace said, moving to stand beside Serendipity. "You know how my sisters feel about spiders."

Wolfe stared at his lady love. What the devil was she up to?

Serendipity cast a wary glance at Grace as if she had sprouted horns.

"I am well aware of the ladies' dislike for them." The butler squared his bent shoulders as if ready to wage war against the beasties. "Where are they, my lady? I shall dispatch them myself."

"I already took the liberty of relocating them to the garden," Grace said, "but do make mention to the maids about paying closer attention to the overhead corners. The spiders feel safe and out of reach when closest to the ceiling."

Walters looked up, scanning the room for the possible invasion of more. "I shall address it with them immediately. Do forgive us for failing in our duties, my lady."

"You never fail us, Walters," Serendipity said. "We know we are well looked after with you. That will be all."

With his thin chest slightly puffed with the praise, Walters bowed and left the room.

"Spiders?" Wolfe asked Grace, unable to contain his curiosity any longer.

"There was one the other day, but I moved it to the garden. Poor Walters sometimes gets confused. The dear old man refuses to take his pension, and as long as he can somewhat perform his duties, Chance has agreed that we should let him do so—as a matter of preserving his pride and as thanks for his many years of devoted service. I saw no reason to muddle his thoughts further, so I brought up the spiders."

"She protects everyone and everything, Your Grace," Serendipity said. "Get used to it."

"As long as her protection includes my heart." He allowed himself the luxury of staring at Grace until Serendipity cleared her throat again. He grudgingly tore himself free of Grace's bewitchment. "Yes. Well. We are still no closer to discovering how word about the goings-on within my household reached this one."

"Let me fetch Nellie," Grace said. "If we have her summoned to the parlor, it will frighten her to no end, and she's done nothing wrong."

"Agreed." Serendipity shooed her onward. "Heaven knows the poor woman has enough on her plate with taking care of you."

Grace rolled her eyes and hurried out to retrieve her maid.

As soon as Grace was well out of sight, Serendipity turned and descended on Wolfe, jabbing the air with her finger. "If you hurt her, I will be the first of my sisters to trounce you. It will not be Chance you have to worry about, Your Grace. I assure you, the Abarough sisters are well able to protect their own."

"I am doing everything in my power to protect Grace as well as the Broadmere family's reputation." Sensing this was far from over, he braced himself for further attack. The air crackled with the woman's frustration.

"You are not, Your Grace. If you were truly concerned about Gracie's good name, you would have remedied your situation before compromising her in the garden while your intended sat in the parlor waiting for your return." Serendipity shook her finger at him, reminding him of Grace. It must be a shared trait they had inherited from their mother. "I can accept that your initial meeting with my sister was quite unconventional. However, that did not give you the right to take advantage of her. Contrary to what you may believe, Gracie is quite sheltered when it comes to men like you."

"Men like me?" He didn't know whether to be insulted or proud, but by heavens, he would defend himself. "Have you ever been in love, my lady?"

Serendipity backed up a step, her shock apparent. "What?"

"Love. Have you ever fallen in love?"

She drew herself up, aloof and insulted. "What has that to do with anything?"

"One cannot control with whom one falls in love. Nor can one control love's timing." He thumped a fist to his chest. "The heart is a fickle thing with a will all its own. I am not its master, but its servant, and it bids me to love Grace for all the rest of my days."

Gastric ambled into the room, spotted Wolfe, and wagged his tail with such vigor that his entire hind end wiggled back and forth.

Wolfe bent and reached for the dog. "Come here, old boy. At least I know I always have a friend in you."

With a happy *woof*, Gastric lumbered forward and bumped his velvety head into Wolfe's hand, grunting with pleasure at the good scratching behind his ears.

"I am not unfriendly, Your Grace." Serendipity huffed, flounced into the hallway, and looked in the direction Grace had gone. "I am simply not pleased with this current predicament that could harm not only my sister's reputation but her heart."

"Allow me to worry about my own reputation and heart, Seri," Grace said from the opposite end of the hall.

Wolfe joined the sisters in the hallway, Gastric at his heels. "Your sister is only concerned about your wellbeing."

Serendipity nodded. "Your heart concerns me more than your reputation. Whether you wish to admit it or not, when you love, dearest sister, you love hard. How many times have I held you while you sobbed with the heartbreak of losing one of your beloved pets?"

Again, Wolfe wasn't quite certain whether to be insulted. He hoped Grace loved him more than she loved Gastric. The dog currently leaned against her skirts, staring up at her with the purest adoration, and when she reached down and petted him, her expression was much the same.

"I am a woman grown," Grace said without looking up from her sweet pet. "My heart is mine to give and to guard."

"I will guard it, my lady," Wolfe said softly as if naught but the two of them stood there. "I swear it."

She looked up at him and smiled. "I know you will. Just as I will guard yours."

Hurried footsteps clattered ever louder, approaching from deeper in the house. Nellie came to a bouncing halt as she rounded the corner. With a hand caught to her throat, she eased forward a few steps. "My lady? Is something amiss? I heard you calling and came as soon as I untangled the bedsheets that girl had in such disarray. Is there a reason everyone waits in the hallway?"

"Perhaps we should return to the parlor." Wolfe stepped aside so the ladies could enter first. After all were within, including Gastric, he slid the doors closed. As he turned, he noticed Grace's maid had gone pale. "You are not in trouble," he told her. "I wished to thank you for warning your mistress about the possible dangers to my brother and sister."

The ruffles on her white cap trembling, Nellie bobbed a nervous curtsy. "You are quite welcome, Your Grace."

"I am also compelled to ask how you came to know about those dangers."

The maid cast a worried look at Grace.

"We need to know, Nellie," Grace said. "For the safety of the children."

With her gaze lowered, the maid whispered, "Jasper spoke of it at the table."

"Jasper?" Wolfe said to Grace and Serendipity. "Is he not the one your butler mentioned earlier? The one sent to the village on errands?"

"Yes," Grace said, then turned to her maid. "Thank you, Nellie. You may go now, and thank you again for helping us keep the children safe."

"They are dears," Nellie said with yet another curtsy, then

scurried from the room.

Wolfe stared after her in amazement. "She is the first servant to ever describe the twins as *dears* and sound as if she truly meant it."

"Many of our servants have been with us since we were as young and high-spirited as Connor and Sissy," Grace said. "They know children need patience and guidance rather than treatment as if they are an annoyance."

"Apparently, I need those in my household to train with yours." Wolfe went to the bellpull and gave it a yank. "Shall we speak with Jasper next?"

"Absolutely," Grace and Serendipity said in unison.

Chapter Twelve

WHILE WAITING FOR Jasper to arrive, all the sisters had returned to the parlor, except for Lady Merry. Wolfe noted how that particular lady had been overjoyed about helping Quill and Rorie's nurses as well as organizing a special tea for Connor and Sissy in the nursery. When Connor had groaned and voiced his boredom, she hadn't batted an eye. Instead, she conquered his disagreeableness with the temptation of the Duke of Broadmere's retired wooden swords and toy armor. The lady hadn't once taken affront with the boy. Instead, she had completely understood Connor's perspective on a proper tea. Wolfe smiled. Connor would want to marry Lady Merry next.

With six of the sisters commanding the conversation in the parlor, Wolfe was beginning to understand their brother's need for more males in the family. The poor young duke was sorely outnumbered. Broadmere and Middlebie, as well as the newly arrived husbands to Lady Blessing and Lady Fortuity, were currently out inspecting the grounds for the lawn party, as ordered to by Lady Serendipity. Wolfe suspected she was the true head of the family's empire even though Broadmere possessed the title.

All eyes shifted to Wolfe as Jasper entered and fidgeted his way to a final standstill in front of the elaborate white marble hearth that lent a regal air to the robin's-egg-blue walls of the parlor.

"The things you repeated about the possible dangers to my brother and sister," Wolfe said to the man, deciding to cut to the meat of it even though it might seem abrupt, "how did you come to know them?"

Young Jasper stared at him while running the brim of his cap through his fingers. "Might I be speaking free, then, Your Grace?"

"Absolutely. I want to know everything, and I appreciate your assistance."

Jasper worked the edge of his hat faster through his fingers, almost spinning it.

"We trust you, Jasper," Grace said, "and know you would never tell us anything false."

The man managed a weak smile and a nod, then looked back at Wolfe. "My sister works in Mr. Caruthers's Treats shop. She be the one who told me 'bout Lady Longmorten and her daughter hissing like a pair of snakes 'bout them children. How they wished them young ones had never come to be, and if they had their druthers, they'd be rid of them afore summer's end. They was sipping their chocolates and talking like they was ready to send those two to the undertaker. It shocked my sister at how much those women hated the bairns. Them two of yours always behaved all polite and proper, Your Grace. My sister went on and on about how fine they always was whenever you brought them to the shop."

A cold, harsh deadliness settled over Wolfe. The same deadliness that had gotten him through the war and strengthened him in every battle. By sheer providence, his brother and sister had been spared a fate he might not have foreseen in time to prevent. "Did your sister overhear anything else?"

Jasper gave him a pained look.

"Speak your mind, man. I would know everything those two said."

"The daughter…" Jasper shuffled in place and wrung his cap between his fists as if it were a rag. "She told Lady Longmorten that the game weren't going to work no more 'cause he was too jealous. My sister said them was her words exact."

"What game and who was too jealous?" Grace asked.

Jasper tipped an apologetic shrug. "Another customer come in 'bout that time, and my sister had to stop wiping down tables and go back behind the counter. All she knew was that Lady Longmorten turned bright red and left so quick her chair tipped over and bounced across the floor. Her daughter hurried out after her. Seemed more angry than embarrassed by her mam's fit of temper."

Grace caught Wolfe's arm and squeezed. Her worry touched his heart. "Thank heavens those women are out of your home."

"They will pay." He didn't know how or when, but he would make them pay. No one threatened his family. "Would your sister be willing to speak to my solicitor?" he asked Jasper. "Relay everything she heard?"

"I can ask her, Your Grace. I feel sure she would, what with them innocents being threatened and all." Jasper smoothed out his hat only to twist it again and hang his head. "None of us knew how to warn you 'bout what we heard—considering your station and ours and what with us not being in your employ." He bowed his head even lower. "Beg pardon for saying so."

"I understand completely." And Wolfe did understand. Few in the aristocracy would ask the time of day from anyone among the lower classes who didn't work for them. What a bloody shame that Polite Society's standards could so easily risk the lives of children.

"Unless there is anything else you feel we should know about," Grace said to Jasper, "you may go now before you wring your poor cap to shreds."

Jasper grinned before shaking it out again and tugging it onto his head. "It's a tough old thing, my lady, but I thank you."

As soon as he left, the sisters exploded, all of them chattering at once until Wolfe was tempted to cover his ears.

"The game they spoke of has to be the engagement," Blessing said.

"Yes," Joy agreed. "Becoming the duchess wins the hand."

"But who would be too jealous?" Felicity asked.

"It has to be her lover," Fortuity volunteered. "It would be her lover if she were a character in one of my stories."

"Do you think she meant to become the duchess for the title and power while keeping the man she loved tethered to her?" Serendipity jumped up from her seat and started pacing. "I know I'd heard she was interested in someone else, but none of the rumors were that nefarious."

"Forgive me, my lady," Wolfe said, "but it is not unknown for both the wife and husband in arranged marriages to take lovers. In fact, it is quite regular and often expected." Perhaps he should not have said that in this room of delicate beings, but these rare sisters didn't strike him as conservatory lilies easily wilted. Still, his conscience demanded he apologize. "Forgive the crudeness of the topic. I would never wish to offend any of your sensibilities."

"Don't be silly," Grace told him. "How do those people live with themselves? Marriage is a…a holy bond."

"It is supposed to be, but in many instances among the peerage it has become a business or political transaction. The closeness your family enjoys is a rare thing, my lady, I assure you." Wolfe helped himself to the brandy decanter. This visit demanded something a great deal stronger than tea. He turned and held it up for the ladies. "Would anyone care to freshen their cups?"

"No, thank you," Grace said before anyone else could answer. "This battle demands clarity. Why did you ask Jasper if his sister would speak to your solicitor? Bringing charges under such circumstances could prove most futile, since the Longmortens never actually took action on their vile wishes against the children. They only spoke of it. And then it is also Jasper's sister's word against theirs, a commoner against a peer." Grace slowly shook her head. "If the Longmortens wished to press the issue, that poor girl might change her mind about sharing what she overheard."

"They may have only spoken about it, but their intentions were strong enough to cause my housekeeper to flee when she feared I had uncovered their plan." Wolfe sipped the brandy, savoring its sweet fruitiness as it warmed his gullet all the way down. "The twins are most definitely safer here until I can review *all* my servants again, secure replacements where necessary, and meet with my solicitor. I expect his arrival as soon as tomorrow. I do hope their staying here is acceptable. Are they behaving?"

"Of course they may stay," Grace said. "You promised them, and promises are important."

Blessing laughed. "They seem like angels to me after chasing my little Rorie. I look forward to talking with them even more."

"As do I," Fortuity said. "I might even coax them into helping me write a story."

"They absolutely must stay," Joy said. "Connor has become quite adept at Hazard, and Sissy is even better."

"They also enjoy testing my new recipes." Felicity snorted a very unladylike laugh. "I know I can always count on Connor for a truthful assessment of whether a treat is a success or a failure."

"As you can see, Your Grace," Serendipity said with the regalness of the eldest of the lot, "your siblings have acclimated quite well to the Broadmere chaos."

"It would seem so." Wolfe found himself quite jealous of his brother and sister. The two had found their way to paradise and left him behind, abandoned to the overly quiet and mismanaged halls of Wolfebourne Lodge.

Grace drew closer, stepping in front of him with her back to her sisters. "What is wrong?" she whispered.

Her intuitiveness to his self-serving emotions both touched and embarrassed him. What would she surely think of his selfishness? "Nothing is wrong, my lady. I am merely pondering all that must be done."

"He is lying," Lady Joy announced to all in the room. "Look at his eyes."

"Joy!" Grace delivered a hard glare to her sister, then looped her arm through his. "His Grace merely needs some air. We shall be in the garden for a bit. Leave us be and talk among yourselves, as I am sure you will, and no, I do not need a chaperone."

"Gracie." Serendipity stepped forward. "You should not—"

"I should not be bothered with useless flummery about compromising situations when I am merely walking in the side garden, in broad daylight and full view of every window and door that looks upon it. Now, stop it. We shall return shortly after His Grace is feeling more himself."

Wolfe maintained his silence, instinct warning it would be the ultimate in foolhardiness to try to mediate this conversation. While he'd never had to deal with so many sisters, he had observed enough of Chance's struggles to learn a thing or two.

Grace ushered him out to the garden and firmly shut the door behind them. "It is clear you are overwhelmed by my family, but take heart. It took Thorne and Matthew some time to find their footing. You will too." She halted then and studied him, wariness in her eyes. "That is…if you still *wish* to find your footing?"

Her insecurities prodded him to reveal his earlier selfish inclinations. He prayed they wouldn't drive her from him, but he couldn't bear her to think he had so easily changed his heart and mind about her.

He remained silent as they ambled deeper into the garden and seated themselves among the roses on a bench warmed by the sun. "I would not describe my feelings as *overwhelmed*, my lady."

"I see." She plucked at the folds of her skirt while staring straight ahead at the fragrant crimson blooms. "Then how would you describe them, Your Grace?"

"Wolfe—please?"

"Wolfe," she repeated softly, but it made his heart sing. "How would you describe your feelings in the parlor, if not overwhelmed?"

"Jealous."

She turned to him and arched a delicate blonde brow. "Jealous?"

"Yes, my lady, jealous."

"I am afraid I don't understand."

"Connor and Sissy have found safe haven. Paradise." He risked taking her hand. Her touch both soothed and inflamed him. "I envy them because while they are free to stay here, I must return to the much-too-quiet halls of Wolfebourne Lodge, with so few servants that it is quite easy to feel as though I am the only soul left on earth."

"Oh." Concern echoed loud and true in that one little word she had so softly uttered. It made him smile.

"Yes." He ran the heel of his thumb across the silkiness of her hand. "I've never been a patient man, and yet this predicament is of my own making because I waited so long to take action. Is that not irony itself?"

"It would seem so." With her head bowed as she kept her gaze on their joined hands, the sunlight illuminated her golden hair, crowning her with a gleaming halo that entranced him.

"Are you truly real, Grace?" he whispered. "Or are you an ethereal being sent to save me from myself?"

She looked up at him, almost startled. Her blue eyes shone like gemstones, sparkling with a sheen of unshed tears. "I fear you will discover I am quite real, and then you will run from me as fast as you can go."

He cupped her face in his hand. With the innocence of her trusting gaze, she transfixed him, drawing him in and making him care about nothing but remaining in her presence. "I will never escape you, my lady. Nor will I ever wish to try."

She huffed and gave him a wry look. "I am fractious a good deal of the time, opinionated all the time, and, as you well know, so unconventional that even my family considers me hopeless at times." She nodded as if to strengthen his defense. "There have been occasions when my sisters pretended not to know me."

"How cruel," he said, while running the backs of his fingers along the soft curve of her cheek. He so very badly wished to kiss her, but she had as much as thrown down the gauntlet to

Serendipity, charging that their time in the garden need not be chaperoned. He had already failed one test by kissing her in the parlor. He didn't need to fail another. "You are perfection, Grace." He couldn't resist a smile. "An ample pairing to my grumpiness, tendency to keep to myself, and hatred of the *ton*'s ridiculous games and competitions with their parties, teas, and making sure they are seen while wearing their finest when walking Rotten Row."

She brightened, her eyes flaring wide with surprise. "I hate those things too and would rather live in the country than ever set foot in London again."

He kissed her hand, then pressed it to his cheek, memorizing the feel of her skin against his and dreaming of even more. "We are well matched indeed."

"If only the way were clear," she said so softly that he almost didn't hear her.

"The way is clear. I shall speak with my solicitor tomorrow and apprise him of all that has come to pass."

"So you are not going to speak with Lady Margaret yourself?"

Wolfe noted that Grace didn't sound jealous. Her tone suggested there was only one correct answer, and it would be in his best interest to choose it. "I intend to speak with her with my solicitor present. From this day forward, I will not deal with Lady Longmorten or her daughter unless I have witnesses to the conversation."

Grace's thoughtful expression made him wonder if he had answered correctly. "A very prudent decision—and a necessary one, I fear. I simply wish Lady Margaret would toss her mother's aspirations to the winds and run away with her lover. That would make matters so much easier."

"Indeed, it would. Or we could run off to Gretna Green and live in Scotland until the *ton* grows bored with us and moves on to tattle about others."

The look she gave him soundly trounced that suggestion. "I do not run. Nor do I leave behind a mess for my family to endure—or, at least, I try not to make things more difficult for them. I have four sisters yet to find love and marry." She shifted on the bench and pondered him as if trying to decide what sort of beastly thing he was. "I can't say that I recommend love, but now that I have discovered you—and the insistent yearning to be with you—I do believe everyone should experience this horribly infuriating sense of happy hopelessness at least once."

"I see." He rolled his shoulders to shake off the barbs sprinkled through her heartfelt sentiment. "'Horribly infuriating, happy hopelessness'? You make a poor argument in favor of love, my lady."

"Happiness and hope should be like sunshine dancing across a fresh green meadow, encouraging it to flourish and bloom with beauty. But it has come to my attention that when love gets involved, worry and fear bite at happiness and hope's heels like hungry wolves ready to devour any hint of a joyful future."

Fearing she was toying with the idea of turning him away, he edged closer and gently drew her into his arms. "Tell me your worries, Grace, and your fears. Tell me so I can be the wolf that hunts them down and devours them."

She rested her hands on his chest and met his gaze, looking so deeply into his eyes that he swore she touched his soul. "I worry that I have this wrong, and it isn't love at all. I worry for Connor and Sissy if we marry and discover we have little to keep us in each other's hearts. I worry for us if we do have it right, but the world makes it so bloody difficult that by the time we win our war, we've lost the love that launched it." She fiddled with his cravat, then twitched an impatient shrug. "I warned you I was fractious. Did I also mention I have the terrible habit of overthinking and charging into battle after everyone else has declared a truce?" She leaned forward and whispered, "Mama and Papa were always telling me to slow down, take off my blinders, and think before battling whatever cause stirred my convictions."

"You are by far the most complicated yet utterly exquisite woman I have ever had the good fortune to meet." He stole a chaste kiss. The chaperone brigade could just be damned. Lifting his head and smoothing her errant tousle of curls back where they belonged, he held her gaze. "I can't promise we will never be unhappy, but I can swear without a doubt that I need you, Grace, and that I love you. Let me help you slay your worries and fears. Together, and with Connor and Sissy's help, I believe we can conquer anything."

With a sheepish smile, she slowly shook her head. "I always thought I would be the last of my sisters to fall in love, but you have well and truly captured me, Your Grace. I love you too."

That declaration warranted another kiss. One not quite so chaste. *Gads alive, I need this woman.* But that could not be until they were wed. With a sigh that was more like a groan, he lifted his head and put a bit of space between them. Already missing her warmth, he tipped his head toward the house. "We really should go back inside and join your family."

"I suppose we should," Grace said, wrinkling her nose at the prospect. "I am sure Serendipity is about to pop the laces on her corset."

They rose and ambled back toward the parlor, neither of them in a hurry to leave behind their comforting solitude in the garden. Wolfe drew in a deep breath and smiled as he hugged her arm closer. Divine Providence and fate had matched him perfectly. He almost chuckled. What would the *ton* think of a duchess who would rather muck about in the fields with her dogs than attend balls at Almack's and every High Society tea?

Serendipity met them at the double doors she had opened wide. Her demeanor suggested she *might* have witnessed at least one of their stolen kisses, and her fierce glare almost made him laugh. "Better now, are we, Your Grace?"

"Indeed. Much better."

Grace patted his arm while giving her sister a daring smile. "He must stay for supper, don't you think? That will give him more time with the children and the chance to get to know our *entire* family."

Serendipity twitched a brow at him. "Well, Your Grace? Who am I to argue, even though I assumed you would wish to leave and tend to the business of procuring another housekeeper? Did you not say yours had fled?"

"I did, but my butler can handle the household well enough until I find another. Feebson has been with the family forever. He knows our needs." Wolfe noted that Grace appeared to be enjoying this back-and-forth immensely. "An evening here is a delight I could never resist."

Peals of laughter, happy barks, and loud thumps like the galloping of horses came from the hallways overhead. Doors slammed and shouts of *hedgie* and *haggis* made the cacophony even louder.

Serendipity stared at the ceiling and slowly shook her head. "Oh dear. Merry has finally taught them the game."

Fortuity laughed and clapped her hands. "I can't wait until Quill is big enough to play."

Blessing caught Fortuity by the hand and tugged her toward the door. "Come. We can carry Quill and Rorie so they can play too."

"The game?" Wolfe asked Grace. He glanced upward, following the raucous sounds coming from the second floor. "Gads, are they herding wild horses up there?"

"No. They are chasing each other." Grace smiled at the ceiling. "Mama and Papa created this game. One person chases all the others, attempting to turn them into either a *haggis* or a *hedgie* with just a touch. If the runner turns you into a hedgie, you have to hug your knees and curl into a ball while grunting like a pig until the runner counts to ten. Then you jump up and you become the runner trying to turn others into a hedgie or a haggis. If you are turned into a haggis, again, you have to curl into a ball and shout *fie, fie, fie* as the runner counts to ten, and then you become the runner."

"I take it your father disliked haggis?"

"Despised it ever since his Scottish cousin tricked him into tasting it." Grace hugged herself while watching the ceiling with a sad, wistful smile. "Papa loved a rousing game of haggis and hedgie. We often played, no matter if we were in the country or the London townhouse."

"I am so sorry, Grace. I can tell you still miss him very much." Wolfe wished it was within his power to take away her pain.

She nodded. "In September, it will be three years since he left us, and I still look for him or think I see him out of the corner of my eye. Sometimes, I even think I hear him."

"I hear him at times when playing cards," Joy said softly from where she stood, looking out the window.

"I often hear him and Mama." Felicity dabbed the corner of her handkerchief to her eyes, then tucked it back inside her sleeve. "They are here—watching over us. I just know it."

"And we are making them proud," Serendipity said, jutting her chin higher. She turned and leveled a wilting glare on Wolfe. "Would you care to join the game of haggis and hedgie?"

He reached for Grace and smiled. "I would be delighted."

Chapter Thirteen

THANK HEAVENS THE Almighty had granted them a pristine day with no more than a few fluffy clouds setting off the sparkling blue of the sky. A teasing but most welcome breeze rustled through the trees and rhythmically swayed the tall grasses. The pristine white tents and table coverings gently billowed as if brought to life by the meadow fairies.

Grace craned her neck, overseeing Carson gathering her hounds and leading them away so they wouldn't be a bother to the guests. The huntsman, which was a ridiculous title for the man, was the only one she trusted to look after her pups. Even poor Gastric, Hector, and Sissy's condescending cat Galileo had joined the ranks of the beasties barred from the festivities. The servants had enough to manage with maintaining the bounty of food and drink that had to be kept either warm or cool, and, more specifically, bug free. They didn't need the additional worry of shooing away the animals.

The long banquet tables sheltered within the tents nearly groaned with everything a discerning guest might desire. Cold joints of not only roasted beef but boiled as well, shoulders of lamb, roasted fowl, lobsters, lettuces, and stewed fruit were just the beginning of the offerings. Additional tables in an adjoining tent held turnovers, cheesecakes, jam puffs, and cold cabinet puddings in molds. Every bread, biscuit, and cake imaginable was artfully arranged where tea would be served.

170

Grace smiled at her sister Felicity fussing over the items she had personally prepared. Dear, sweet Felicity adored food, both eating it and preparing it. Thank heavens for the talented seamstress from the village who had already repaired several of her gowns whose seams had given way.

"What did Felicity make this year?" Joy asked as she came up beside Grace.

"I managed to find out right before she ordered me out of the tent," Grace said, then counted off on her fingers. "Salmagundi with the freshest shallots from Cook's garden. Of course, she used chopped chicken and duck, so I won't be trying that. Cold pigeon pie, and I can't imagine how she could be so heartless to those poor little birds. Rout cakes and fool—both blueberry and raspberry. I'll most definitely try those."

"Did Connor approve them?" Joy asked with a laugh. "That young man has become quite the connoisseur."

"I believe he did." Grace pointed the child out, running down the hillside with his sister and a few children of the same age from the village. Everyone was invited to the Broadmere picnic, no matter their station in life. "Do you not think he's grown since staying with us? It must be from taste-testing Felicity's recipes."

"Possibly." Joy made a show of glancing all around. "And where is your intended?" she asked with a coy wink.

"Joy!"

"Do not scold. Everyone knows." Joy adjusted her gloves, straightening the seams between her fingers. "Has His Grace's solicitor spoken to *you know who* yet?"

"I wish I knew." And that was the crux of it. Until matters were handled as delicately as possible, even though Wolfe and the ladies Longmorten were not on speaking terms, Grace had to play the part of nothing more than the Duke of Wolfebourne's neighbor. She could hardly be seen walking with Wolfe and behaving as though they belonged to one another, and that also made overhearing any pertinent information about his engagement to Lady Margaret a great deal more difficult.

"We could go welcome the Longmortens," Joy suggested with a wicked grin.

"Chance and Serendipity are welcoming the guests as they arrive—remember?" Grace scanned the grounds, making note of who was where and talking to whom. She spied the Longmortens and their ever-present guard, Sir Andrew. "Our persons of interest are over there beside the willow, already seated at one of the tables. Lady Longmorten looks ready to bite through iron spikes, Lady Margaret appears to be misery itself, and Sir Andrew is either angry or taken with a fever. Have you ever seen so much color in the man's cheeks before?"

"He is her lover," Joy said with such conviction that Grace turned and stared at her. Usually quite adept at reading individuals, almost to the point of being labeled as gifted, her sister almost always knew more about people than they knew about themselves.

"Did Lady Margaret confide in you?"

Joy rolled her eyes. "She didn't have to. All you need do is watch her. *There.* Right there. She looked at him again as if wishing they were anywhere but here. See it? And if you wait but a few moments, she will repeat the action, as will he."

"He does appear to be smoldering a bit whenever he looks at her." Grace studied the pair. What a miserable way to live—denying your love for another all in the name of riches and social standing. "I wish we could help her."

"Help her?" Joy swatted Grace's skirts with her closed parasol. "Not two days ago you were ready to thrash the woman and her mother for threatening Connor and Sissy."

"I still am." Grace swatted Joy back with her own lacy parasol that matched the regal blue of her new spencer. Far be it from her to allow her younger sister to get the better of her. "But if we helped Lady Margaret run away with Sir Andrew, would that not get both the women permanently away from Wolfebourne Lodge?"

"Must you two pick at each other as if you were still children?" Serendipity asked as she came up behind them. "I mean, really!"

"Calm yourself," Grace told her. "The picnic looks to be a roaring success, and everyone is enjoying their outing and has you and Felicity to thank for it. Joy and I were just discussing Lady Margaret and Sir Andrew. She claims they are lovers."

Serendipity opened her pale yellow parasol and rested it on her shoulder, shielding that part of her face not protected from the sun by the brim of her matching bonnet. She nodded at Grace and Joy. "Your creamy complexions, ladies. Parasols up, please." Then she casually turned and studied the Longmorten women and their knight. "I believe you might have something there, Joy. They do keep glancing at each other when they believe no one sees."

"It's a wonder Lady Longmorten has not had an attack of apoplexy," Joy said while twirling her parasol on her shoulder. "She came here today to do battle. See the murder in her eyes?"

"Well…" With her parasol properly in place, Grace caught up her white skirts so she might walk faster without staining her hem on the green grasses of the meadow. "I say we make the first move by going over and speaking with them. What say you, sisters?" But she hadn't taken two steps before she was blocked by Connor and Sissy, hopping up and down and chattering at the same time.

"Calm down, sir and madam," she told them, bending to bring herself to their eye level. "One at a time. I can't help you if I can't understand you."

"Wait," Serendipity said. She and Joy casually moved around and placed themselves and their parasols so the Longmortens couldn't see the children. "Carry on."

"Lord Middlebie is foxed," Sissy said in a worried whisper. "He's shouting all sorts of things."

"Jug-bitten badly," Connor added. "And even louder than usual. He's done told all the men that you didn't give him a second glance 'cause you got your sights set on a duke and couldn't care less that the man's already promised to marry another woman—the woman he feels *he* should rightly have."

"Oh, dear heavens, what a mess." Serendipity stretched to look around the area. "I told Chance to watch that man. We all know how Middlebie gets when he overindulges. It is beyond me why our bacon-brained brother even invited him here for the summer after I expressly asked him not to."

"Give over, Seri," Grace said, searching the sprawling picnic for the drunken Scot. "You know as well as I that Chance wants us all married off and probably thought if an eligible male stayed under our roof, one of us might surrender."

"Not bloody well likely," Joy said. "We all know what Middlebie is like."

"Joy! Language!" Serendipity gathered the children closer. "Where is Lord Middlebie putting on his show?"

Connor pointed. "On the far side of the pond. Over there, behind them trees. He even stripped off his shirt and started picking up big rocks and throwing them in the water to show everyone his strength."

Serendipity looked ready to collapse in a dead faint, and Joy snickered so hard her face went red as a boiled beetroot. Both the children turned to Grace.

"What you want we should do?" Sissy asked her. "We don't want him to spoil Lady Seri's party."

"No, indeed," Grace said. "We wouldn't want that." She waved Connor forward. "I need you to find Chance and fetch him as quick as you can. Bring him to the pond. Joy, you and Sissy come with me. It will take all three of us to keep Lord Middlebie confused and distracted until Chance comes to lead his sotted friend away."

"What should I do?" Serendipity asked, looking so lost and despondent that Grace's heart hurt for her poor sister who always had the answers.

"Start the lawn games and keep the rest of the guests as far away from the area around the pond as you possibly can."

"I shall hang Chance by his braces if this day is ruined." Serendipity left in a flurry, muttering about everything she intended to do to her brother if Middlebie soured the picnic.

"How are we going to distract a drunkard determined to put on a show?" Joy asked. "And if he sees you, he'll probably get even louder. Did you happen to consider that?"

"You are not helping, Joy. If you don't have positive suggestions, keep your thoughts to yourself." As they rounded the copse shielding the pond from the rest of the guests, Grace groaned. The half-dressed Middlebie stood knee deep in the edge of the pond, his pale skin glistening like a fish's belly freshly pulled from the water.

"I could hide in the reeds and throw rocks at him," Sissy suggested. "Reckon he might think it was midges come to get him."

"It depends on how much and what he's had to drink." Grace wasn't an expert on drunkards, but she remembered Mama remarking once that whisky tended to make men sillier a great deal faster than wine or ratafia. And with Middlebie being a Scot, his preferred spirit was whisky. She held to the little girl's shoulders, reluctant to have her hide in the reeds. What if something went awry, like a stray creepy-crawly? "Is there nowhere else you could hide and throw things at him? I don't like the idea of your wading into the reeds."

"If I use my sling, I could hit him from those bushes on the other side of the water."

"Your sling?" Grace tore her attention from the drunken Scot putting on an entirely too loud exhibition and stared down at the child. "Are you fairly accurate?"

Sissy grinned. "I'm better than Connor, even though he always lies and says I'm not."

"Then, by all means, have at it. Good hunting—just try not to put out his eye or do him any serious harm." As the little girl skipped away, Grace hoped she hadn't erred in permitting Sissy to open fire on a living target. She caught hold of Joy's arm and hurried along beside her. "Why aren't any of those men stopping him?"

At least five gentlemen of questionable manners and uncertain social standing stood on the banks of the pond, cheering Middlebie on. If they'd had any decency about them, they would've taken him away so he wouldn't be an insult to any of the women and children attending the party.

"I am not acquainted with any of those men." Joy tugged her arm free, caught hold of Grace, and pulled her to a stop. "I am none too certain we should go over there. They all appear to be well fuddled themselves."

"Sissy is getting ready to open fire by my command," Grace told her. "We can't *not* go over there."

"True." Joy looked back in the direction from which they'd just come. "Connor should come along with Chance at any moment too so, I'm certain we'll be all right."

"Others are meandering this way as well," Grace said. "Either Middlebie's noise or the rumors have carried across the meadow."

"Both, more than likely."

"In for a penny, in for a pound." Grace snapped her parasol shut and brandished it like a sword as she charged forward. "Middlebie! Shame on you. Out of the pond, I say. Out and to the stables with you until you recover from your imbibing. My brother will have your hide for this! Such disgraceful behavior at my family's annual picnic. Shame on you, my lord!"

The questionable gentlemen finding Middlebie's antics so entertaining disappeared, fading into the tree line like morning fog burned away by sunshine.

"Cowards!" Middlebie shouted after the men before twisting back and forth in the water. He sputtered unintelligible obscenities while staggering in the pond's sticky mire until he fully lost his balance and went down with a monstrous splash. "Bloody hell!" Sitting in the waist-deep muck, he smacked the back of his neck. "Ow! These damnable English midges bite hard."

"Come out of there this instant, Lord Middlebie," Grace said. "Your behavior is most unacceptable. Dress yourself and leave."

"I'm not coming out till she agrees to be off to Gretna Green with me." The stubborn Scot jutted his stubbly chin higher with such a jerk that he almost fell backward in the muddy water. Then he lurched forward a bit, squinting at Grace with a disturbing intensity as he swayed back and forth like a cobra about to strike. He snorted and threw a hand at her in dismissal. "Off wi' ye! Chance said ye already promised yerself to that duke what will never take ye down the aisle. If ye dinna believe me, just ask the woman he's been tied to since he was a bairn. Is that her standing there beside ye? Feckin' hell. Where is she? Tell her to stop her foolishness and come along. I need her dowry, and her too. She's no' so bad once ye give her a chance to prove her own worth."

"Who the devil is he wanting to take to Gretna Green? I'm going to help Seri hang Chance by his braces," Grace said to Joy. "I can't believe our addlepated brother confided in someone like Middlebie, and how dare he give that drunkard the slightest hope that one of us would be silly enough to marry him. I wonder if Sissy could incapacitate him from there?"

"I doubt she has any stones large enough over there in those bushes." Joy huffed, snapped her parasol shut, and smacked her palm with it as if ready to brawl. "I've always questioned our brother's ability to reason. Papa would be after them both with the buggy whip if he were still here. Shall we do Papa proud?"

"And do what? Knock the man over and have him drown?" Grace turned once again and looked back. "Oh dear heavens, Seri is surely going to swoon. Look at that group headed this way." She squinted and looked closer at the tallest man in the lead. "Heaven help us. That's Wolfe at the front of them. We asked Connor to fetch Chance, not Wolfe."

"Perhaps he couldn't find him, and I daresay that doesn't matter now. If we don't quiet that fool Middlebie, who knows how much damage he'll wreak on Wolfebourne's plans to break the engagement?" Joy picked up a rock and threw it at the wailing Scot. "Be quiet! What would your mother say were she to see you now and witness your behavior? Why would any woman wish to be with you when you are so determined to play the part of the fool?"

Surprisingly enough, Middlebie went still and stared at Joy as if she had cast a spell and turned him to stone. Without a word, he drew himself up from the muck, slogged his way out of the pond, and started fumbling with his shirt, trying to pull it on.

"Middlebie!" Wolfe bellowed, his deep voice rolling across the grounds like thunder. "What the devil is wrong with you?"

Middlebie didn't answer, just kept his head bowed as he struggled into his shirt, then retrieved his neckcloth from the ground and draped it around his neck.

Wolfe reached the man and caught him with a hard right to the jaw. The Scot reeled back, landed hard on the ground, and stayed there—motionless.

A tug on her skirt made Grace turn and discover Connor.

"You better get to Wolfe, and in a hurry," the boy told her. "He found me afore I could find His Grace to tell him 'bout his friend." The child's eyes brimmed with fear. "I never seen Wolfe so angry. He might hurt that man something fierce. Hurt him so bad he might even die."

Grace rounded on her heels, tossed her parasol aside, and reached Wolfe just as he yanked the limp man up from the ground to hit him again. "Your Grace! That is quite sufficient." She pushed in close and put a hand on Wolfe's heaving chest. His unbridled rage almost made her retreat. But no, she couldn't. This situation needed calming. "Wolfe," she said so softly that she knew only he would hear, "it is done, and all is well. Let him go. Let…him…go."

"He could have harmed you," he said through bared teeth, growling like a cornered beast. "May have already harmed your reputation."

"But he didn't, and now you saved me. Leave him to the

stable lads. They'll watch over him until he can sort himself and leave the estate." She risked touching his cheek, smiling as the raspiness of the day's stubble brushed against her fingers. "All is well. Let him go."

Wolfe released his hold on the unconscious Scot and let the man drop. He took a step back but kept his gaze locked on Grace. The intensity of his stare burned through her until she struggled to breathe.

The slightest movement to her right caught her attention. Serendipity gave the barest nod at the trio of guests standing slightly apart from the rest of the crowd, on a higher point up the hillside. The Longmortens and their knight observed the most unsavory situation with the interest of buzzards about to descend upon the battlefield dead.

Chance chose that moment to appear, looking slightly worse for the wear and making Grace wonder which guest he had treated to what appeared to be a very intimate tour of the more secluded areas of the grounds. "Fred, Jasper," Chance said with a snap of his fingers, "get Arnold and Louis to assist you in seeing that Lord Middlebie finds a clean stall in the stable in which to ponder his poor choices once he opens his eyes and returns to the living."

"Yes, Your Grace." The men nodded and hurried to complete their assigned task.

Even though it was the last thing she wished to do, Grace avoided further eye contact with Wolfe and did her best to help Serendipity and Joy encourage the guests to return to the indulgences of the picnic rather than revel in the excitement of a drunken, misbehaving lord. The best way to tamp down any rumors was to behave as if all was now well.

Connor and Sissy clustered around her, staying as close as frightened chicks around a mother hen. Somehow, she got the sense that they feared they were in trouble. Pulling them aside to a nearby fallen log, she had them seat themselves on either side of her. "What is wrong with you two? Why haven't you returned to playing?"

Both children stared downward and remained silent while swinging their feet and bouncing their heels against the log.

"I can't help you if I don't know what's troubling you. I'm not like Joy. She can look into people's minds, you know." She nudged Connor, teasing him with an eerie whisper. "Shall I call her over and have her look in your ear so she can tell me what you're thinking?"

Connor squinted up at her, studying her with an expression so serious that she immediately dropped all pretense of levity. "Sissy and I did some sneaking around before Lord Middlebie stirred up all that trouble. We felt it our duty to do some discovering."

Grace braced herself, uncertain what the two would confess to next. "Sneaking around and discovering, you say?"

Sissy nodded while nervously chewing on her bottom lip, and Connor bobbed his head.

Grace folded her hands in her lap, not at all sure how to continue. She'd always been on the other side of these conversations, where she was the one confessing sins in the hopes of receiving a lighter punishment. She wondered if Mama and Papa had ever been unsure of what to do when their children were a little too adventurous or naughty.

After pulling in and releasing a deep breath, she settled herself more comfortably on the log. "And what did you hope to accomplish with your sneaking around and discovering? I take it this is something I should know about, since you brought it up?"

"Jake and Willie told us Wolfe's solicitor met with Lady Longface...er...I mean...Lady Longmorten and Lady Margaret this morning," Connor said.

"Firstly, who are Jake and Willie?" Grace asked, trying to remain calm and logical—mannerisms with which she always struggled. "And how do they know about your brother's solicitor and who the man is?"

"Jake and Willie are the smithy's sons. They know everyone

who comes and goes in the village." Connor pointed at his sister. "And Sissy's friends saw him too."

Sissy nodded. "Anne, the vicar's daughter, and Jenny. Her mama and papa run the inn where Lady Longmorten and Lady Margaret are staying."

"I see. That still doesn't answer how they knew for certain that this morning's visitor was your brother's solicitor."

"That's what we thought too at first," Connor said. "But then Jenny told us about his name in the book her mama has people sign whenever they take a room. He signed *Mr. Horace Beeksbie.* I remember Wolfe saying that name before when he was telling us about not only being our brother but also our guard. He's got papers that say he's supposed to protect us till we get older."

"You mean your guardian?" Grace gently corrected him.

"Yes." Sissy bounced in place. "Wolfe is our guardian till we get old enough to take care of ourselves."

Grace nodded, lacing her fingers together and clenching her hands tighter in her lap. She had never been the patient sort, and keeping the twins on track to get to the meat of the confession was proving to be most trying. "So, your sneaking around discovered that the solicitor had spoken to the Longmortens this morning? That's good. Your brother intended for him to speak with them at their earliest convenience."

"But they told the solicitor that they was going to ruin Wolfe," Connor said.

"Then Mr. Beeksbie told them he had signed papers from folks in the village who had heard them talking about getting rid of us in terrible ways." Sissy hopped to her feet, unable to sit still any longer.

"How on earth did the two of you learn all of this?" Grace looked all around to ensure no one else was close enough to overhear. "It's almost as if you were in the room with them."

"My friends was there with them," Sissy said, beaming proudly. "The sitting room at the inn has big cupboards all around the room. Jenny and Anne was in one of them having a tea party with their dolls."

"I see." Grace clenched her hands so tightly that her nails threatened to tear through the seams of her gloves. "And you are quite certain they heard all of this as you stated?" After all, children had active imaginations. Were these two and their compatriots reliable sources of such life-altering information? "And how did the Longmortens react to the news that Mr. Beeksbie gave them?"

Both Connor and Sissy ducked their heads, and their little shoulders sagged. "They said if they couldn't ruin our brother, then they would do their best to ruin you 'cause they know you are the one Wolfe really likes," Sissy whispered.

"And how do they know that?" Grace hazarded to ask, even though she suspected the culprits stood before her.

"We might have told her," Connor said, mumbling so softly that she had to lean forward to hear him. "But that was afore her and Lady Margaret moved out. We told them right afore we runned away and went to the rock gorge where you and Wolfe found us and took us to your house."

Sissy rubbed her upper arm and flinched as if in pain. "Lady Longmorten caught hold of me when I ran too close to her table earlier. She twisted my arm something fierce and said she would do worse than that the next time she got the chance."

"What?" Grace pushed up the child's sleeve and discovered red, finger-shaped stripes already purpling into angry bruises. Rage consumed her as she gently drew Sissy into a hug. "I want you and Connor to find Merry, Blessing, or Fortuity and stay close to them while I deal with this. No one harms a child on Broadmere land, and more importantly, no one ever harms a friend of mine."

"Are we in trouble?" Connor asked with a wistful glance at the herd of children playing off in the distance.

"Absolutely not," Grace said. "You have done nothing wrong. I simply want you with my sisters because I want you safe and have no idea what that pair of cruel harpies may try next when I escort them to their carriage." She rose, shook out the folds of her white walking dress, and tugged the wrinkles from her blue spencer with its bronze buttons. She was ready to wage war. The Longmortens and Sir Andrew had returned to their table and sat sipping their tea as if they were royalty. Teeth clenched, she nudged the children toward her sisters. "Off with you, now. I will be along shortly after I see to the rubbish that has blown into our picnic."

Without another look back, she charged forward, her fury fixated on Lady Longmorten. How dare that woman hurt Sissy! As soon as she reached her, she grabbed her by the arm, in the same way the cruel hag had handled the child. "To your feet, Lady Longmorten," Grace said, barely managing to keep her tone even. "Allow me to escort you to your carriage." She dragged the dowager countess up from her chair.

"What on earth?" Lady Longmorten stumbled a few steps, then wrenched her arm free. "How dare you! No one handles me in such a manner."

"No one handles children in such a manner either," Grace said, loud and bold. "Yet you left bruises on little Sissy's arm when she drew too close, and then you threatened her with what you hoped to visit upon her later."

The old woman's mouth fell open, and she clutched her white-gloved hands to the base of her throat. "I have never been so insulted in all my life."

"Then I am proud to be the first to call you out for your cruelty." Grabbing hold of Lady Longmorten's arm again, Grace turned to Lady Margaret. "As far as I am concerned, you're no better. I suggest you gather your things and accompany your mother out the gate, or I'll be more than happy to drag you out as well."

"Now see here." Sir Andrew rose, red as fire and sputtering like a boiling teakettle. "You will remove your hands and your rudeness from our presence immediately."

"Might I suggest you remember where you are, Sir Andrew?"

Grace offered the fool her sweetest smile. "This is Broadmere land, and your welcome here has run its course. Leave. Now. And might I suggest you sleep with one eye open and never turn your back on these two? They can't be trusted. Any person who mistreats children is capable of anything."

A collective gasp all around filled Grace with a mild twinge of regret—not because she had confronted Lady Longmorten but because she had ruined Serendipity's picnic.

She yanked on the old woman's spindly arm again. "Come along, you. Or shall I summon the constable to cart you out?"

"You round-heeled little chit!" Lady Longmorten squawked like an insulted peahen. "Causing a scene merely to draw attention away from your whoring after the man my daughter is engaged to marry."

"The engagement is off," Wolfe said as he descended upon them with long, purposeful strides. "Why would I marry a woman intent on doing my brother and sister harm? A woman whose mother would gladly see to their disposal as if they were nothing more than scraps from the dinner table?" He glared at Sir Andrew. "Why would I want a woman who thinks me such a fool that I wouldn't even notice her lover living under the same roof as us?"

Both Lady Margaret and Lady Longmorten paled while Sir Andrew became even more red-faced. "You insult me, Your Grace," the knight said. "I demand satisfaction."

"Any time. Any place. Any weapon. Have your second contact mine." Wolfe swaggered closer. "And while I'm at it, would you also be insulted to learn that Lady Margaret intended to leave for Gretna Green with the Earl of Middlebie on the morrow? He drank himself into delirium because he wished her to leave with him today."

"What?" Sir Andrew looked not at Lady Margaret but at her mother. "Did you know of this?"

"Of course I did not know of this, you fool. And how could that be true? The drunken ape was bemoaning his inability to snare a Broadmere daughter and her dowry." Lady Longmorten shook a finger at Grace. "You ruined everything. Everything! But my daughter and I shall prevail. You can have Wolfebourne. Keep him in good health. But we shall have everything but his entailed properties. The two of you will be the Duke and Duchess of Paupers."

"You are a pitiful creature," Grace told the bitter woman. She barely restrained herself from clawing out her eyes and snatching off her hair. The only thing saving Lady Longmorten from a robust thrashing was Grace's delayed regret for ruining Serendipity's picnic. "And you have spoiled an otherwise lovely day. Get off Broadmere land, out of my sight, and tell your solicitor he best study his facts well, because the attempted murder of a peer's brother and sister far outweighs something as ridiculous as a breach of promise. As a matter of fact, I am sure there must be a clause in there somewhere regarding your daughter's purity. There usually is. Shall we ask the village doctor to examine her? I'm sure we can clear one of the tents to grant her some privacy."

"Gracie!" Serendipity stood nearby, eyes flashing and cheeks as crimson as roses.

A deeper regret swept through Grace. *Poor Seri.* Perhaps she *had* gone a bit far with that one. But if they were going to entertain their guests with a show, they might as well offer them an exemplary spectacle they wouldn't soon forget. "Is Lord Middlebie awake yet? Perhaps he would like to leave with the ladies, since he is so anxious to get to Gretna Green."

"They are mine!" Sir Andrew roared, reacting with more passion than the man had ever exhibited before.

"*They?*" Grace asked as loudly as possible to ensure none of the guests missed it. "Are we to understand that you share mother *and* daughter?"

Sir Andrew stormed toward Grace, only halting when Wolfe stepped in and blocked his way. Wild eyed, the knight bared his teeth. "They are mine. Both of them."

"Silence yourself, you fool!" Lady Longmorten told him.

"Oh, Mama, please," Lady Margaret said with a pitiful wail.

"My solicitor made you an offer this morning, my lady," Wolfe said to Lady Longmorten. "Shall I send him back around with the papers you and Lady Margaret refused to sign?"

"Yes!" Lady Margaret snapped before her mother could answer. "Please do, Your Grace. Freedom will be a refreshing change." She turned and glared at Lady Longmorten. "As will Scotland and the attention of a man who wishes to be a real husband to me."

"Do not dare defy me," Lady Longmorten said. "You can't marry that empty-pocketed Scot!"

"As soon as he recovers from his whisky, we set off for Gretna Green, and I shall sign over my properties and allowance—over which you have no authority."

"Walters!" Serendipity clapped her hands. "Have the footmen escort the Longmortens and Sir Andrew out."

"And throw Middlebie in the carriage with them," Chance said.

Grace clenched her fists to keep from latching on to Lady Longmorten again. She so badly wanted to punish the woman for hurting Sissy. But a glance at Serendipity stayed her hand. It would be a long while before Serendipity forgave her for such a spectacle.

———✦———

Chapter Fourteen

WOLFE STOOD BESIDE the fence row, watching Grace tromp across the field with her hounds. She appeared to be trying to instill some semblance of discipline into the seven half-grown pups that would probably never go to different homes—especially if Grace, Connor, and Sissy had their way about it.

He propped his arms atop the wooden rail and leaned against the fence. He didn't care if they ended up with a thousand dogs at Wolfebourne Lodge as long as Grace was his forevermore.

She had fought like a lioness, protecting his brother and sister with no thought to the rumors her actions would trigger. Gratitude and adoration did not begin to describe all he felt for her. The woman amazed him, humbled him, and he loved her with a terrifying fury. If he'd had his way about it, they too would have eloped to Gretna Green and returned to Binnocksbourne as man and wife.

But she wished to wait because of the damage she'd done to the annual Broadmere picnic. The gossips would retell the story about this year's event for ages to come, and his softhearted wife-to-be felt guilty about spoiling her sister Serendipity's perfect day even though it was not entirely Grace's fault. If any one person should shoulder the blame, it was him. He was the common thread running through the entire tapestry of all that had gone wrong that day.

At his feet, Gastric groaned and rolled over, turning the other side of his pink belly toward the sun. Galileo perched atop the nearest fencepost, the stoic feline war general overseeing the troops' training. Hector bounced alongside Grace, attempting to help her keep the puppies and older hounds herded in some semblance of order.

Connor and Sissy were enjoying a day with their friends in the village. The vicar and his wife had invited all the children known to have taken part in spying on the Longmortens to enjoy a day of serving the church by sprucing up the grounds, followed by a much calmer picnic that was not fraught with such astonishing gossip. The couple had also promised to instill a proper biblical sense of that which was right and that which was wrong in the young ones, but Wolfe suspected the vicar and his wife also wanted access to any additional *on dit* that the children might not have already shared about his former fiancée, her mother, and their lover, Sir Andrew. The man of the cloth and his spouse had been quite entranced by all the truths that had come to light at the Broadmere picnic.

A glance back at the line of great, sprawling oaks shading the outskirts of the manicured grounds surrounding the manor house revealed the remainder of the Broadmere family and extended families. They were not about to grant Wolfe and Grace any compromising time to themselves, and from the look of it, they fully intended to guard her virtue en masse.

He didn't care. Well, he did, but he was still grateful for any time spent with her.

"Marry me today," he called out to her when she and the dogs circled close enough to hear him.

She halted and shot him a disbelieving look. "I thought I made my position about eloping to Gretna Green quite clear, Your Grace."

He patted his pocket. "We do not have to elope. Our special license is right here in my pocket."

She meandered closer but kept a disappointingly respectable distance between them. Her hesitant smile and watchful demeanor both teased and worried him. "I thought we were going to have the banns read starting the first Sunday next month?"

"What are you afraid of, Gracie?" he asked quietly so her family couldn't hear.

She tossed her head. "I have no idea what you are talking about."

"Grace."

"What?"

"The other evening, in the drawing room, Joy tutored me on how to read people. What I read now is that you are afraid—and I need to know why, so I might correct it."

She ignored him, concentrating instead on the multitude of dogs milling around her.

"I am not going away. You might as well answer."

She gave him a curt huff, then flounced down and sat in the tangle of billowy grass that covered that part of the meadow. "Are Connor and Sissy not back yet?"

"They'll not return until well after tea, remember? The vicar's wife was most clear on that." Bending his tall frame, he snaked through the fence, daring to close the distance between them and sit in the grass beside her. The dogs clambered and bounced all around until Grace convinced them to calm themselves and sit.

He reached over and took her hand in his. "I thought you wished to be my wife. Was I mistaken?" He held his breath, praying she had not changed her mind after all that had happened.

She refused to look at him. Instead, she kept her head bowed, hiding behind the wave of golden-blonde curls that had worked loose from her hairpins. "I do wish to be your wife."

"Then why do we delay embracing our wedded bliss? From all I know of you and all that your sisters say, you have never given a whit about what the gossips tattle on about." He let go of her hand, swept back her hair, and gently turned her face to his. "What is it, Grace? What is wrong?" He grazed his thumb along the fullness of her bottom lip. "You frighten me, my lady," he said. "You make me fear I am about to lose you."

Uncertainty welled in the sapphire blue of her eyes, fueling his fears even more. "What if…"

He waited for her to finish, holding his breath again as all the terrible *what ifs* she might utter raced through his mind. "What if?" he prompted her when she still didn't speak.

"I am not a usual…lady." She cringed as if confessing a most egregious sin. "You may think you already know that, but taking a wife such as myself is quite a different matter entirely."

Rather than reassure her or allay her fears with smiles and platitudes, he forced himself to remain solemn. "Name off your sins, my lady. Even though we have done this before, name them off so I might know of all your vile ways."

"I am not toying with you, Wolfe. I am quite serious."

"As am I. Name them."

"I do not eat meat."

"Dishes with meat will not be offered to you nor placed on your end of the table. I, however, will continue to enjoy a good cut of beef or whatever meat Cook has prepared."

"I do not approve of hunting either. Fox hunts are particularly cruel, and I can't abide them. Are you willing to respect my wishes on that?"

"I have yet to see a fox since arriving in the country, my lady, and closing Wolfebourne land to hunting is not an issue. There is still the sport of breeding thoroughbreds and hounds, supervising the maintenance of crops, and filling our manor with children for Connor and Sissy to recruit for even more mischief."

She stared at him, the heightened pink of her cheeks sorely tempting him to kiss her. "You know of my adventuring clothes."

He allowed himself a heavy sigh. "Indeed, I do. Might we come to the same agreement that you and your father had? No riding near the roadway or wearing them into the village. You only wear them while on Wolfebourne or Broadmere land?"

"Yes. I believe that only fair."

"What else?" He was winning, and with any luck, they would be happily married by week's end. Struggling not to gloat, he nodded for her to continue. "You already told me you are opinionated and fractious, that you speak your mind, and I have witnessed your protectiveness over those you care about firsthand. All of which, if anything, makes me love you even more." He dared to kiss her cheek and lingered close to the silkiness of her hair as he whispered, "I want you as my wife, Grace. Within the next hour would not be soon enough."

"I am afraid," she whispered.

"My fearless defender of animals and children? My amazing warrioress who rushes into the fray without hesitation? What could possibly strike fear into your valiant heart? Tell me so I may slay whatever demons still trouble you."

She lowered her gaze, making him realize she was quite serious.

"Grace—my heart is yours forevermore. No matter what. Tell me what you fear."

"You do not care that some might say you married a tomboy or a hoyden? You won't change your mind about marrying such an unconventional lady?"

"My only care is for you, my love."

She patted his chest. "You truly have a special license?"

"I do."

She fiddled with his cravat, the way she always did when feeling particularly anxious. "Then perhaps we might marry this coming Saturday. Would that do?"

"Well." He struggled not to smile and pull her into his arms—instead, he remained quite serious. "I suppose Saturday would do, if that is what you have your heart set on."

"If not Saturday, then what day would you prefer?"

"Yesterday would not be soon enough, my lady."

Her pensiveness melted away, replaced with a wry smile. "I do not manage teasing well, either, unless I am the teaser."

"So I have come to realize. Is there anything else I should

know?"

She pushed up from the ground and laughed. "Loads more, I would imagine, but I suppose there should be some surprises to keep you from growing bored with me."

"I doubt very much that boredom with you will ever be a problem, my lady." He rose and primly offered his arm. "Come. Let us tell your family so your sisters can plan the battle."

"Plan the battle?"

"If I have learned anything since meeting your family, it is that your sisters plan all major events much like generals wage war. In fact, the Crown would do well to commission Serendipity to train the commanders for each branch of the service."

Grace laughed as she lithely slipped through the fence, even though she was wearing her walking dress rather than her adventuring buckskins. "I am sure Seri would be most proud to hear that."

"Seri would be most proud to hear what?" Serendipity asked from where she and Blessing were fishing a wildflower out of little Rorie's mouth and prying another one out of her fist.

"There is a wedding breakfast to plan for this Saturday," Grace said with a pointed nod at Felicity, who immediately jumped up and clapped with joy.

"*This* Saturday?" Serendipity repeated, looking aghast. "Oh dear heavens, this is Wednesday. There is your dress to be sorted. Our dresses to be sorted. The food." She came up short and looked at Wolfe. "I assume you have a special license and the ceremony will be here?"

He almost retreated a step but caught himself in time. "Yes to the special license, and I have no preference as to where we have the ceremony, as long as we have it."

"Well done, you," Fortuity said from the blanket spread across the ground where she sat beside her sleeping son.

Chance strode forward and clapped him on the back. "Welcome to the family, Wolfebourne, and may God have mercy on your soul."

"Don't worry, Gracie," Merry said with a narrow-eyed glare at her brother. "Joy and I can manage the frogs and eels for Chance's bed."

"Are we not all getting a little too old for that prank?" Chance asked.

"We will stop that prank when you cease behaving like a horse's arse," Blessing said.

"Exactly," Joy agreed.

Blessing's husband, Thorne, and Fortuity's husband, Matthew, stepped forward with wide grins.

"Congratulations, Wolfebourne," Thorne said, "Trust me, you will never regret it."

Wolfe smiled at Grace. "I know I won't."

"And if you ever need reinforcements," Matthew said with a wicked wink, "do not send for us. Neither of us are foolhardy enough to test the sisters' alliance."

"It sounds as though there will be a need for a great many frogs and eels for the men," Grace said as she started toward the house. "And now, if you will excuse me, I feel the need for an outing with Pegasus before Seri confines me to my room with innumerable preparations."

"Gracie!" Serendipity stared at her walking away, huffing when she didn't slow. She looked back at Wolfe as if he would be silly enough to try to stop Grace. "Today is Wednesday. She needs to start preparing *now*. Speak with her."

"I shall," he said, seizing on the opportunity and starting toward the stable. "Tenebrae and I will ride with her and do our very best to convince her she should be doing other things."

"Your Grace!" Serendipity fisted her hands on her hips while the other sisters giggled.

"Leave off, Seri," Chance said. "They are marrying on Saturday."

"It is most inappropriate," Serendipity said with a tight-jawed look at her brother.

"When has Gracie ever been appropriate?" Joy asked, then

went uncharacteristically serious. "She is not a lightskirt, Seri, and you know it. Leave her be."

Wolfe smiled to himself and kept walking, the sisters' lively conversation and the men's chuckling fading away as he neared the stable. A private ride with Grace was a treasure he was not about to miss.

By the time he and Jasper had his lively black stallion and Grace's equally exuberant Pegasus ready for the ride, she joined them wearing her adventuring clothes—as he had known she would.

She halted and looked all around. "Well?"

"Well, what?" Wolfe launched himself up into the saddle, knowing it would be unwise to offer Grace any help with mounting her horse. In her mind, that would be akin to his saying she possessed the poorest imaginable skills of horsemanship.

"Where is everyone else?" She settled into the saddle and patted her steed as he pranced back and forth, excited to start the outing.

"I believe Lady Joy and your brother convinced the others that since we are marrying this Saturday, our enjoying a ride without benefit of a chaperone was irrelevant."

Grace feigned a shocked demeanor. "How scandalous," she said with a laugh, then took the lead, her lovely behind bouncing up and down in a most suggestive way as she became one with her horse's gait.

"Indeed." Wolfe would be more than happy to make the outing as scandalous as she wished. The lady had but to give him the command. He adjusted his seating, attempting to lessen the discomfort of the hardened ridge she had awakened.

They galloped across the meadows and cleared several fences, giving their horses their heads. They didn't slow until they reached the fateful ravine that had caused them to meet after Grace rescued poor Hector from the deadly grip of the woodbine.

Pegasus and Tenebrae seemed contented enough to meander side by side for a while, so they encouraged their horses to amble alongside the tangled overgrowth bordering the deep gully.

"This is nice." Grace closed her eyes and lifted her face to the sun, as Pegasus required no guidance. "You do not mind a wife with freckles, do you?"

"Not so long as you allow me to kiss them."

She smiled before opening her eyes and nodding at a point up ahead. "Just beyond that gentle rise is the main road to the village. We daren't ride past it or someone might see my attire."

"What say you to dismounting and walking for a while?" Yes, he had an ulterior motive. Nothing so unchivalrous as making her his wife ahead of their wedding on Saturday, but a heated embrace would not be amiss. At least, he hoped she felt that way. The choice was entirely hers.

Rather than answer, she alighted with the grace of a butterfly flitting down to perch on a blade of grass. "Will Tenebrae stay with Pegasus? They seem friendly enough now that they have been around each other for a while, and there are no mares here to stir their competitiveness."

Wolfe dismounted and patted his horse. "Yes, Tenebrae has always been an even-tempered old man, and I feel certain they can sense our relationship."

"I think so too." The smile she gave him made him ache to pull her into his arms. "You are the first person I've ever known— other than Mr. Carson—who believes animals take as much notice of human behavior as we do of theirs."

"When I think of all the people I have met in this world, I do not necessarily agree with the assessment that we humans are the more brilliant of the species the Almighty ever created."

"You are most definitely the right man for me." She went to him, slid her hands up his chest, and tiptoed for a kiss.

He gathered her close, crushing into the warmth of her soft curves. She molded against him, making him groan and toy with the idea of stripping them both naked and consummating Saturday's vows here and now in the grassy field. Cupping her face between his hands, he kissed her deep and with every ounce of urgency pounding through him. She tasted of the berries they'd eaten earlier, but even more importantly, she tasted of need.

He worked his way lower, nibbling along the satin of her throat and the ticklish ridge of her collarbone. Cupping the perfect fullness of her breasts nearly undid him. With his face buried in the sweetness of the valley between them, he slowly lowered himself to his knees. She knotted her fingers in his hair, then tugged and pulled in time with her groans as he worked his mouth down her torso, forcing himself *not* to lift her shirt but nibbling her through it. As he nuzzled more and breathed her in, he ran his hand lower and rubbed her most intimately through her buckskins. The warmth between her legs pulled a yearning growl free of him.

"Oh my." Once again, she filled her hands with his hair, yanking and groaning as she stumbled and almost lost her balance.

Another growl escaped him as he caught her and lowered her to the ground. His senses raged into a blinding haze of need. But he would not take her. Not today. He was determined to reserve that ultimate pleasure for after they said *I do*. "When we join, it will be the perfect sealing of our vows," he rasped as he nuzzled her breasts through her clothing.

Hovering over her, he opened her legs with his knee and jutted his hips forward, nudging and rubbing his hard length against her warmth that would soon be his. Both of them remained infuriatingly clothed. Keeping their garments in place was the only way he knew of to set himself a boundary that would make him stop and think rather than reel out of control and bury himself in her, as he so badly needed to do.

"I swear I will not take you until Saturday." He rhythmically ground himself against her. "I will not take you until you are my wife."

"I will surely die by then." She groaned, arching to meet his rubbing thrusts, clutching at him and wrapping her legs around his waist. "This aching…this wonderful aching will kill me."

He understood completely. The feel of her, the smell of her need, was driving him past the point of reason. He plundered her mouth with his tongue as he slid his hand down between them and massaged her between her legs harder and faster, tickling her sex through her clothing with an insistent steadiness he knew would soon send her into oblivion. Oh, what he wouldn't give to rip off every thread she wore and join with her. But not yet—not today.

She shrieked and shuddered beneath him, moaning and thrusting hard against the pressure of his fingers. Then it was as though she melted, relaxing and letting her legs slowly slide from around him and come to rest on the ground. She barely shifted beneath him with slow, deep breaths, but her heart pounded against his chest.

"How in the world did you do that?" she asked in a lazy whisper without opening her eyes.

"I am a very gifted man."

"You have no idea."

"It will be even better after we are wed." He rose and kissed the tip of her nose.

"I fail to see how that could be remotely possible," she said, her eyes still closed.

"Trust me, my love. It is very possible."

She barely cracked open an eye and smiled. "On this, I will always trust you, my very gifted man."

"I rather like the sound of that." He nibbled a slow, leisurely kiss along her jawline, noticing with some pride and a great deal of satisfaction that her lips had gone a delightful shade of cherry red with his attentions. Even though he still painfully ached for relief, her nearly boneless state of relaxed bliss made his suffering well worth it. He could tend to himself later.

"I suppose we just proved we do, in fact, require a chaperone." Her lighthearted tone revealed no remorse or regret whatsoever.

"I think we did quite well." He locked eyes with her, losing himself in the twin pools of blue that had grown so much darker with her passion. "You remain a virgin, and we have yet to see each other unclothed."

She didn't respond, just held his gaze and caught her bottom lip between her teeth. The faintest puckering between her brows worried him.

"Grace?"

"What?"

"You look as though you dread what I am about to ask."

"That is because I do."

He remained on top of her, propping himself on his forearms to keep from crushing her. "I am not moving until you tell me what is wrong."

She struggled to look anywhere but in his eyes. "You know I often ride astride? The only time I ever ride sidesaddle is in the park in London."

"I fail to understand how that is a problem." He twitched the slightest shrug, then pecked another kiss to the tip of her nose. "You may still ride astride after we marry. Here in the country. On our land or the Broadmere estate. I feel you should still ride sidesaddle in front of others, of course, and absolutely no riding once you get with child." He gave her a stern look that he prayed she took to heart. "I will not have you or our children endangered in any way."

"You obviously have no idea of what I am attempting to tell you in as delicate a way as possible."

Her expression became so terse that he wondered what he had missed. He wasn't normally thick when it came to understanding hints and innuendo. "Just tell me, Grace, since you are quite right. I have no idea what you are trying to tell me."

She shifted beneath him with a deep breath then released it as a heavy sigh. "Mama warned that if I insisted on riding astride that my husband might be taken aback on my wedding night if I did not inform him and make it quite clear that I had never lowered my guard and allowed a man any liberties." Tears welled in her eyes. "And yet here I am, unmarried and lying beneath you after allowing you a great many liberties. I'm afraid you won't believe me when I tell you that no man has ever *known* me—as in the biblical sense of the word."

It finally dawned on him that in her roundabout way, Grace was attempting to tell him that her maidenhead might not be intact due to her habit of riding astride and usually at a hard gallop. He had heard of that happening. Never had he come across it, but he knew it to be a possibility.

He framed her face in his hands and forced her to look him in the eyes. "Stop looking for things that will make me stop loving you, because I swear upon my life that no such thing exists."

Her bottom lip quivered in a most heart-wrenching way. "I merely thought you should know."

"Thank you, my lady. I now know, and do not give a rat's arse that your maidenhead may have given its life to your saddle rather than my cock." He couldn't resist a devilish grin. "The rest of you is mine, and I consider myself a truly blessed man in that regard."

"Such language, Your Grace!" But the laughter in her eyes made the scolding fall short.

"You, my dear one, are my heart mate, the other half of my soul, and, very soon, my wife." He nibbled a tender kiss across the sweetness of her lips before lifting his head and smiling down at her. "Forgive me for the coarseness of my words, my love. I merely wished to impress upon you their sincerity."

"Oh, I am quite impressed, Your Grace. Quite impressed, and I can hardly wait for whatever else you wish to impress upon me."

"Saturday, my love. After we have said our vows—I swear to impress you to the very best of my abilities."

Chapter Fifteen

"YOU PROMISED, FELICITY. How could you not keep your word when you know how much this means to me?" Grace couldn't believe her sister had betrayed her, and she refused to allow Felicity's teary-eyed shock to convince her to look aside just this once.

"You said *no meat*." Felicity pointed at the wedding breakfast menu. "Kippers are fish. They are not meat. Everything is in accordance with your wishes. No animal was harmed in the making of your feast!"

"Except for those poor smoked kippers." Grace thumped on that particular item on the menu even harder. "Have you ever looked into the eyes of a herring? A fish is a living thing that hatches, grows to find another suitable fish, then lays eggs to bring little herrings into the world and protects them until they mature enough to make little herrings of their own. Papa showed me once in his book about fish. It's still in the townhouse's library in London, if you don't believe me. Those poor, tortured fish are not bushes that bloom, produce berries, go dormant in the winter, and wait for the gardener's pruning and the bees pollinating to begat more berries the next season. Berry bushes are not sentient beings. Fish are."

"You are impossible." Felicity snatched the menu away and marched back to the door. "Fish do not have *feelings*, Gracie. They are fish." She snapped the creamy-white square of parchment as if it were a whip. "But far be it from me to argue with Lady Grace, Mother Nature's most devoted servant. I shall keep the kippers on the sideboard in the kitchen. If anyone wants them, they will have to ask Walters to fetch them."

"Fine." Grace glared at her younger sister, determined to hold her ground on this day of all days. She was already a bundle of prickliness. Could Felicity not understand that?

"Yes, fine!" Felicity stamped her foot, then slammed the door on her way out.

"What in heaven's name did you say to Felicity?" Joy asked as she entered the dressing room.

"She put kippers on the menu." Grace glared at Joy, daring her to side with Felicity.

"Oh, dear heavens." Joy made a dramatic show of pressing her hand to her forehead. "Not kippers for Gracie, the protector of anything that might look back at you from the plate."

"Exactly!" When Joy put it like that, it did indeed appear as if she might have overreacted, but Grace wasn't about to admit it. Fish were living things. How did one know they did not have any feelings? She preferred to err on the side of caution. "Felicity is usually much more understanding. I can't believe she did this to me, and on today of all days."

"Speaking of which, you're not handling this day well at all. You never make Felicity cry. You're always the one to protect her."

And that was another thing. Grace felt absolutely horrid for being so bloody impossible to her sweet sister, who always took such pleasure in making things perfect for others. "I'll apologize to her the next time she returns, as I'm sure she will. She has asked me innumerable questions this morning that could well have been handled yesterday or the day before."

"There's the spirit. How could she possibly remain distraught with you when you positively overflow with such genuine remorse and understanding?"

"Sarcasm is very ugly on you, sister." Grace flounced down

and sat cross-legged on the floor in nothing but her shift. What on earth was wrong with her? She was barely tolerating her own presence, and if her stomach churned any harder, it would surely turn itself inside out.

Joy circled her while toeing a path through the utter disarray of the dressing room. "I saw Nellie in the kitchen fetching your third pot of tea. Do you think that wise? What happens when you need the chamber pot or bourdaloue at a critical juncture in your vows?"

Grace dropped her head into her hands. "I will more than likely need a bucket in which to cast up my accounts."

"I have never seen you like this. You're the fearless one." Joy dropped beside her and rubbed her back. "You love Wolfe. Correct?"

"Correct."

"You love the twins, and they love you. Correct?"

"Again—correct."

"And Wolfe is even more unsociable than you are, preferring the country over Town. Am I correct on that as well?"

Grace lifted her head and stared into her sister's eyes, which were the same shade of blue as her own. "You are correct on all counts, Joy, so why am I still so bloody miserable?"

"Is it becoming a duchess and overseeing a household that has you in such a state? You're never this thorny. Not even on your worst of days."

Grace flinched. Joy's words stung like a slap. "I know nothing about *duchessing* or running a household," she said in a desperate whisper. "I can run a stable and see that every animal on the estate is properly tended to, but I have no idea how to even plan what meals to feed a husband." She dropped her face into her hands. "I can't very well order a bag of oats tied to his face, now can I?"

"Well...you could." Joy gave her an affectionate shake. "I doubt, however, that your intended would appreciate that." Laughing, she pulled Grace into a tighter hug. "Your new housekeeper will help you. You know Mrs. Perridone. She's Mrs. Flackney's sister and would never let your home sink like a scuttled ship."

"Since when do you use nautical terms?"

"Unfortunately, most of the books in the library here are about ships and the sea. You know how that was one of Papa's passions. A visit to Creary's Bookshop in the village for something to read other than Fortuity's romances or the Royal Navy is definitely in order." She gently shook Grace again. "As I was saying, Mrs. Perridone was a housekeeper for the Portenses for as long as we've had Mrs. Flackney. Consider yourself fortunate that Wolfe was able to coax her away on the recommendation of Mrs. Flackney."

The dressing room door swung open, and Nellie sidled in bearing a large tray with two round-bellied teapots, multiple cups, and an assortment of biscuits, scones, and sweet buns. "Your tea, my lady, and I also brought your morning chocolate and favorite breads." The maid gave Grace a pointed look. "Then we *must* get you ready for your ceremony. It's already half past seven, and the wedding is set for nine."

"I am leaving you to it, then." Joy pushed up from the floor and shook out her skirts. "I shall send in Gastric and Galileo. Those two will make you feel better."

"Thank you, Joy—for everything." Grace already felt somewhat better after her sister's encouragement. She accepted a cup of chocolate from Nellie, took a sip, then realized she had run the poor maid in circles since before dawn. "Nellie, pour yourself a cup of chocolate and sit for a little while. I've been an absolute beast this morning and feel terrible about it."

The maid turned to her with an open-mouthed stare, then tilted her head. "Beg pardon, my lady?"

"You heard me. Things can wait long enough for you to have a nice cup of chocolate and a bread or two. These past few days have been extra hard on you, what with packing my things and sending them over to the lodge. Don't think I haven't noticed, and I do appreciate you."

The maid tucked her chin and smiled, obviously over-whelmed by the praise. "It was my pleasure, my lady. It truly was." She poured herself a half cup of chocolate.

"Fill it to the brim," Grace said. "You deserve it."

Still smiling, Nellie filled the cup the rest of the way. "Mrs. Flackney wrote to London. Your things should arrive from there within a fortnight, she said, and she already sent a note to Mrs. Perridone advising her of such." The maid sat on a trunk, dipped a biscuit in her chocolate, then delicately nibbled at it. "Thank you, my lady."

"You are quite welcome." Grace cradled her cup between her hands, pulled in a deep breath, and resolved to do better toward those around her. Her worries gave her no right to be an unruly tempest with everyone else.

The dressing room door creaked open wider, and Gastric ambled in, followed by Galileo. If anyone had ever told Grace that her favorite hound would someday take a surly orange cat as a best friend, she would've asked them if they'd been into the brandy. The fluffy, pumpkin-colored feline rarely left Gastric's side, and the hound had even been caught snuffling the cat's ears and occasionally giving them a good wash with a swipe of his tongue.

The dog flopped down beside her, propped his nose on her leg, and looked at her with adoration and obvious pleading for a biscuit. His chocolate-brown eyes and faint whine were impossible to resist. Galileo sat in front of her, pinning her with a judgmental, unblinking stare.

After giving Gastric a biscuit, Grace offered one to the cat, who sniffed it, then recoiled as if it were poison. "I don't know what you want, Galileo. Biscuits, tea, and hot chocolate are all I have, and I don't believe anything other than the biscuits would be advisable for you to nibble."

The feline gave an aloof flick of his ear, then turned his back to her as if to dismiss her presence. She was half tempted to tug on his slowly flipping tail just to aggravate him.

"I don't understand cats," she said to Nellie as the maid took her cup away and gently but firmly urged her to stand.

"As I see it," Nellie said, "you are much like a cat, my lady. Independent. Know your own mind. Determined to go your own way. Perhaps that is why Master Galileo sometimes takes umbrage with you. Maybe he fears you will overshadow him." She wrapped the stays around Grace and pulled them snugly while tightening the laces. "Are you still wearing the blue silk, or have you decided on another?"

"I promise not to change my mind again, Nellie. It's still the blue silk." Besides, all Grace's other gowns were packed and ready for the footmen to load onto the wagon bound for Wolfebourne Lodge. "I know I've been a terror, and I am sorry."

"Every woman has a right to be a bit fractious when preparing for her wedding." Nellie nodded for her to bend forward so she could put the petticoat on over her head and tug it down in place. The maid went round to the back, tied it shut, and anchored it with hooks and eyelets. "Have a seat, my lady, whilst I fetch your silk stockings. Lady Serendipity had new pairs delivered for everyone just yesterday."

The maid idly chattered about absolutely nothing. Grace smiled and nodded as though taking in every word, but her mind was on what was about to happen in the garden at nine o'clock. She rubbed Gastric's velvety ears, wishing she could wear her buckskins, and that she and Wolfe could be wed beside the ravine.

The ravine. Good heavens, she should never have thought about the ravine and rekindled that deliciously uncomfortable aching her husband-to-be now triggered whenever in her presence. She cleared her throat and took another sip of tea, thankful that the liquid had cooled.

"And now the gown," Nellie said as she expertly held the garment so that Grace had but to stand and bend a little to wriggle up into it. "My goodness, you've gone a bit flushed. Have a seat again, my lady. I can fasten your gown just as well while you sit before I tend to your hair. Are you feeling faint?"

"I'm fine," Grace hurried to say. "And no feathers or silly frippery in my hair, please. I wish it simple." She pressed a hand to her chest, noting the redness in her cheeks had spread there as well. She wondered if she should wear a fichu, since her fair skin was determined to betray her. "Is this neckline modest enough for a bride? I don't wish the vicar and his wife to think any poorer of me than they already do."

Nellie blew out a curt huff. "The vicar and his wife adjust their opinions by the weightiness of the coins in the offering plate. Donations for the upkeep of the kirk and the vicarage also sway them, my lady. Since you will soon be a duchess who intends to spend a great deal of time in their parish, I feel certain they will be most generous in their thoughts about you and His Grace." She held out the tray of necklaces and earrings. "What gems will you wear on this special day, my lady? Your mother wished each of her daughters to have something from this collection on the day they married. Lady Serendipity said so when she brought the tray to me."

Grace knew without hesitation which of Mama's precious collection was meant for her. She had always told Mama that the topaz crosses were her favorite, and Mama had said she should wear them on her wedding day, since topaz symbolized love and good fortune. All the sisters knew which pieces Mama wished each of them to have—she had told them just before she died. "The topaz crosses. Mama wanted me to wear them today."

Nellie smiled as she affixed the delicate cross earrings onto Grace's pierced ears, then fastened the gold necklace bearing the simple topaz cross around her neck. "Lady Serendipity thought those would be the ones you chose." She carefully closed the velvet case and placed it on the dresser. "You are ready, my lady, and may I say, you've never looked lovelier."

"Thank you, Nellie." Grace rose, fidgeting with her long gloves, tugging at their hems where they clung well above her elbows. She hated the silly things. They reminded her of the formal balls she had never liked. "Are you certain it would be wrong to wear my lacy, short gloves?"

"A wedding is a formal occasion, my lady." Nellie fussed with Grace's curls and plumped her short, puffy sleeves trimmed with ivory lace. "They are most becoming with your gown and will let your husband know you care for him so greatly that you'd wear something you despise—since you rarely wear gloves around him, as you should."

"You're getting wilier, Nellie."

The maid offered a smug nod. "One can but try, my lady."

"Shall I go down now or wait until closer to nine?"

Nellie ratcheted her eyebrows so high, they disappeared beneath the ruffle of her white cap. "The clock already struck that hour quite a bit ago, my lady. It's nearly half past."

"Pray for me, Nellie."

"Always, my lady."

After a deep breath that failed to calm her pounding heart or the fluttering in her middle, Grace swept out of the room, down the hallway, and down the stairs.

"At last," Chance said from where he perched on the edge of the bench beside the double doors to the parlor. "Wolfebourne had us check outside your window twice and listen to your dressing room door to ensure you hadn't run away."

"The trellis is gone, remember?"

"I reminded him of that, but he said you would find a way if you wished to escape badly enough." Chance took her hand and placed it on his arm. "And I have to agree with him. You always find a way—even if it might be foolhardy." He halted and leaned down to look her in the eyes. "Seri says you love him. Do you, Gracie? You know I wanted you married because of that infernal will, but I want you happy because you're my sister, and I care about you."

"I do love him, Chance. I'm merely suffering from what Nellie assures me are *bridal vapors*." She hugged her brother's arm tighter. "I care about you too, even though you irritate me to no end."

"Thank you, sister. I always strive to do my best." He escorted her through the parlor and out into the garden.

As they followed the stepping stones that led them deeper into the vibrant assortment of rosebushes in full bloom, she concentrated on her breathing and swallowed hard. *Do not be ill,* she silently repeated over and over. She loved Wolfe. Covering him with a disgusting wash of tea and hot chocolate would not be the way to show it. They passed between the fragrant white and pink roses that were Mama's favorites, and she found herself unable to take another step.

Up ahead, Wolfe was stunning. His dark hair with its touches of silver still needed trimming, but it made him even more handsome in a wild, untamed way. Most men would've worn a hat, but he didn't, and she was glad. His best dress, a cutaway coat as black as his polished boots, buff-colored pantaloons, and a crisp white cravat set off his broad shoulders, narrow waist, and long, muscular legs. Heaven help her. This wondrous man was about to be hers forevermore.

"Gracie?" Chance tugged on her. "Come along, now."

She found it impossible to move, completely captured by her future husband's dark-eyed gaze.

"Gracie?" Chance tugged again.

"I can't—I don't know why, but I can't seem to move." It was as though her body was not her own. Someone else controlled it.

Wolfe slowly moved toward her, closing the distance between them. With gentle understanding and love shining in his eyes, he took her hand from her brother's arm and placed it on his. "Come, my dear one. You can do this."

His deep voice washed over her, filling her with such joy that she almost cried out. Tears stung her eyes, threatening to break free and roll down her cheeks. Whatever had frozen her in place released her. With her gaze locked with his, she walked with him to where the vicar waited.

"All right now?" Wolfe asked ever so softly.

She nodded. "All right now."

"Thank goodness," Connor whispered entirely too loudly to Sissy. "I thought she'd changed her mind."

Sissy elbowed him. "Hush!"

Wolfe gave Grace an apologetic shake of his head, and she accepted it with a squeeze of his hand. If anything, the twins strengthened her, and she was not only grateful for their presence but for her sisters' quiet giggles and acceptance of the rowdy pair attending the ceremony rather than remaining in the nursery with baby Quill and little Rorie.

Mr. Donaldson, the vicar, cleared his throat and swept a smiling gaze at everyone gathered in the garden. "It has been made abundantly clear to me that all gathered here wish a more abbreviated service than that which is written in the *Book of Common Prayer*. Therefore, I shall do my best to shorten it while still keeping in accordance with God's will."

Grace nervously chewed on the inside of her cheek, wishing the man would simply get on with it. She felt quite certain that the Almighty had already heard the *Book of Common Prayer* so many times that He might very well be sick of it too. She flinched as the vicar drew in a deep breath, as if about to recite the entirety of the Holy Bible.

Wolfe squeezed her hand, a subtle and silent reassurance that while he felt the same, they must bear this.

Mr. Donaldson adjusted his spectacles, then bent his head and squinted at the open book in his hands.

Grace curled her toes with impatience. Why didn't the silly man simply move it closer to his face?

"Dearly beloved," Mr. Donaldson began, "we are gathered together here in the sight of God, and in the face of this congregation, to join together this man and this woman in holy matrimony; which is an honorable estate, instituted of God in the time of man's innocency, signifying unto us the mystical union that is betwixt Christ and his Church; which holy estate Christ adorned and beautified with his presence, and first miracle that he wrought, in Cana of Galilee; and is commended of Saint Paul to be honorable among all men: and therefore is not by any to be enterprised, nor taken in hand, unadvisedly, lightly, or wantonly, to satisfy men's carnal lusts and appetites, like brute beasts that have no understanding; but reverently, discreetly, advisedly, soberly, and in the fear of God; duly considering the causes for which matrimony was ordained."

Heaven help us. Grace stifled a groan. If this was the abbreviated version, she couldn't imagine standing through the service word for word from the *Book of Common Prayer.* Her stomach gurgled loudly enough for all to hear even over the endless droning on of the vicar. She clenched her teeth and whispered, "Sorry," to Wolfe.

He trembled against her side. She prayed that meant he was silently laughing.

Mr. Donaldson lowered the book for a moment and glared at them before continuing. "Wilt thou, Romulus Adalwolf Craigston, Duke of Wolfebourne, take Grace Elena Daisy Abarough to be thy wedded wife, to live together after God's ordinance in the holy estate of matrimony? Wilt thou love her, comfort her, honor, and keep her in sickness and in health; and, forsaking all others, keep thee only unto her, so long as you both shall live?"

"I will," Wolfe said.

Romulus Adalwolf? How could he not have told her his Christian name before now? Romulus as in Romulus and Remus? The twins raised by a wolf? The myth about the city of Rome's namesake and origin? And what was the origin and meaning of Adalwolf? Good heavens, and here she thought her three names were a bit excessive.

Wolfe cleared his throat and nudged her while pointedly arching a brow at her.

Oh dear. The vicar had asked her something. Surely he had just repeated the same question to her. "I will," she said, with a little more exuberance than she intended.

The twins snickered, as did her sisters, her brother, and her brothers-in-law. In the distance, her hounds had started a racket that sent a shiver of alarm through her. They sounded as though they'd escaped the pens they only stayed in whenever their liveliness might prove a bit overwhelming to guests. Behind her, a muffled *woof* and scratching at the closed parlor doors told her that Gastric wished to join the ceremony as well.

Wolfe took hold of her left hand and slid a gleaming ring of gold onto her finger. "With this ring, I thee wed, with my body, I thee worship, and with all my worldly goods I thee endow: in the name of the Father, and of the Son, and of the Holy Ghost. Amen."

"Amen," she repeated, even though she wasn't quite certain she was supposed to.

"Let us pray," Mr. Donaldson said.

They bowed their heads just as her herd of adoring hounds poured into the garden, and Gastric managed to force open the parlor door.

Carson, winded and gasping for breath, crashed in behind them, their leashes in his hands. "I beg your forgiveness, my lady," he shouted over the cacophony of happy yips and barks. "I've never seen them act this way before."

Grace split the air with a sharp whistle, then pointed at the ground to her left. "Down and quiet, if you wish to remain for the rest of the ceremony."

Every hound, including Lucy's seven half-grown pups, lay down and watched expectantly, seeming to smile with their long red tongues hanging out. Gastric lay at the front of the group with Hector and Galileo on either side of him. The cat appeared to be surveying the dogs as if deciding which of them to execute first.

With a decisive nod, Grace turned back to the vicar. "Continue, Mr. Donaldson. They will behave now."

Wolfe turned aside with a coughing fit that Grace suspected was supposed to cover his laughter. After a moment, he composed himself and gave her hand a squeeze. "Yes, Mr. Donaldson. After all, we are about to cross the finish line."

"Uhm…yes." The vicar frowned down at his book while flipping a page. "Forgive me—I seem to have lost my place."

"It would seem you covered everything," Wolfe said, "except the very last bit."

Mr. Donaldson shook his head and snapped the small prayer book shut. "Forasmuch as Romulus Adalwolf and Grace Elena Daisy have consented together in holy wedlock, and have witnessed the same before God and this company, and thereto have given and pledged their troth either to other, and have declared the same by giving and receiving of a ring, and by joining of hands; I pronounce that they be man and wife together. In the name of the Father, and of the Son, and of the Holy Ghost. Those whom God hath joined together let no man put asunder. Amen."

"Amen!" Connor shouted, then jumped up from his seat and ran to hug them.

Unable to contain her joy, Grace laughed and hugged the boy close as she held out a hand for Sissy to join them.

"Please forgive his lack of manners," Sissy said. "Sometimes he just can't help himself." She poked Connor in the shoulder. "Wolfe looks like he wants to hug her now. Give him a turn, as everyone wishes to congratulate them."

Connor glared at her. "How do you know? This is the first wedding where we made it to the end. Father died in the middle of his."

Merry clapped her hands. "No such talk allowed today! It's bad luck. Come. Let's see what the buffet holds. Maybe we can sneak a treat." She caught hold of the twins and steered them inside.

"I took the liberty of bringing the register," Mr. Donaldson said before Grace had a moment to look into her new husband's eyes. "If we could proceed to the library with the designated witnesses, we can enter the marriage lines, and sign the original and the copy for the bride."

Mrs. Donaldson nudged in close, reminding Grace of her dogs when they wanted to be petted. "Such a lovely ceremony. Very lovely, indeed."

Grace forced a smile and hooked her hand through Wolfe's arm as they obediently fell in step behind the vicar and his wife to complete the legal proof that the wedding had taken place. "Sorry about the dogs," she whispered for Wolfe's ears alone.

"If not for them," Wolfe whispered back just as quietly, "I feel certain the vicar would still be praying over us even though he promised an *abbreviated* service."

Grace held her breath to keep from giggling as they stepped into the library and approached the desk bearing the oversized parish register book. She touched the cross at her throat and sent up a silent prayer of thanks. She had indeed found the perfect man to marry.

Chapter Sixteen

B RAEMER, WOLFE'S VALET, paused in collecting his master's things and glanced at the door connecting the duke's bedchamber and suite of private rooms to the duchess's chambers. "Should I send the new housekeeper to Her Grace to inquire if anything is amiss? That last thud seemed quite loud."

"No, Braemer. I am sure everything is fine." Wolfe resettled his stance, trying not to fidget as the valet assisted him in changing into his usual state of undress when lounging: a worn pair of buckskins and a shirt open at the throat. He never wore a banyan, considering them too pretentious. Gads alive, he and his new wife had just arrived home for the first time in their wedded bliss, and the servants behaved as if it were just another ordinary day. He shooed the man away. "That will do, thank you."

"Yes, Your Grace." The man tipped a formal nod, gathered Wolfe's discarded clothing, and disappeared from the room with the silence of a shadow.

"At last." Wolfe went to the connecting door and knocked.

A deafening chorus of barks and howls filled the air as Grace swung it open and shyly waved him in to her side of their private rooms. "Please forgive me. Pete, Moses, and Ferdinand aren't quite settled yet, and I didn't have the heart to put them out in the stable. As you can see, Gastric has made himself quite at home. I've left the hallway door open a little so they can go exploring if they get too fidgety. They've already introduced themselves to the kitchen and found their way to Connor and Sissy's rooms."

All four dogs were on the bed, with Gastric commandeering the choicest spot on the pillows against the upholstered head-board.

Wolfe made a show of stroking his chin as he meandered back and forth in front of the four-poster bed with its ivory cloth hangings neatly tied back with gold cording. "There appears to be no room in your bed for you, my lady." Which was quite perfect, in his opinion, since she belonged in his.

She ducked her head, but not before he noted the lovely, rosy blush highlighting her cheeks. "I'm sure I could wiggle in among them. They often slept with me back home."

"This is your home now, my love," he said ever so softly while drawing her into his arms.

She slid her hands up his chest and tenderly tapped his chin with the tip of her finger. "*You* are my home, Wolfe. Wherever you are, that is where I shall be."

He cupped her face and sampled the sweetness of her mouth. "My wife—my home."

A soft whine came from the bed, making Grace gently pull away and turn to the dogs. "I will be in the next room. Be good lads and behave." She picked up an armload of what appeared to be old clothes and placed them on the bed. "Here you are. Familiar smells, see? All is well."

The dogs nosed through the garments, each of them circling through them three times before settling down and seeming to relax.

She caught hold of Wolfe's hand, led him back into his bed-chamber, and closed the door behind them. "Thank you for your patience. I'd be so uneasy if they weren't settled in." She twitched a cringing shrug. "Please don't be jealous. This"—she made a sweeping gesture that encompassed the room—"all this takes some getting used to for them...and me."

He went to her, determined to put her at ease. "I will not lie and say I'm not jealous." Ever so gently, he slid his fingers along her jawline, then up into her hair, smiling as he loosened and flicked away the hairpins holding her upswept curls in place. Her tresses fell down her back in a golden waterfall. "Your caring when it comes to your animals and for my brother and sister is one of the many things that warmed my cold, cynical heart and brought it to life once more. I never thought myself capable of love—until you captured me and pulled the blinders from my heart and mind." He needed her to know how much he adored her. Not just for her beauty. Or her wit. But for her unique, unconventional spirit that made her so wonderfully her.

"I love you, Gracie," he whispered, then sealed the declaration with a more passionate kiss.

She molded herself against him, holding him as if determined to never let him go. When he lifted his head, she slowed him with a gentle touch of his cheek. "Nellie said she would help me into my fresh chemise. All I need do is call her to aid me."

"I am unwilling to let you go even for that short amount of time." He ran a fingertip along the neckline of her dress, smiling as she shivered. "I propose we be as unconventional as ever. Are you willing?"

With a coy tip of her head, she fiddled with the open folds of his collar, smoothing them as if they needed ironing. "I agree to nothing, Your Grace, until I know the terms in full."

"Your rooms," he said while brushing kisses from her temple to her earlobe, "are for your dressing, whatever necessary personal time you desire, and, of course, your beloved animals. But I shall see to your undressing." He ran the tip of his tongue along the salty sweetness of her throat. "And the bed in this room, our bed, will be shared every night. I want to sleep with you draped across me after we've loved ourselves into oblivion, then wake with you in my arms every morning so we may love each other even more."

Gracing him with a suitably impressed look, she nodded. "Those terms sound most acceptable. Therefore, I shall agree to them fully. The only time my parents didn't share their bed was when Mama was giving birth—and at the end, when she was ill." She untucked his shirt and slid her hands underneath it. "Oh my, you are so…"

He waited for her to finish. When she didn't, he laughed. "I am so…what?"

"Your body ripples with hardened muscle, yet your skin is smooth and supple like velvet." She wet her lips, bringing him to an almost painful hardness. "You're as powerful and sleek as a prize stallion."

Ever so gently, he swept her hair out of the way and rained kisses along her neck, then down across her shoulder, baring it even more with a tug on her dress as he turned her and deftly unfastened the buttons in the back. "You took my breath away when you joined me in the garden for our vows."

"You did the same for me," she said as her gown fell into a puddle around her feet. "In fact, you made it impossible for me to move, I was so taken by you."

Still nibbling along her shoulder, he untied her stays and allowed them to join the dress on the floor. "I must say, you did give my poor old heart a bit of yank when you halted. I thought surely you were about to flee."

She turned in his arms and gathered his shirt up to his shoulders. "Off with this, Your Grace, and tell me—if I ran, would you catch me?"

"Without a doubt, my love." He tossed his shirt aside, then scooped her up into his arms and carried her to the bed. "And I would never let you go." He untied her slippers and flicked them away. Her suddenly pensive look made him pause. "Gracie? What is it?"

She chewed on her bottom lip, eyeing him as if afraid to share her thoughts.

With her ankle in his hand, he gently tapped on her stocking-covered toes. "Tell me, my love. What is wrong?"

"I have read a great many things," she said, then wrinkled her nose. "But none were as detailed as I needed them to be."

"Things?"

"What am I supposed to do to *please* you?" She folded her hands atop her stomach and nervously tapped her thumbs together. "You treated me to unimaginable pleasure at the ravine that day, but I did nothing for you." She frowned, worry in her eyes. "I don't want you wandering because I don't make you *happy* in this room."

"Firstly, I would never wander." He slid his hands up her leg, untied her garter, then slipped off her stocking and tossed it. "You are mine as I am yours. Never will there ever be another for either of us."

That seemed to please her, but he still read uncertainty in her face. He made short work of her other stocking, then stepped back and stood at the side of the bed.

"What are you doing now?" She rose and propped herself on her elbows, her golden curls tumbling across the pillows and the subtle curve of her breasts teasing him through the thin material of her chemise.

"I am divesting myself of my clothes."

"Oh." She glanced down at her shift. "I suppose I should rid myself of this, then?"

As he unbuttoned his falls and let the buckskins drop, he held her eyes with his. "I would consider that not only an honor, my lady, but the perfect wedding present."

Her gaze boldly raked down his body, and her eyes went wide. "Oh my—you are nothing like the statues."

"Is that good or bad, my lady?" He climbed in next to her and gently tugged on the chemise she had yet to shed.

"Uhm…good. I suppose. Might I get back to you on that particular point, since I have no experience with such things?"

He laughed as he helped her wiggle out of her shift. "You may, indeed, my love." The sight of her in all her glory threatened to undo him before he even got started. Leaning over her, he teased her with a slow, tender kiss, growling with pleasure as she pulled herself closer and pressed the length of her body against his.

"Warm silk," he whispered against her mouth as he ran his hands across her. Never in a thousand lifetimes would he get enough of her. He kissed his way lower, reveling in the taste of her.

She arched against him as she had done at the ravine, wrapping her legs around him and squeezing. Her little noises of delight as he explored her guided him along. Every time between them needed to be special, but this first time especially needed to be perfect, properly melding their vows.

"I adore you," he said as she cried out and clung to him, achieving the first of the many pleasures he intended to give her this evening. It was a long time before dawn, and they had much loving to do. He kissed his way back up to her mouth and settled his hips between her legs, gently prodding as though tenderly requesting admission to her bliss.

"Make me your wife," she rasped, wrapping her arms around him and pulling him closer. "Fully and completely."

"Gladly." He slid in, forcing himself to go with care and grant her the time he knew she needed to adjust. Clenching his teeth, every muscle tensed, he fought the need to plunder her fully with every ounce of raging lust pulsing through him.

Her breath coming in quick little gasps, she slid her hands down his sides and gripped his buttocks. "Oh my—now I know what I needed so badly at the ravine."

"And what I needed so badly to give you," he answered with a groan. With his forehead pressed to hers, he forced himself to hold. "Was the pain terrible, my love?" He had only deflowered one other virgin, and that lady had carried on as if he had cleaved her in two with a dull sword. He ached to move, to continue on, but refused to do so until he knew his precious wife was all right.

"The pain is still terrible," she said in a desperate, gasping whisper. "The aching is much worse than before, and I need relief. What do we need to do?"

While he wanted to throw back his head and roar, he didn't. He should have known his beloved, fearless Gracie would match him in passion. After all, she perfectly matched him in everything else. "We do this, my love."

He started slow, increasing the rhythm and building the fury with every thrust. She met him each time, arching and drawing him in faster and faster. Then she split the air with a throaty shout and clung to him, pulsing with wave after wave of rapturous shudders.

Unable to maintain control any longer, he gave in to the relentless need to bury himself and release, filling her as she emptied him. He buried his face in the curve of her neck, a groan escaping him as he gasped for breath.

"That was…unimaginable," she said, her voice ragged as she combed her fingers into his hair.

He smiled and pressed a kiss to her throat. "In a good way?"

"In a most delightful way." She shifted and kissed his forehead. "How do people not do this all the time?"

He rumbled with laughter, unable to keep from it. "Indeed. I have often wondered that myself." He propped himself up on his forearms and smiled down at her. "We are now one, my lady. In every sense of the word."

She reached up and pushed his wild hair back from his face. "I can't possibly imagine life without you."

"Good, my love. Because I can't possibly imagine life without you either."

Epilogue

Wolfebourne Lodge
Binnocksbourne, England
April 1823

"THEY LOOK THE same to me," Connor said. He pointed at the cradle to the right and then at the one to the left. "I bet the dogs don't even know which is which."

"The ribbon on that headboard plainly says *Remus Jamison,*" Sissy said, "and that one says *Gwyneth Jennette.*"

"Dogs can't very well read, now can they?"

"They don't have to read. The babies smell different. Grace said so."

Wolfe knew if he didn't quiet those two, his beloved infants would soon scream their displeasure at being disturbed to all of England. Then poor Grace would have yet another nap interrupted, since she had yet to find a nurse or nanny she trusted. He hurried into the nursery and caught hold of his brother and sister by the shoulders. "If you two awaken the little ones, I shall inform Mrs. Perridone that you volunteered to help the maids scrub the chamber pots."

The twins stared at him in horror, then Connor pointed at the crowd of dogs with their noses propped on the cradles, avidly watching the babies sleep. "What about them?" he asked in a loud whisper.

"They help Remy and Gwynnie sleep," Grace said from the doorway, "because they make them feel safe."

"Gads alive, my love." Wolfe hurried to wrap an arm around his exhausted wife so she might lean against him. "Forgive us for waking you."

"You didn't wake me." She meandered closer to the cradles and smiled down at her children. "I'll need to feed them soon. *That* is what woke me."

"Does your stomach growl or something when theirs gets empty?" Connor asked.

"Something like that," Grace told the child while giving Wolfe a pointed look.

"Why don't you two run along now?" he suggested, taking her hint to heart. "See if Lady Merry's carriage is anywhere in sight. Her letter said she should arrive today to see the babies and also bring along a prospective nurse and a nanny Lady Fortuity found for us to interview. A nurse and nanny that successfully survived the Broadmere gauntlet."

"Last one to the gate is a warty old toad," Connor said before shooting out the door.

Sissy rolled her eyes. "Since we have Remy now, can we please send Connor off to boarding school? I truly believe he needs it."

"No one is sending anyone off," Wolfe said as he escorted her out and closed the door behind her. Turning back to Grace, he asked, "Are you certain we didn't wake you?"

She had already stretched out on the sofa in front of the windows beside the cradles. "You didn't wake me. This uncomfortable fullness did. Hand me Remy. He's already wolfish with hunger, working his little feet back and forth and getting red in the face." She loosened the ties on the makeshift robe she'd had the village seamstress create for her.

Wolfe picked up his squirming son. "Hush now, young man. Don't wake your sister if you wish to eat your fill first."

The baby grunted and growled even louder, making Wolfe laugh. He couldn't remember ever feeling so content, complete, or exhausted.

"While I know you enjoy being unconventional," he said as he settled the babe in Grace's arms, "a wet nurse would be a godsend for you. Don't you agree? Doesn't an entire night of uninterrupted sleep sound absolutely decadent?"

"It does."

But Wolfe could tell by her tone that she was not yet ready to hand off the feeding of her babies to another, no matter how socially expected it was for her to do so. "It's entirely your decision, my love. Whenever you are ready."

She hitched with a jaw-cracking yawn, then smiled at the babe rooting at her breast. "Soon, perhaps. When they are a little older. Two weeks just seems so early." She patted the cushions beside her. "Come sit with us before Gwynnie needs you or Gastric beats you to the spot."

Wolfe eased down beside her, then rubbed a finger across the velvety softness of his son's dark hair. "I believe he's doubled in size since he came into the world."

"The way he eats, I'm not in the least bit surprised." She looked up from the babe with concern. "Don't you need to return to Parliament? The session just started a few weeks ago."

"They can go to the devil," he said, meaning every word. "My family needs me."

"So, you don't miss the quiet of your life before? The carefree routine of an unmarried duke?"

He cupped her cheek and gently stroked his thumb across it. "That was no life, my love. That was sheer and utter loneliness."

She leaned into his hand and smiled. "I'm so happy." She added a teasing wink. "And I promise to give Nellie time to run a brush through my hair today. I'm sure I look like something that should live in the bushes."

"You are more beautiful every day, my love." He leaned across his grunting son and kissed her. "Remy and Gwynnie are fortunate to have been born to a most glorious woman."

"I'm blessed by all of you."

An indignant yowl rose from the cradle. Gastric and Hector

yipped sharply, and the remainder of the hounds darted back and forth between Wolfe and the baby's bed.

Grace laughed. "It appears someone has realized her brother is eating without her."

"I'm coming, Gwynnie." Wolfe wove his way through the dogs. "Apparently, I do not move quickly enough for her or her guardians." He scooped up his impatient daughter and cradled her to his chest. "Yes, dearest. I know Papa is slow, but grant me some grace. I've never been around such a tiny beauty before." He settled her to Grace's other breast, then gently nudged a pillow beneath each of the babes to make things easier.

"You've become quite adept at this, Your Grace."

The regret in her eyes gave him pause. "What is it, my love?"

"I need to find a nurse, a nanny, and a wet nurse to help me. For your sake, more than mine. Keeping you here at my side is like caging a wild animal."

Her eyes filled with tears, as they often had for little to no reason at all since the babies came. Thankfully, Mrs. Perridone and Nellie had both assured him that was sometimes the way of it with new mothers.

He knelt at her side and stroked her mess of curls back from her face. "I love you, and there is no other place in creation I would rather be than at your side."

Her tears overflowed, and she leaned her head into his hand. "I never ever used to cry, and now I weep when the wind changes. What the devil is wrong with me?"

"Nothing is wrong with you, my love, and if it makes you feel better to cry, then do it."

"You are a most patient husband."

"With such a wondrous family, patience is easy." He kissed his son's head and then his daughter's. "Merry will be beside herself with these two. I'm surprised Joy, Felicity, and Serendipity aren't coming, too."

"Marriage Mart. Remember?" Grace arched a brow. "Chance gains a percentage of the coffers upon the happy marriage of each sister, but not the entirety until all are married. Since Merry is the youngest, she is the safest—for now. Joy is next on the chopping block, and the Season is now in full swing."

"What about Serendipity? She's the eldest."

"She promised Mama she wouldn't wed until the rest of us were firmly settled in our happily-ever-afters. When Mama passed, Seri became the matriarch, seeing to everyone else." Grace twitched the slightest shrug. "Since Joy is a year younger than me, Chance will set his sights on getting her matched next. If he finds a man able to beat her at the gaming tables, he should be set."

"Somehow, I doubt that. I don't see Joy taking well to losing." Wolfe huffed a soft laugh to keep from disturbing the peacefully nursing babies. "Heaven help the man who ever challenges Joy and wins."

Grace grinned. "They used to say that about me, and just look at us."

He stretched and kissed her cheek. "Yes, my love, just look at us now."

"Yes," she said softly. "We've both won."

"Indeed we have."

THE END

About the Author

If you enjoyed GRACE'S SAVING, please consider leaving a review on the site where you purchased your copy, or a reader site such as Goodreads, or BookBub.

If you'd like to receive my newsletter, here's the link to sign up:
maevegreyson.com/contact.html#newsletter

I love to hear from readers! Drop me a line at
maevegreyson@gmail.com

Or visit me on Facebook:
facebook.com/AuthorMaeveGreyson

Join my Facebook Group – Maeve's Corner:
facebook.com/groups/MaevesCorner

I'm also on Instagram:
maevegreyson

My website:
https://maevegreyson.com

Feel free to ask questions or leave some Reader Buzz on
bingebooks.com/author/maeve-greyson

Goodreads:
goodreads.com/maevegreyson

Follow me on these sites to get notifications about new releases, sales, and special deals:

Amazon:
amazon.com/Maeve-Greyson/e/B004PE9T9U

BookBub:
bookbub.com/authors/maeve-greyson

Many thanks and may your life always be filled with good books!
Maeve